TWDI

TROUBLE WITH A DREAM I

Cowboys, Bikers and Madmen

by Penelope Wells

A tale based on the life and times of the artist Penelope Wells

GALVANIZED GROUP INC.

In order to protect the innocent, as well as the guilty, I have changed names and locations and am compelled to say that portions of the book are fictional. Some characters have been combined and time frames altered; therefore, any similarity to persons living or dead is completely coincidental.

This is my story, written in my own words. I'm not what you'd call a professional writer, but I have been asked to recount the tales of my adventures to captivated friends and acquaintances ever since I was a tot.

After I was offered a movie deal and told that Hollywood was desperate for me, I decided that it was time to put pen to paper, and this is it… my story….

THE LETTER

Dear Pat,

I'm writing to let you know that I'm on the run. I've shot four men, members of an outlaw motorcycle club, it was self-defense, but I doubt that the truth matters much right now. Things are chaotic, I'm certain that a hit man is on my trail and probably the FBI as well.

I'm headed for a safe place; you know that I can survive. I'll see you when it's over.

Love,
Sissy

TABLE OF CONTENTS

RATTLESNAKES AND RACEHORSES

I had just turned thirteen years old when my father decided to pull up roots and move the family East, to a big city across the country. We sold nearly everything we owned, loaded a U-HAUL trailer with necessities and started the long journey into a mysterious new world.

I rode in the back seat of the family car with my brother, Pete, and sister, Pat; father was driving while mother read the road map.

As we traveled along, I looked out the car window at the countryside and saw the cattle and horses peacefully grazing in the pastures. The scenery made me smile, as I began to think about my life and what it had been like.

Raised on a ranch in the Wild West, I was driving cattle and helping with the yearly branding by the time I was five years old. I, like most country kids was innocent and naïve, but tough as rawhide. Ranching was a lifestyle that I took to naturally and enjoyed.

My mind began to wander back and I thought about the first time that I had ever ridden a horse. I remembered looking at the massive animal stomping its feet, snorting and ripping up grass with his big teeth. "He's a giant!" I said, "his head is as big as me!" Standing on the ground, I couldn't see up past his belly.

My father picked me up and put me in the saddle; it was a long, long way from the ground. Then he handed me the reins and said, "Kick him when you want to go, pull back when you want to stop and neck rein him to the left or right."

The horses name was Buckshot, a gentle animal beloved by the whole clan. I bravely sat in the saddle, held the reins and kicked the horse, but he didn't move, he just kept eating grass. So I kicked harder. Then I noticed something; I was so tiny that my feet didn't clear the saddle and I wasn't actually kicking the horse at all.

I called to my father who wasn't watching, "Daddy, Daddy," I yelled to get his attention, "my legs aren't long enough to kick him."

"Click your tongue like this, click, click." He made a sound with his mouth and then added, "Show that horse who's boss!"

I clicked my tongue two times, let out a loud, "Yah!" and we were off. It was exciting the big horse was actually listening to me! I trotted him down the driveway, out the gate, and started up the road; and when no one stopped me, I kept right on going. Buckshot and I took a long ride all the way to the foothills.

I remembered the way his mane felt in my hand and his earthy smell. I patted him on the neck and said in my little voice, "You're a good horse Buckshot."

The leather saddle went squeak, squeak, squeak, as Buckshot walked along, and his head moved up and down with each step. The sound of his hooves clacking on the pavement made a rhythm, it sounded as though he was dancing in tap shoes. I made up a little song and sang it to him as we plodded along. I was the happiest girl in the world and had fallen in love with a magical animal.

Every night, before I went to sleep, I said my prayers and then thought about my plans and dreams. I called it my Dream List and that night, I added a horse at the very top. I wanted a horse more than anything in the whole wide world. I recited my list as I counted on my fingers:

Number one: Horse.

Number two: Artist.

My mother was an artist and I knew that I wanted to be one too. I enjoyed coloring in my coloring books and expressing myself with bright bold colors on big sheets of paper.

Number three: Husband.

I had never gone through a stage like most little girls and disliked boys; I liked the boys and the boys liked me. I planned to marry a rugged handsome, older man, perhaps one of the Kindergarteners in my Sunday School class. But I knew that I was still a little young for marriage, so I decided to put off that dream for another year, or maybe even two.

Number four: House.

Now with the new addition of the horse to my list, I would need land for it to run and play. So I changed number four.

Number four: Ranch

Number five: Family.

I planned to have a baby that would be even cuter than my favorite rubber baby doll!

Yep, that was my complete plan, a plan that I had made from the start. But was it too much to ask for?

After recalling the memory of my Dream List and my pleasant ride with Buckshot, I tried to go all the way back to the beginning of my life. What was the very first thing that I could remember?

A picture began to come clear, I remembered riding in the back seat of a car. Cousin Annabelle was sitting beside me and Daddy and Uncle Harley were in the front seat as we traveled along a country highway.

I'm not sure how old Belle and I were at the time, but we must have been quite young because I remembered that we were both wearing pretty

7

panties with rows and rows of ruffles across the back, and that we had complimented each other on how pretty they looked.

There were no seatbelts back then, the cars were big and roomy and Annabelle and I were full of energy, and playing loud and wildly. We lay on the ledge under the back window and rolled down onto the seat and then to the floor, then we jumped up and down and giggled and did it all over again.

Suddenly, Uncle Harley slammed on the brakes. Annabelle and I quickly stopped what we were doing, "Uh oh, we're in trouble!"

"That silly joker cut us off!" I heard Daddy shout. Then Uncle Harley said, "They gave us the bird, and in front of our daughters!

"The bird?" I looked at Belle and she shrugged her shoulders. We hadn't seen any bird, we didn't have any idea what was going on, but we knew that the bird must have been very bad because Uncle Harley hit the gas pedal and raced after the men.

Belle and I were thrown back into the seat, we tightly held hands as the car weaved back and forth. The tires screeched and we lurched forward. Uncle Harley ran the other car off of the road and it came to an abrupt halt. It was a sunny hot day and the dry powdery dust billowed into the windows from the shoulder of the worn country highway.

Our angry fathers jumped out of the car. "Wait here girls," they ordered.

I stood up on the seat and looked through the back window as Daddy and Uncle Harley stomped toward the men.

Even though I was only a toddler, somehow I knew that there was going to be a fight. "Get 'em Daddy! Get 'em!" I shouted. I jumped up and down and pounded my tiny fists on the back of the seat. "Get up Belle, our daddies are going to get those guys!"

Annabelle didn't get up she stayed down in the seat covering her eyes. "No, no, I don't want to see!" she cried.

The men in the car were shouting at our daddies, words that I had never heard before. Daddy and Uncle Harley didn't say anything, Daddy walked on one side of the car and Uncle Harley the other, they reached in through the windows and yanked the men halfway out... POW! The blood went flying, splattering on the windshield. Daddy and Uncle Harley tossed the men back into their car, their heads flopped loosely like rag dolls.

"That will teach them not to disrespect our daughters," I heard Daddy say as he and Uncle Harley walked back toward us.

Yes, I'm certain that the men surely had been taught a lesson...Nobody messed with my daddy.

The next thing that I could remember was Thanksgiving, the year that Uncle Henry raised the turkey.

Our mothers planned to cook the meal together, so everyone arrived early in the morning with their special recipes and seasonings. I helped Mommy carry in the big pot, it was nearly as big as me, but I was determined to help out and managed to wrestle it into the kitchen.

After everyone had arrived, Uncle Henry went out to the coop to catch the turkey. My cousins and I could hear the gobble, gobble, gobbling and we ran outside to see what was happening. Uncle Henry was chasing the turkey and it was funny watching the big man trying to catch the huge fat bird. We laughed and giggle and jumped up and down, clapping our little hands.

We were shouting at Uncle Henry, trying to help him out, "Twy to get him in the cono Unco Henwy!"

After about ten minutes of the comical show, Uncle Henry caught the bird and began to carry it to the barn. "Come on kids, you want to help Uncle Henry get the turkey ready?"

"Yes, we will help you Unco Henwy," and we followed him inside.

There must have been about ten of us, all tiny little kids, gathered in the barn to help Uncle Henry with the turkey. He closed the barn door and latched it shut, then without delay, Uncle Henry walked to the chopping block and, WHAP! The big headless bird started running around the barn, its neck flailing and spouting blood. We were running in panic waving our little arms, screaming at the top of our lungs, blood splattering us from head to toe. Uncle Henry was laughing and watching as we ran wildly from the headless menace.

"What's going on here? I thought you wanted to help me," he chuckled. "Catch the turkey kids! Catch the turkey!"

Finally, the turkey stopped running and Uncle Henry picked the bird up by the neck and unlatched the barn door. "Now, who wants to help me pluck the turkey?"

"No! No! No plucking! No plucking!" we all screamed and bolted for the door. We blasted out of the barn, all at the same time. Little Buck's diaper fell down he kicked it off and kept on going keeping up with the rest of us.

I don't remember anything else about that day but later, I found out that the whole thing had been filmed and the movie was played occasionally at family get-togethers. I'm sure that the turkey wouldn't agree, but I suppose that it was funny, in a Wells family sort of way.

Our family was very close, in fact, Daddy and his brothers even worked together, they owned and operated a packaged-home company. The houses were built at the factory and then the walls were stacked on trucks and shipped to the site where they were then erected. The company shipped homes all over the country.

Daddy had a small plane and he used to fly to different job locations to check on progress and scout new sights. I was Daddy's girl and I went everywhere with him.

I adored my father and everything he did was alright with me. I thought that he was the smartest bravest man in all the world. Daddy's soft blue eyes reminded me of a brightly-lit sky, his skin as white as snow, and hair as dark as night. With a cleft in his noble chin, there wasn't another man as handsome as my daddy.

I hadn't started school yet, so Daddy could take me to work with him. I loved to fly and go really, really fast. I remembered the excitement each time we were headed for the airport, as I would soon be soaring in the sky with my daddy. I couldn't remember my first flight because I was too young, but Daddy told me about it. He said that he had just gotten his pilot's license and bought the plane, and he took Mom and me for the very first flight.

Before we went up, Daddy told me that he held me in his arms and walked around the plane explaining things to me, "This is the wing and this is the propeller;" then he pointed to the sky, "and that's where the plane is going to take us Puppy, way up in the clouds."

He said that I wasn't impressed with anything but the shiny chrome letters of the plane's model, Challenger. I couldn't say many big words yet, but I could say, "Chal..len..gerr." I thought that it was the plane's name and from that point on, I called it "Mr. Challenger."

We had a nice flight that first day, sightseeing and enjoying the bright sunshine, but when it came time to land there was a strong updraft and Daddy had to circle the airport three times before he could finally land.

During the time he was circling my mother went hysterical, but Dad said that her reaction didn't bother me in the slightest, I just kept my eyes on him. If Daddy was in charge I had no fear, and from that day on he couldn't keep me out of the plane.

Early one morning, Daddy woke me and asked if I wanted to go to work with him. I excitedly jumped out of bed and was ready to go within minutes. Daddy and I loaded the car and while we headed for the airport, he explained that we were taking a load of brass to a job site, high in the mountains, and that Uncle Glen was coming along.

Uncle Glen was the oldest of my father's many brothers, and he was bigger than life! He wore a big cowboy hat with a jeweled band, made especially for him by a beautiful Indian princess. His boots were shiny alligator skin and the story was that Uncle Glen had wrestled the gator and killed it with his bare hands. Uncle Glen had a big shiny, silver belt buckle that he had won in the Rodeo, and he rode his horse with a spangled silver saddle and bridle and people called him, "The King of the Cowboys."

My Uncle Glen and I had a lot in common he was just as horse-crazy as I was.

Even though I loved my Uncle Glen, I didn't want him along; I preferred to fly alone with Daddy, that way, I had all of his attention. I knew that the men would be talking business and ignoring me, but I still had fun watching the view from the window. The world was so tiny from up there, everything on the ground seemed like cute little toys.

When Daddy and I arrived at the airport, Uncle Glen was already there with the brass, and he and Daddy began to load it into the plane. I tried to help out, but the brass was too heavy for me to lift. "Stay out of the way Puppy," Daddy told me, "you just sit there and look beautiful."

I patiently watched as the men loaded the brass. Challenger was a little plane and the brass was heavy, I could see that it was being weighted down heavily as more and more brass was placed onboard. Then, I looked at Uncle Glen's big belly. Uncle Glen was too heavy! "Oh no! We'll never get off the ground!"

"Too fat, too fat!" I started hollering at my father and pointing to Uncle Glen.

"What's wrong Pup?' Daddy asked.

"He can't go, Uncle's belly is... too fat!"

"Hey Glen, did you hear that? Penelope says that you're too fat."

"Now isn't that just like a woman," Uncle Glen laughed. He picked me up and walked to the plane and put me inside. "You better be nice to your Uncle Glen, my big belly might look pretty good to you later on when you get tired, it makes a nice soft pillow," he chuckled.

I was insulted, "I'm too big for naps."

There were only two seats in the plane, one behind the other; Uncle Glen climbed in behind the pilot's seat and put me in his lap.

When Daddy started the engine, the excitement began to build. I loved flying so much that I could barely contain myself as we taxied to the runway. Soon we would be in the sky! I clapped my little hands with anticipation, "Yay! I'm going flying!"

The highway ran parallel to the runway, with a fence in between, and there was another fence that ran across the end of the runway, with power lines above it. Planes had to be high enough to clear the power lines before they reached the end of the runway.

We started down the runway, faster and faster, trying to pick up enough speed to take off. The wheels left the ground, but when Daddy pulled up he couldn't get enough altitude; we weren't going to clear the wires!!

"Stop! Stop!" Uncle Glen shouted.

"I can't brother we're going too fast, the brakes on the plane aren't good and we'll crash into the fence!!"

Daddy kept his head and banked to the left toward the highway, we were flying sideways, one wing up and one wing down. Uncle Glen held me tight against his belly while he yelled at Daddy. I was being smashed and I kicked and wiggled to get a view out the window, and when I did, I could see that the lower wing wasn't going to clear the highway fence. "Daddy! The fence! The fence!!" I shouted at the top of my lungs.

Daddy tipped the wing up, we missed the fence and flew within inches over the top of the cars on the highway..... RERERERERER!

Daddy began to pick up altitude we were finally free, flying in the sky! I felt a rush of excitement and clapped my hands for joy; I bounced up and down in Uncle Glen's lap, "Yay! We're flying!"

Our destination was in the opposite direction, so Daddy banked sharply to the left and headed back toward the airport.

Uncle Glen wasn't holding me as tightly this time and when the plane tipped sideways again, I plopped down on the window with my hands and face pressed against it.

Uncle Glen was still yelling at his younger brother, "Take it easy Paul, quit playing around! This is dangerous!"

I looked through the window, down at the ground and I could see the people on the highway; they had stopped their cars and gotten out to watch the "air show."

Daddy noticed the attention that he was getting and he buzzed down low over the enthusiastic crowd. RERERERERERERRR!

It was like a rollercoaster ride, I put my hands up, "Weeeeeeeeeeeeee!"

I could see the audience roaring with excitement, they were waving scarves and handkerchiefs, cheering us on.

Uncle Glen was a tough guy and nothing ever rattled him, but he was a little shook up, and Daddy decided to take advantage of the rare opportunity to tease his older brother. He began to fly the plane almost straight up, climbing higher and higher in the sky.

12

"Stop playing around Paul, this isn't funny, we're going to stall!"

When Daddy reached the altitude he wanted...he looped around and we were flying upside down. "Hooray! Daddy! Upside down, upside down!"

"Paul stop being such a show off, that brass is liable to break loose!"

Uncle Glen had me tightly around my waist, "Weeeeeee! Go Daddy go!" I giggled and waved my arms and kicked my chubby legs.

Daddy made a complete circle and when he leveled off, Uncle Glen finally calmed down enough to notice me cheering and laughing and clapping my hands, "Hooray Daddy!"

He began to chuckle, "Paul you're scaring your kid," he joked.

Daddy tipped a wing to say good-bye to the crowd and we were off to the job site. My daddy was a superstar!

It was a long and treacherous flight through the mountains to reach the job site. I watched out the window as the landscape changed from a sunny and friendly country valley to a dark and stormy scene. The rugged craggy mountains were covered with snow and a powerful wind was slamming into the small plane in unrelenting bursts. We were flying against a strong headwind and even though the speed indicator registered at eighty miles per hour, we were barely moving ahead and burning fuel at an alarming rate.

"How's the fuel holding up brother?" Uncle Glen asked.

"It's always close through these mountains, but we'll make it, we always do," Daddy answered.

We had to stop for fuel at the half way point. The company had set up a small makeshift airport for refueling on the mountain jobs.

Despite the turbulent jolting ride, I began to get sleepy and snuggled down on Uncle Glen's belly for a nap. He was right, it did make a great pillow.

Uncle Glen had fallen asleep too, but we were suddenly startled awake by a jolt and a loud BOOM!

"What's wrong?" Uncle Glen asked.

"It's just the wind, but take a look down at the airport."

Uncle Glen and I looked out the window, the runway was narrow and small, nestled in a cleft closely situated between two ominous mountains. The planes on the ground were tightly tied down to prevent the wind from flipping them over and blowing them away. The men at the airport had hung out a rag to act as a windsock, but it was tangled around the pole and completely useless for telling the wind direction. Without a windsock to help with calculations, it was nearly impossible to land in the blustery snowy storm.

"Can we make it to the Connelly job without refueling?" Uncle Glen asked.

"No, we barely made it this far, but don't worry brother, I'll get her down."

"I hope Ma's praying for us today," Uncle Glen said hopefully.

Daddy bravely tried to come in for a landing, but when we got close, a gust of wind blew through the cleft and swept us up the side of the mountain. It felt as though a giant was pulling us up like a toy on a string, but Daddy got control of the plane and broke away.

The runway was situated so closely between the slopes that we had to fly all the way around the highest peak to get lined up again for the landing. Fuel was low, we had to make it this time, it was now or never.

Daddy flew around the perilous stormy peak, preparing to make another attempt to land the little plane. The wind was whipping and I heard the engine sputter… we were out of fuel!! But Daddy did the impossible, and glided in for a safe landing.

After we came to a stop, Daddy got out of the plane and reached in to get me. I jumped into his arms, "Good job Daddy!"

Then Uncle Glen started to climb out, he had one foot on the ground, when the wind caught the plane and Challenger started to tip up and blow down the runway! "Get back in the plane Glen!" Daddy hollered.

It was a struggle, but Uncle Glen managed to get back into the moving airplane before it blew away. He sat inside and waited while we refueled.

There were snacks and drinks inside the nearby shack and I took a candy bar for Uncle Glen. Daddy and I walked back to the plane and he lifted me inside. I sat back on Uncle Glen's lap, reached around his big belly and gave him a giant hug. "You saved the day!" I proudly told him, "and here is your reward!" I gave him the candy bar. "We better take care of that belly, it comes in handy."

Uncle Glen gave me a solid pat on the back. I snuggled down with him and started to go back to sleep. I hadn't wanted Uncle Glen along, but now I was glad that he was here.

Daddy started the engine and we were soon in the sky once again; we flew out of the stormy weather and safely reached the Connelly job.

The last time that I flew with Daddy was just before I started Kindergarten. We were in the big company plane flying four of Dad's brothers to a rush job, just south of San Diego, and we got lost. I was sitting beside Daddy, we didn't say anything to my Uncles, they were napping and we didn't want to stir things up.

I was keeping a sharp eye out for the small country airport, but didn't see it. It was a clear sunny day and we had plenty of fuel so we weren't worried.

Soon, we saw a windsock flying at a landing strip. "This must be it," we concluded, and decided to go in for a landing.

It was an easy landing on the clear calm day and after we had come to a halt, I climbed in the back and woke up my Uncles. We all got out of the plane and stretched and began to look around... the area was deserted.

"This doesn't look right. Where in the world are we?" Uncle Harley asked.

There were no paved roads and in the far distance were rows of partially-built, little shack houses. "From the looks of those houses, I'd say that we're in Mexico," Uncle Buck reasoned.

POP! POP! POP! POP! It sounded like firecrackers, but in a cloud of dust rushing toward us, was a beat-up, old pick-up truck full of men. They were shooting at three police cars that were in hot pursuit. The sirens wailed and the police relentlessly fired back at the men in the truck.

"Paul, get us out of here!" my Uncles all shouted.

Daddy picked me up and quickly threw me back into the plane. He tried to start the engine as his brothers all piled back inside. The engine sputtered, "Don't fail me now baby," Daddy urged.

"Paul, they're heading this way! Let's get going brother!" Uncle Slim hollered.

The engine turned over and the propeller began to spin, we started racing down the runway with the truck chasing after us. The men in the pickup were shouting and waving.

Uncle Lee knew a little Spanish and could understand some what they were saying, "Those silly jokers think that we're here to pick them up!"

The Mexican Police started shooting at us and when the men in the truck realize that we were leaving them behind, they began to shoot at us too!

We were picking up speed, but hadn't left the ground yet, when my uncles pulled out the guns that they had stowed on the plane, and opened fire. "BANG! BANG! BANG!" holding off the angry Banditos. Then our wheels left the ground and we were soon out of range.

"Whoa howdy! That was a close one!" Uncle Lee exclaimed.

"I figure it to be some kind of drug deal gone bad," Uncle Buck reasoned. "Yep musta been," he added as he rubbed his jaw.

"We've got to find the dang job and get to work! Paul, which way are you going?"

The brothers put their heads together, and figured out where we had gone wrong; seems that someone had neglected to give Daddy some key information. We flew north and the jobsite was actually quite easy to find.

Getting lost was no surprise, it was a common thing in our family. Fact was there was never a Wells born with a good sense of direction. There are stories in the family history books about it, and here's one of 'em...

Three of the Wells brothers were making the treacherous trip West, across the country with a wagon train.

Battered by harsh weather and merciless conditions, the group found themselves deep in the wilderness and out of food. Game was scarce and the Wells brothers, who were excellent hunters, went to get meat for the hungry pioneers. After killing a buck, they headed back to their group, but were noticed by a band of fierce renegade Indians who wanted the buck for themselves, and they attacked!

The brothers weren't about to give up the only thing between them and starvation and even though they were three against many, the mighty brothers fought and won the battle.

After the bloody fight, the boys got turned around and lost their direction. For three days, they were hopelessly wandering in the rough unfamiliar territory. Dangerous animals and Braves on the warpath lurked around every corner, but the brothers kept going, carrying the buck on one of the horses and searching for their desperate starving friends in the wagon train.

The brothers saw a familiar landmark and in an attempt to get their bearings, they got off their horses to view a rough handwritten map. Suddenly, a bear, smelling the bloody deer meat, came up behind them. "ROARRR!" The horses bolted, and the bear, after easier prey, attacked the brothers. The fight was on and the brothers were out of ammunition.

Everyone knows that you can't outrun a bear, but too late for pretense, the boys broke free and hightailed it out of there! When the three cleared the thick brush... Halleluiah! There was the wagon train! The brothers ran full speed toward their family and friends, they were a-yelling and a-shouting with the bear close on their heels.

A redheaded teenage girl, named Maggie, in petticoats and a pink bonnet, heard the shouts and saw the Wells brothers running for their lives. While the others scrambled around in a panic trying to figure out what to do, Maggie reached into her wagon, grabbed a big rifle and... BOOM! With the inaccurate old weapon, the little gal hit the lumbering bear right through the eye, and dropped it at over a hundred yards.

Once the bear was down, the Wells boys whistled for their faithful horses, and the horses came galloping out of cover. Everyone was happy to see that the boys were still alive and between the buck and the bear, there was plenty of meat for the duration of the trip.

The group didn't have any more trouble with the natives either; after their battle with the Wells brothers, the Indians had respect for the strong fierce warriors and didn't attack again.

But things weren't exactly happily ever after. After seeing the way that Maggie had downed the bear, all three of the brothers wanted to marry her; she was their kind of gal. They fought over Maggie, practically killing each other in the process and great-great-grandfather won. Little Maggie was my great-great-grandmother. I never met her of course, but I heard that she was as beautiful as she was strong, and I'm proud to say that some think that I favor her bit.

My grandma and grandpa were both wonderful people, but they didn't live together. Grandma lived at home and Grandpa went from family to family, helping his children wherever he was needed. It was always a thrill whenever I saw Grandpa walking up our driveway. He was a very wise and patient man and the time that I spent with him was precious to me. Grandpa was an old time cowboy, and in the spring and summer months, we had rattlesnake and scrambled eggs for breakfast. When the weather warmed up, the snakes came out and Grandpa killed the ones that came near the house. He used a tool that he made himself; it was spear-like, similar to a frog-gigger.

Grandpa told us kids to stay inside the house with the doors shut when he went out to kill snakes; but I loved Grandpa and I wanted to be with him all the time. So one day, when he went out to kill rattlers, I wanted to go with him. Grandpa didn't discourage me, we simply walked into the mudroom together and he gave me one of his spear-like weapons, then we went outside and hunted for snakes. I wasn't afraid because I was with Grandpa.

It didn't take long before I found a snake hole and Grandpa told me to jab my spear inside. I hesitated for a moment, got up my courage and thrust the spear into the rattlesnake hole. I hit something and quickly pulled back on the spear. I was not prepared for what I was to encounter arising from that dark black hole; I had pulled up a squirming hissing demon, straight from the pit of hell! The snake was twisting around and striking at my spear; poison ran down the wooden pole. Then the snake spotted me, our eyes locked and a shiver went down my spine. Its head rose up and it began to rattle its tail.

I looked into the face of that rattlesnake; it was the meanest ugliest thing that I had ever seen. It hissed and spit and opened its mouth wide. I saw its big fangs and its evil forked tongue, but the thing that frightened me more than anything else were those black B-B eyes, they looked like the devil was looking at me right through them.

I knew that the snake was preparing to strike, it wanted to kill me. I hoped that it didn't have enough slack to reach and I stood strong, firmly holding my spear.

It never got a chance to strike at me, Grandpa was quicker than that ol' snake; he pinned down its head, "Finish it off!" he shouted and I chopped off its head.

The body squirmed around like it was still alive. I knew that it was dead and that it was just the nerves making it move around, but I couldn't help being afraid that it was still gonna get me somehow.

"Throw it in the sack," Grandpa instructed. I did, but not with my hands, I used my spear.

"Now look for another hole," Grandpa said. "You push harder this time; really drive that spear home before you pull it back out."

"Another one, Grandpa? I think I've had enough."

"Okay," Grandpa laughed. "You did good, go on in the house with the other kids."

I was relieved that he had let me go and I hoped that he didn't think that I was a sissy, but I never wanted to see an ugly snake face again. Those hideous eyes looking at me, I could never get them completely out of my mind and I was haunted by them at night, for years to come.

As it turned out, Grandpa wasn't disappointed in me, he said that I was the only girl who had ever hunted rattlesnake with him and he bragged about how brave I was.

Grandpa skinned the snake and we fried him up. I ate that ol' sidewinder and he tasted pretty good too.

Grandpa made me a hatband from the skin, positioning the snake's head in the front with the mouth open wide, exposing the fangs. It was my trophy and it meant a lot to me; I put it on my cowboy hat and I wore it everywhere.

Spending time with Grandma was very different than it was with Grandpa. Grandma came from a wealthy highfaluting family. She attended the best schools and met Grandpa while she was in college. Grandpa had gotten into college on a football scholarship; he was a rough-and-rowdy cowboy.

Grandma had been sheltered all of her life and she had never met anyone like him before. They say that opposites attract and it was certainly true in this case; Grandma, the petite elegant lady and Grandpa the big rough tough guy. They fell in love and were soon married.

Grandma was a strong God-fearing woman, a woman with a true mother's heart. She devoted her whole life to her family and she cared for all of us. There was never any jealousy or competition among the grandchildren in the family, vying for her attention, there was plenty of love for us all.

Grandma called us all by the same pet name, Weezie. And strangely enough it didn't matter how many of us Weezies were grouped together, when Grandma called a Weezie, somehow we all knew to whom she was speaking.

Grandma didn't have to take us to amusement parks or do any of the things that most kids find exciting, because just being with her was special. She taught us how to bake and even showed us the secret ingredients to her famous recipes, things that she never let anyone else know. Grandma had been cooking and baking for so many years that she simply measured ingredients by the hand full. "Your hand is smaller than Grandma's so you put in one and a half handfuls," she would say.

Grandma taught us how to sew by hand and we worked on beautiful quilts with her and listened intently as she unveiled the secrets of life.

When Grandma was a young mother, she had a powerful life-changing experience with God and was blessed with the gift of second sight. It was never clear to me exactly what second sight was, but I did know that Grandma knew things about the future that no ordinary person could have ever known.

Grandma was an intercessor, and would sometimes fast and pray for weeks at a time when God laid a burden on her heart. I believe that she was combatting evil forces, to alter a dark future for someone that she loved.

Grandma rarely spoke of her special gift, but one time, and one time only, did she tell me a secret about myself. I remember it vividly, just as if it were yesterday. I was sitting across from her, holding a quilt piece in my hand when grandma began to speak. I always listened to every word that she said, but by the tone of her voice I knew that this was something very important. "Penelope," she said in a serious tone, "there is something that you are meant to do, a mission for you and you alone. When you find it, the world will open up to you. But don't get ahead of God, your timing must be right, or you will fail."

"I'll do my very best, Grandma," I promised.

Grandma's words were burned into my mind. Would I be able to find

19

the special thing that I was meant to do? Would I be able to fulfill my mission in life? Only time would tell. But I was a mere child, there was certainly no hurry, I had the rest of my life to discover it.

As far as I was concerned, my grandma was the greatest woman who had ever lived. There was nothing in this world that I wouldn't do for her, and one day, that devotion was put to the test.

One special weekend, my cousin, Linda Lou, and I both got to spend the night at Grandma's house together. That was something that rarely happened, and we were so excited that we could hardly stand it.

We arrived at Grandma's after lunch, on a Saturday, and spent the next hour happily sewing on a brightly colored quilt while we listened to Grandma explain to us about prayer.

"When someone comes to your mind and you feel concern for them," Grandma said, "that's God's way of telling you to pray for that person. Don't worry about them; worry is of the devil, you pray until the burden lifts. Then, you trust God to do the rest."

"That's enough for now," she said as she began to pick up the sewing and put it away, "you girls need some fresh air and exercise, go on outside and play for a while."

"We don't want to play Grandma, we want to help you. Is there anything that we can do to help out around here?"

Grandma sent us into the backyard to pull weeds. She showed us what a weed looked like and gave us a bucket to put them in. The backyard was a full acre and Linda Lou and I decided that we would pull all the weeds from the entire yard, not just the small bucket full that Grandma had asked for. If Grandma needed something done we were ready to do it for her; that, and much, much more.

Linda Lou and I worked hard until we had cleared the whole acre of weeds. We proudly marched into the house and showed Grandma all the weeds that we had picked. She praised us and told us what a good job we had done and Linda Lou and I were beaming with pride. Grandma sent us to the bathroom to clean up and when we had finished we started working on the lovely quilt again.

A short time later, we could smell the aroma of fried chicken cooking in the kitchen. Grandma sure did know how to fry up a chicken! Lou and I were extra hungry from working so hard in the yard and our mouths were watering like a couple of old hound dogs. It seemed to take forever before Grandma finally called us in for dinner.

Grandma started putting the food on the table, and what a spread! Fried chicken, biscuits and gravy, corn on the cob, mashed potatoes and a big glass of raw milk with the cream floating to the top. What more could a hungry kid ask for?

I quickly said grace and Grandma started piling food on our plates. Yum, yum, and just when I thought that it couldn't get any better, I heard Grandma say, "Grandma made apple pie and ice cream for dessert."

(Not once in my life did I ever see my grandmother eat; she was always busy caring for everyone else, making sure that they had everything that they wanted during a meal.)

Linda Lou and I were using good manners, but we were practically in a feeding frenzy. Then it happened... Grandma came walking to the table holding a bowl, and with the big silver spoon she plopped a whopping helping of weeds on our plates! What in the world was going on? Why was Grandma feeding us weeds? Was she okay?

Linda Lou and I looked at our plates and then at each other; what were we going to do about this? "Grandma, we don't like weeds," Lou told her.

"Oh my," she answered, "Grandma worked very hard making these greens for you."

Well, if Grandma worked hard, there was no way that we were going to hurt her feelings and we started to eat the weeds that we had picked from the yard.

When Grandma went back to the stove for a minute I asked, "Lou, do you think that they're poisonous?"

"I don't know," she answered, "but I'm not going to hurt Grandma's feelings, even if she did go crazy."

Linda Lou and I choked down every last weed and hoped we didn't die. We made it through the rest of the evening without dying and when bedtime came around, we were happy that we were still alive.

Grandma put us in the big fluffy bed and tucked us in for the night. She always rubbed our backs and prayed for us until we were fast asleep. I tried to stay awake and feign sleep, but I was just too tired and I dozed off. I woke up later, and checked on Lou and found that she was still breathing. All through the night, Linda Lou and I continued to check on each other. When the sun came up the next morning, we knew that we had made it, we had eaten the weeds and lived, and we hadn't hurt Grandma's feelings!

Later that day, when Uncle Slim came to pick us up, Linda Lou told him of our concern for Grandma. Uncle Slim walked into the kitchen where Grandma was serving us up some pie. "Ma, what in the world are you doing, feeding these girls weeds? They're afraid that you've gone loco."

Grandma explained that she had fed us dandelion greens. "You girls have had dandelion greens," Uncle Slim said, "they're good for ya. What in the world are you complaining about?"

We were relieved that Grandma hadn't gone crazy, but we were upset that Uncle Slim may have embarrassed her, or that we had hurt her feelings. "We're sorry Grandma, we didn't know that it was okay to eat weeds."

"Not all weeds," she said. "You ask your fathers before you eat anything from the yard, some plants are poisonous."

"We know that some plants are poisonous Grandma and we were hoping that the ones we ate weren't."

"You mean that you thought I had gone crazy and may have been feeding you poisonous weeds; and you ate them anyway?"

"We didn't want to hurt your feelings Grandma."

"So, you'd rather eat poison and die than hurt your old Grandma's feelings," she said lovingly with a smile.

Grandma was sitting in her big stuffed, rocking chair; she pulled us up into her lap and rocked us in her arms. Lou and I leaned on Grandma's chest and closed our eyes, we loved her more than we loved our own lives.

I never heard Grandma say the words, "I love you." Instead, she showed me love and she taught me how to love. Grandma built a strong foundation for me and had a love so powerful that it continues to live on and hold me up, even to this very day.

One of the yummy ways that Grandma showed us love was baking. She made a terrific blackberry pie and my cousins and I were willing to do whatever it took for a piece of it. We would carry baskets and go off on a mission to get enough berries for her to make a pie.

Unfortunately, the berry bushes were on Old Man Woodman's property, the meanest man in the valley; but cousin Anna Belle and I weren't about to let that stop us. Old Man Woodman's blackberry bushes were at least eight feet high and twice as wide; they trailed on down the property for about a half an acre and the berries were big and juicy. When we approached the barbed wire fence, the danger began. Old Man Woodman had six hound dogs and they could hear and smell everything. Making sure that we were downwind from the dogs, we separated the barbed wire and carefully climbed through. Then like soldiers in the battlefield, we crawled on our bellies until we reached the berry bushes.

Using the wooden planks that we had left there on our previous heist, we leaned them on top of the bushes. Then oh... so... carefully... we walked out on the shaky wobbly planks and begin picking berries. Every step would sink us deeper into the thorny vines, and each reach for that big juicy berry was a balancing act without a net.

Seeing the crooked prickly vines twisting under and around the plank, I wondered what would happen if one of us lost our balance and fell. We would be eaten by the massive razor-toothed monster and ripped to shreds, never to be seen again. I couldn't see how anyone could ever escape such a peril.

We had only filled our baskets about half way when Anna Belle stumbled. Luckily she caught herself, but the hounds heard her gasp. "Run! Run!" she screamed. And run we did, as fast as we could, the pack of hounds howling and barking, frenzied, racing to attack us, the invaders.

We could hear the old man shouting, "You kids get off my property!" Then it sounded like the sky burst open, BOOM! A shotgun blast cracked through the air. The dogs were gaining fast, the old man kept yelling and shooting the shotgun. BOOM! BOOM! BOOM! And we ran even faster.

"Anna Belle, do you think we're out of range yet?"

"Just hold on to the berries!" she screamed back.

We clung to the baskets full of our precious loot and when we reached the barbed wire fence, we leapt clean over it. One of us usually took some rock salt in the behind, but that was the price we were willing to pay.

Of course Grandma never knew what we did to get the blackberries, but I'll tell ya what, blackberry pie never tasted so good!

Christmas was another great family holiday. Like most kids, I looked forward to Christmas, but I thought that Christmas, for my family, was more special than for any other, as it was always magical. Every year my mother would take me shopping and buy me a beautiful new Christmas outfit. The year that I was seven or eight years old; Mom and I selected a green satin and chiffon dress. It had puffy sleeves and a sash that tied in a big bow in the back. I had lots of stiff petticoats underneath to make it full and fluffy. I got shiny patent leather shoes with a cute little purse to match and a white fur cape. The thing that I liked most of all was the fur muff; I slipped my hands inside and it kept them toasty warm. I usually hated dressing up, but I loved this outfit and couldn't wait to wear it to the family Christmas party and show it off.

Mom had attended a prestigious finishing school and was a professional fashion model. She had incredible and rare eyes which were a sharp bright yellow and they became her trademark. Mom always made sure that we looked our best whenever we went out, as keeping up appearances was very important to her.

I was a tomboy and Mother didn't like it, especially when she was trying to fix my hair. It seemed to take hours as she pulled it up and pinned and arranged the curls. Before she was done, she usually had cracked me in the head with the brush a few times because I whined and wiggled and complained, but when she finished I looked like a princess.

Today was the day! Christmas Eve had finally arrived and it was time for the family Christmas party!

We were in the car driving to Uncle Buck's house and I sat in the back seat of the car, rubbing the bumps on my head from being cracked by the hairbrush. I was careful not to muss my hair, I knew better, but nothing could get me down today, it was Christmas time.

When we arrived at Uncle Buck's, everyone else was already there. Grandma and my aunts had made our favorite dishes and we all sat at the long dining table. Grandpa said grace and thanked God for our many blessings, then we feasted on the delicious food.

After dinner, my cousins and I played and had a good time, but always in the back of our minds was the lingering question, when was Santa going to arrive?

Finally, we heard jungle bells and the sound of reindeer hooves stomping on the roof. "Santa's here! Santa's here!" we all shouted with glee as we ran wildly through the house.

"HO, HO, HO!" There he was, it was Santa, in person, coming through the front door with his big bag of toys. Santa couldn't get into the house; he was carrying so many toys that his bag was stuck in the doorway!

"HO, HO, HO," the jolly Santa laughed again as the bag burst open; toys scattered as he pressed through the doorway.

"Santa! Santa!" we all rushed to circle around him. "We love you Santa!"

"Are there any good little children here tonight?" he asked.

"Yes, yes!" we all chimed in together, our eyes bright with anticipation.

Santa sat on a chair and his helper called out the name of each child. The air was wild with excitement as we waited to hear our names and sit on Santa's lap, to receive a gift. We anxiously watched as our brothers, sisters and cousins opened their presents. It was a wonderfully exciting time.

As a rule we usually played with the cousins who were closest to our own age. In my group there were six girls, all born within four months of each other. Santa had given all of the girls in my group, an adorable little baby doll, equipped with bottles, cute tiny clothes and buggies. My cousins and I were busily feeding our dolls and pushing them in the

24

buggies through the rambling old house.

The girls and I considered the older group of cousins, the big kids. That year, the big kids got boxing gloves. When cousin Travis opened up the his gift, he immediately slipped on the gloves and cousin Johnny grabbed the other pair. My Uncles and the other big kids formed a circle around them in the family room and... the fight was on!

The girls and I stopped what we were doing to watch the excitement. Some of the Uncles and cousins were cheering for Travis, and others were for Johnny.

It was brutal watching my cousins boxing, they were punching each other hard and I soon realized that this was no game, it was a fierce fight. It was horrible, but still, there was something about boxing that excited me.

When I saw Johnny knock Travis down, I thought that the fight was over, but all it did was heighten the excitement. "Get up! Get up!" Uncle Slim shouted at his son as he pounded the floor by Travis' head.

Travis got to his feet then, the bell rang, "Saved by the bell!"

It was like a real boxing match, both of the boys went to their corners and their fathers coached them, planning the strategy for the next round.

Ding!... the bell rang and the fight was on again. Travis had an opening and hit Johnny in the nose, Johnny staggered and I thought he might go down, but then he surprised us all and punched Travis square in the face. Travis fell to the floor, and he wasn't getting up this time.

Johnny sighed and shook his head, then he wiped the blood from his nose with his shirtsleeve. "The winner!" Uncle Buck announced as he raised Johnny's arm.

I was worried about Travis, but no one else seemed to be concerned, they were all busy congratulating the winner.

I was watching Travis lying on the floor, but I couldn't get to him through all of the commotion. He soon shook it off and sat in a chair; when I got closer, I could see that he had a split lip, but seemed okay otherwise.

Uncle Slim patted his son on the back, "You kids have it easy," he told Travis. "When I was your age we boxed to the knockout, every time."

I wondered why Grandma and my aunts were allowing such a thing, and I came to find out that they weren't anywhere in the house. None of the girls knew where they had gone and more fights commenced.

The big kids never cried and they never complained, they stepped into the ring and fought like warriors. It was the way that we had been raised, tough to a fault.

The truth of the matter was, that the big kids really weren't that big at all, they were only ten to twelve years old. I was happy that I was the oldest child in my family and that my brother wouldn't be expected to fight, as he was way too young.

All of the big boys in the family had fought until they could no longer stand. Then I heard it, it was mean Uncle Henry, "Let's see what these girls are made of," he loudly clamored.

Then someone answered him, "I'll put my Pup up against any of yours!" It was my dad and he meant me!

Uncle Henry shouted back at Daddy, "You think that that scrawny little girl can fight? Let's see how she stands up against my Cupcake! Come on Cupcake, get in there and show these sissies how it's done."

"Oh no, not Cupcake!" Cupcake was bigger and stronger and faster, and she always beat me! Of all the kids in the family, why did it have to be her?

I guessed that Dad must have seen this as a chance for me to finally defeat Cupcake. He had been the boxing champion in the army, and started me boxing as soon as I learned to walk and had solid footing. Dad didn't want me to grow up to be a defenseless, helpless female; he wanted me to be able to take care of myself. He would get on his knees and teach me how to throw a punch and guard. Later, I learned how to take a punch and handle the pain. He had taught me well, and now my skills would be put to the test.

Uncle Henry's challenge had been accepted. Dad put the gloves on me, and as he laced them up the excitement began to build. I felt energy racing through my body and I bounced from one foot to the other.

"You know how to box Pup, don't let her intimidate you, use your jackhammer jab and wait for an opening."

Cupcake and I walked into the center of the ring and she whispered to me, "Penelope we don't really want to hurt each other, let's pull our punches and just put on a good show. Okay?"

It was true, I didn't want to hurt my cousin. "Okay," I agreed. Then we tapped gloves and returned to our corners.

Ding!... The first round began; Cupcake and I punched each other on the gloves and moved around the ring looking each other sternly in the eye. One, two, three, punching one another in the arms and shoulders. We were putting on a good show, and no one was getting hurt.

"Come on Cupcake!" Uncle Henry shouted to his champion.

"You can take her Cupcake!" Grandpa yelled. (Grandpa had learned from experience not to bet on me against Cupcake.)

My father didn't give up, he was faithful and cheered me on, "You look good Pup….. looking good!"

I did everything that Dad had taught me to, but I pulled my punches just like Cupcake and I had agreed.

The crowd of cousins and uncles began to roar, they wanted action! "Let her have it Cupcake! Now!" Uncle Henry yelled at the top of his lungs.

I wasn't too concerned since this wasn't a real fight, but Cupcake didn't honor our agreement and she let me have it, right in the gut! She hit me so hard that it knocked the wind out of me and bent me over. I went down on my knees trying to catch my breath. "That blasted Cupcake! I never could trust her!"

The count began, "One, two, three, four…."

"Get up! Get up!" all the little cousins in my group shouted to me in their tiny voices. "Cupcake you're horrible!" they screamed and jeered at her. "Get up Penelope, you've got to get up!" They knew what Cupcake was like, she was a mean-spirited kid who always cheated, and one of us usually ended up getting hurt.

When I heard my little cousins cheering me on, it practically pulled me to my feet and I caught my breath. What Cupcake had done was wrong and I raised my fists and began fighting again… for real this time, and I was fuming mad.

"Don't get rattled; don't lose your head," Dad warned, "keep your guard up!"

Cupcake wildly threw one punch after another, pow, pow, pow, she knew that she had knocked me for a loop and she was moving in for the kill. Cupcake was good, she made contact every time. I was taking a beating, but I wasn't hurt, I had managed to block everything that she could throw at me.

The girls were appalled at the viciousness of her attack, "Stop it Cupcake, you're a jerk!"

The bell rang and I hadn't hit Cupcake, not one time.

When we went to our corners, I noticed that the sleeves on my special dress were ripped; chiffon doesn't hold up well in the boxing ring. "Oh no; my dress!"

"Don't worry about your dress Pup, you're doing a good job out there, she's getting tired. How you holding up? You feel alright?"

"I feel great Dad, I'm gonna get that Cupcake this time, you just watch, she's going down!"

My little cousins were in my corner, "You can do it Penelope, you can get that mean ol' Cupcake."

Ding!... It was round two and I had already been knocked down once. Negative thoughts came into my mind, "Cupcake always beats you, you can never win at anything against her, especially not in a fight; she's stronger and much bigger than you."

"Come on Penelope you can do it... you can do it... you can do it!" my little cousins chanted as they jumped up and down cheering me on.

I pushed the negative thoughts from my mind, I was determined, this time I was going to win! Cupcake was fierce and strong, but I wanted the victory more. She was confident, but she wasn't going to beat me, not this time!

Cupcake and I were chubby-cheeked little girls, but we fought with all our might in our frilly little dresses. Our long curls bounced and our fancy hairdos fell as the pins came loose when we were punched in the face and head.

I survived the second, third and fourth rounds. Cupcake was definitely the stronger fighter, but my jackhammer jab was taking a toll on her. I knew that I was fighting out of my league, but I wouldn't give up no matter how hard she pounded me.

When the bell rang, I went to my corner. I had taken some hard shots to the face; my eye was bleeding and beginning to swell. Anna Belle was prepared and iced it right away.

"Have you had enough? Do you want me to throw in the towel?" Dad asked.

"No Dad, whatever you do don't stop the fight! The cut's not that bad, I can still see."

Blood ran down my satin dress and dripped in a puddle on the floor. Linda Lou looked at me, "You better stop, your eye is really swelling up."

I could feel the pressure and the pain, and my eye was partially closed. "No, I'm not giving up!"

"Okay Puppy, knock her out!"

The bell rang, I didn't look good, the cut was bleeding worse and my eye kept swelling, closing it more and more, but my dad and the girls stuck by me.

I had to take Cupcake down, not just for myself but for the girls and my dad as well. I was tired of Uncle Henry making fun of my father every time that Cupcake beat me at something. I was tired of Cupcake taking cheap shots at the girls, hurting them and always getting away with it. She was a sneak and a bully and it was up to me to teach her a lesson; everyone was counting on me.

Cupcake was fighting harder than she ever had before. I was trying to protect my eye and that was what she was aiming for. It was difficult for me to see on that side and she was taking full advantage.

I heard Uncle Henry, "She's done Cupcake, take her out!"

Cupcake opened up and blasted me with everything she had, but she got careless and left herself wide open. This was the opportunity that I had been waiting for, Cupcake was finally mine! I cocked my fist to give her the knockout punch…. Suddenly the door burst open, it was Grandma, "You stop this fighting, right now!"

"Match over!!" Grandpa announced.

Cupcake and I put down our hands and I walked slowly toward her, "Well, maybe next time Cupcake,"…………POW!!! Cupcake sucker-punched me square in the nose. I fell to my knees, blood sprayed from nostrils, my eyes teared up and pain shot through my head.

That stinkin' Cupcake threw her head back and started laughing at me. The loud hideous laughter rang through my ears, it was maddening. I pulled myself together and stood up. I could see just enough through the blood and tears to make out Cupcake's outline, and I let her have it, full force, right in that big fat mouth of hers. CRACK!!! Her head whipped back, and then she fell forward, right on me. I caught her in my arms and held her for a moment. "Fight's over Cupcake," I said, and I threw her to the floor. She was out cold.

Dad scooped me up and put me on his shoulders, the girls were cheering as I was carried around in a victory parade. My mind was hazy and I was bleeding from my eye and nose. I couldn't even see, but it was one of the happiest moments of my life!

The rest of the day is kind of foggy, but I do remember Aunt Bessie cleaning me up. By the time she got hold of me, one of my eyes were swollen shut and both of them were starting to blacken. While she was trying to get my nose to stop bleeding, I could hear my mother screaming at Daddy, "That dress is an original, and it's completely ruined! You don't know how hard I worked to make that kid look nice! And her face, she'll never look the same! Boo hoo hoo!"

Mom was right, I didn't look the same, from that day on, I had a bump on the bridge of my nose; but to me, the victory was well worth it.

My father didn't treat me like a girl, and I thank him for it. It may sound cruel to some people, fighting little girls in the boxing ring, but without Dad toughening me up, I would have never survived the hardships of a cruel and unforgiving world.

I had finally defeated Cupcake, but there was one thing that I wanted even more, that didn't get for Christmas that year, a horse. I wanted a horse more than anything else in the world. Every night when I said my prayers, I asked God for a horse; every birthday when I blew out the candles I wished for a horse of my own. And every Christmas, I asked Santa to bring me one thing, and one thing only, a horse.

One hot summer night, I saw a falling star and like always, I wished for a horse, hoping with all my heart that it would come true and the next day it did! Daddy brought home a rowdy little horse that he had named Dynamite! When I saw the stunning jet black animal being unloaded from the trailer, I was so happy that I felt as though I were walking on air.

Later, I found out Dynamite's story; she was out of a well-known racehorse, but was a bit small and it was assumed that she wouldn't be fast enough to compete with the much larger horses. Dynamite was never given a chance to prove herself and was sold as soon as she was weaned.

Sleek and beautiful, Dynamite was bought by a highfaluting family who wanted to make a polo pony out of her. A high-spirited racehorse, Dynamite wasn't suited for polo. She was too wild and unruly; she couldn't settle down enough to play the game and was soon sold again.

Selling Dynamite was an easy task as she was an exceptional looking animal. But as soon as her new owner rode her and tried to hold her back, Dynamite blew up; she took off with him and found herself for sale once again.

Dynamite went from owner to owner and finally ended up at the end of the road, working in a string of horses taking city slickers on afternoon trail rides.

Working the string didn't last for long either, Old Lady Snodgrass, who owned the business, soon realized that her new horse was a lawsuit waiting to happen. Dynamite would never allow another horse ahead of her, she always had to be first and would go to any extreme to get there.

The old lady put a sign out on her gate, "horse for sale," and when Daddy spotted the stunning animal, he bought her for me.

"This horse has had a hard time finding a home," Daddy told me, "maybe it's because she was meant for you. When this baby runs, she blows up like a keg of Dynamite," he said patting her on the neck and looking at her admiringly. "This is a hot-blooded animal Pup, and she's not been trained properly so don't run her too fast until the two of you have had the time to get to know each other." Then Daddy handed me the lead rope.

Dynamite held her head high and flashed her eyes about. She was nervous, wondering what was in store for her. I caringly led her around

30

the ranch and introduced her to all of the other animals. She met the dogs and the chickens and the cows, and then we took a casual ride by the creek and had a cool drink of water.

It was starting to get late so I put her away in a stall. "You get a good night's sleep Dynamite, and tomorrow we'll go for a real ride and have some fun."

The next morning, I got up early and Dynamite and I went out riding. I did what Dad had told me to, and I took it nice and easy. But hours later, in the afternoon, Dynamite and I came upon the wide open flatland. She tossed her head, and snorted and began to prance and breathe heavily with excitement. I knew that she wanted to run across the plain and so did I… Yah! Let's go girl!

Dynamite made a powerful lunge forward…KA…BOOM! Almost instantly, she was at top speed! Dynamite ran like the wind, like I had never seen an animal run before. "Go girl! Go!" I urged her on. I could feel the pulsing pounding of her powerful heart; Dynamite was doing what she had been born to do…run. We raced through the grassy fields until we had crossed the entire plain, and when we got near the fence… "Come on girl, let's go!" Over the fence she went, as graceful as a deer, she hit the ground running and kept up the fast pace.

When we had gone a little further, I pulled back on the reins, "Whoa." Dynamite didn't want to stop, she was excited and she fought me. "Easy girl, take it easy."

Dynamite bowed her neck and snorted, jumping and trotting sideways. I stroked her neck, "Easy girl, settle down now."

Finally, Dynamite did settle down and I walked her slow the rest of the way home to cool her off.

When we got back to the ranch, I jumped out of the saddle and when I reached to take off her bridle, Dynamite nuzzled my neck. It tickled and I started to giggle, then she rubbed her nose all over my head. I thought that she was going to try to eat my hair, but she didn't, she just breathed in my scent. I wrapped my arms around her and patted her sleek shiny neck. We both knew it, Dynamite and I were two of a kind!

Every day we ran the countryside together, free and wild. We jumped the creeks and fences, nothing could hold us in. Dynamite was the most exciting thing in my life.

It was only a month later, when Uncle Glen invited me to ride my fabulous new horse with him on the Sheriff's Posse Annual Trail Ride! It was especially exciting for me, as kids weren't usually invited.

The day of the big event, I wanted to look good enough to ride with my

Uncle Glen; after all, he was The King of the Cowboys. I cleaned and polished my bridle and saddle and gave Dynamite a special grooming. Then, I dressed in my cowgirl best, suede chaps, shiny new cowboy boots and my hat with the rattlesnake band. I stood and admired my hat it in the mirror, "You look real mean rattlesnake, hisssssss." I made a face as I hissed at the snake in the mirror. I was ready to ride.

Uncle Glen picked me up and we were off, trailering our horses behind us.

The trail ride was held on private property, and what a spread! The scenery was magnificent and we couldn't have asked for nicer weather if we had ordered it ourselves.

There were about a hundred riders on the trail that day, and Dynamite wasn't the lead horse; she didn't like it, and was continually trying to bolt ahead and pass the other riders. It was hard holding her back, she was snorting and prancing sideways and making me look bad.

With Uncle Glen being The King of the Cowboys and all, some of the other riders started to poke fun at us. It didn't faze Uncle Glen, but it embarrassed me.

About halfway into the ride, we came to a small bog and the horses and riders began to cross over. As the horses crossed the muddy ground, it became softer and murkier and each horse that followed sank in deeper.

The horses crossing the bog, jumped and bucked up in panic, they thrust back and forth struggling to break free of the deep mud, and as they did, their riders were being thrown off left and right.

When it came time for Dynamite and me to cross, I was a bit nervous. Dynamite stepped in and sank in deep; she jumped, lunging forward and back, struggling to free her legs from the strong suction of the mud and cross the bog.

But Dynamite was different from the other horses, she loved me, and every time that I started to fall off of her, she stopped and stood completely still until I had regained my balance. Each time that Dynamite stopped for me, her feet would sink into the mud again, but it didn't seem to matter to her how unsafe she felt for herself, she put me first and wouldn't allow me to be hurt.

After we had crossed over, Dynamite and I stood and looked at the other riders scattered on the ground, moaning and complaining about their backs and knees.

Some of them had managed to get to their feet and were running willy-nilly, calling and trying to catch their expensive, highly-trained horses. These horses were happy to be free of their strict riders, grabbing a bite or two of grass as they trotted away from them.

"Who's embarrassed now?" I laughed to myself.

Dynamite and I worked for hours helping the other riders catch their unconcerned wandering horses. It was hard, but I resisted the urge to poke fun at the mud-covered abandoned riders.

I've had mean horses try to crush my leg against the fence and I've even had them run under low tree branches to try and brush me off of their backs. A good horse will never try to harm you, but Dynamite was much more than a good horse; no matter how wild and crazy things got on our many adventures, I never once fell off of her, she wouldn't let me.

After the trail ride, Uncle Glen bought me a fancy new bridle; it had long braided reins with a strap at the end. "Use the strap when she acts up and fights to take the lead," Uncle Glen told me, "break her of that bad habit."

Uncle Glen was always very good to me. I loved my new bridle and I thanked him with a big hug and a kiss on the cheek.

I would do my best to train Dynamite. She couldn't always be first, and she would have to learn to deal with it.

The valley where my family lived was a peaceful and beautiful place to grow up. With tall trees, crystal clear streams, and fresh clean air, it was the picture of a perfect childhood dream. But there was a dark shadow that was always looming, and ever-present hatred... the feud.

People know what a feud is and I'm certain that most think of it as a joke, but let me assure you that a feud is dangerous and very real. Even as children we were always aware of the imminent violence that could erupt at any moment if someone crossed the line.

Back in the day, we had our own law in the valley. The ranchers were the law and they executed swift punishment the way they saw fit. A beating or fistfight would sometimes settle it, but there are scores of dead men buried in shallow graves in the hills.

People had been divided since the beginning, when the territory was first settled and it was a free range. The cattlemen came first and then the sheepmen, but cattle and sheep can't graze the land together, and the trouble soon began. Cattle wrap the grass around their tongue and pull it up into their mouth to eat. Sheep bite the grass off all the way down to the nub, leaving nothing for the cattle to feed on. Sheep destroy the pastures and leave the cattle to starve.

Through the years the ranchers fought, cattlemen against sheepmen, battle after battle. Eventually, the sheepherders were driven from the fertile valley and the boundaries were drawn, but not until after much bloodshed. Fathers and sons and brothers had been killed, the resentment and hatred ran deep. Even though fences were up and the range war had been settled many years before I was born, it was still a heated issue and very much alive.

My cousins and I had pictures in our young minds of the sheepherders who lived outside the valley. We were certain that they had horns on their heads, carefully hidden by their hair and maybe even fangs and claws that came out at night! Those evil monsters who wanted to kill our cattle and destroy us.

We all knew to tell the menfolk immediately if we spotted a sheep near our property. Missing sheep or cattle could lead to a quick accusation and maybe even death, or another war.

As children we accepted the situation as normal and merely stayed away from the sheepherder monsters, their sheep and their land. We never crossed the line, not even in fun, we all knew better. It didn't concern me most of the time except when I was near sheepherder territory in the unfenced pastures of the southern foothills.

It had been a long hot summer, the tenth year of my life. The land surrounding the ranch was overgrown and dry as a tinderbox, and it posed a serious fire threat. We had been taking turns herding the cows out beyond the fence line to graze and eat down the overgrown grasses. The cows were the best of the livestock to take in the unfenced areas as they were friendly and easy to handle.

Our cows were special and they knew it; they acted as though they were members of an exclusive club. They gave the best milk in the county and it made me feel special just drinking it. Rich thick cream and sweet butter, our cows gave it all to us. As a child, I was amazed by them and thought that they were magic.

It was Saturday, my day to take the cows out to the wild pasture. After they had been milked, I saddled Dynamite and "escorted the girls" off for a day of special grazing. I enjoyed those lazy days, out alone with Dynamite and the cows. I relaxed under a big tree and chewed on a twig while I watched them all feed.

When the cows would get too close to sheepherders land, I would jump on Dynamite and herd them back, closer to our property. I was careful never to cross the line.

I loved all of the cows, but my favorite one was Moo Moo. I think Moo Moo thought that she was responsible for me because she was always near. It was comforting, the sweet cow standing by watching over me with those big brown eyes, adorned by the long luxurious lashes; she was

34

a real beauty.

It was early fall and the weather had been sunny and warm, so I left the house without a jacket. But a few hours later, a cold damp wind came whipping through the valley and I was getting miserable. I huddled on the ground and pulled my knees to my chest, trying to stay warm. I was shivering hard and my teeth were chattering, but I couldn't leave my post.

Moo Moo came slowly walking over and lay down beside me to block the wind. I moved up against her warm body and leaned on her shoulder. Moo Moo wrapped her head around me and covered me with her big neck. Instantly, I was warm as toast and I relaxed and sighed in relief. I wrapped my arm around the huge cow and gave her a few pats. "Thank you Moo Moo," I said as I stroked her shiny coat.

I was cozy, safe and warm and before I knew it I had fallen fast asleep. I remember of dreaming pleasant childhood dreams about castles and clouds, when Moo Moo nuzzled me awake. The bell was ringing; it was milking time. I yawned and stretched and got to my feet. Then I took a quick glance around and I didn't see the other cows! "Oh no! Had they wandered too far?"

Fear gripped me as I jumped on Dynamite. I had to find the cows; this was serious, as serious as anything could ever be. The bell at the barn was steadily ringing and I hoped that the cows would hear it and come running for their grain. I frantically flashed my eyes from one end of the pastures to the other as Dynamite and I raced along, but the cows were completely out of sight. If the sheepherders had my cows they might already be dead. Would I ever find them?!

I galloped over a small hill and into a canyon, and there I saw the cows peacefully grazing, ignoring the supper bell. I quietly called to them, but like the bell, they ignored me too. The chubby cows were enjoying the wild oats that they had found.

I worked my way past them and began to drive them home. We were headed for the ranch when I heard someone or something in the bushes. I was close to sheepherder property and my first instinct was to run, but I couldn't leave my cows behind.

I decided to face whatever it was and I quickly zeroed in on the noise. It was a boy, about my age, hiding in the brush and in his hands… a B-B gun!

Our cows had been shot by B-Bs before and here he was, the perpetrator; I had caught him red- handed! "He's not going to shoot my cows again," I said to myself through clenched teeth.

I was angry and I turned Dynamite toward the boy, grabbing my lasso

35

as we dashed ahead at a gallop. I was quickly upon him and the boy was shocked. "Put that gun down, boy!" I shouted as I made a pass by him.

There was so much brush in the way that I couldn't lasso the kid, so I hit him hard with the lasso and knocked him down. When the kid fell, the B-B gun went off and shot me in the arm. It stung like the dickens and blood squirted from the wound, but it just made me more angry. "Knock it off, you jerk!" I shouted.

I had to act fast, before the boy had a chance to get his bearings and shoot me again. Even though it was just a B-B gun, it could still put an eye out.

I turned Dynamite around and when we got close I leapt from her back on top of the kid and we wrestled, rolling around in the brush.

At that age, there isn't much difference between boys and girls, girls are equally strong. I managed to get on top of the boy and pin him down on his back. I was straddling him, holding his arms down with both of my hands. We were face to face, just inches apart, "Don't you move a muscle, you dirty sheepherder."

This was the closest that I had ever been to a sheepherder and my chance to solve the mystery. I took my hand and pushed the boy's hair back and found that he didn't have horns.

The boy looked up at me and a big smile appeared on his face. "Wow," he said in amazement, "you're a girl."

"Yeah that's right, I'm a girl alright, a girl who's gonna kick the guts out of you if you don't do what you're told. Now gimmme that gun!"

"Sure, anything you say," he willingly agreed.

When he loosened his grip on the gun, I took it away from him. "Don't you ever mess with my cows again!" I was out of breath and held my fist in his face as I shouted at him, but he just kept smiling at me.

When I got up, I slammed the gun against a rock and threw it as far away as I could, then I scattered the B-Bs. "You won't be shooting another cow with that gun!" Then, I stomped away from him toward my horse.

"I'm sorry I shot you," the boy apologized, "when you hit me, the gun went off accidentally."

"Yeah, sure it did sheepherder," I said as I climbed up on Dynamite, "and I suppose that you aren't the one who's been shooting my cows either."

"It's true, I wouldn't shoot your cows, I wouldn't shoot any animal; I was just target practicing, shooting at that old log over there. Check it and see for yourself, it's full of B-Bs.

I glanced toward the log and from where I was sitting I could see a paper target and it did look like it had B-B holes in it.

"Even if you did shoot at the log, it doesn't mean that you weren't going to shoot my cows too. You aren't supposed to be over here anyway, sheepherder, stay in your own territory!"

Just then, I heard the sound of a man's voice; someone was looking for the boy. I was sitting on Dynamite and I could see him clearly; he was carrying a shotgun and walking through the brush toward me. He saw me too, "Who are you?" he shouted.

He was coming from the direction of sheepherder property and I hightailed it out of there. The cows were well on their way home and I quickly caught up to them. "Come on girls, let's get home for supper!" I prompted, and drove the cows home.

On the way home I thought about the sheepherder boy. I hadn't seen any horns on his head and he didn't even cuss me out when I broke his gun and scattered his ammo. He actually seemed like a nice kid, some might even call him handsome. Maybe he wasn't a monster at all. Could it be that I had misjudged him?

When I arrived home, I hid my arm, bloody from the B-B wound. The boys were waiting, ready to milk. "What took you so long?" they asked.

"Aw quit hassling me," I answered. "Tell Ma that I'm heading out to Linda Lou's."

I was finished working for the day, and that night Lou and I had planned a sleep over at her house, so I rode Dynamite straight over.

When I arrived, Linda Lou was waiting for me in the driveway and we put Dynamite away in the barn. "Lou, let's go to the secret fort, I've got to tell you something."

We snuck to our secret fort, making sure that no one saw us. By the time we got there, Linda Lou had noticed the blood on my shirtsleeve. "Oh my gosh, what happened?"

I rolled up my sleeve and showed her the wound. Lou got the first aid kit and while she dug out the B-B I told her the story. "I probably should have left the kid alone," I said. "Ouch! But I was sure that he was the one that's been... ouch! Shooting the cows, and I had to stop him. What do you think Lou, will the sheepherders come after me? What should I do? Should I tell?"

Lou and I discussed it, it was a big decision. "The man saw you huh?"

"Yes, he asked me who I was."

"Well, sure he knows that you're a cattlemen's daughter by now, and you broke the kid's gun. That man is bound to find out what you did, unless the boy plays it smart and keeps his mouth shut."

After the discussion, we were quiet for a moment. We knew how our fathers would react if they found out that someone had shot me, especially a sheepherder and there would be trouble for sure. We decided to keep it a secret and hope that the boy with the B-B gun would do the same. We walked slowly to the house dreading what might happen in the next few days.

When we walked through the front door, Aunt Bessie had a nice supper prepared. "I was just about to call you girls," she said, "now get in there and get washed up," she instructed, and shooed us into the bathroom.

When Uncle Slim said grace that night, Lou and I prayed extra hard that God would stop the trouble with the sheepherders. We quickly finished eating and when the dishes were washed we went to Lou's room and found a nice surprise. Aunt Bessie had bought both of us new pajamas and quilted robes with slippers to match. We took our baths and put on the new pajamas; they were lovely, soft pink with satin ribbons and bows.

We decided to play beauty parlor and set each other's hair in sponge rollers, to look nice for church the next morning. Everyone knows that you can't play beauty parlor without having the full treatment, so we snuck into Aunt Bessie's vanity and used her cosmetics. Lou and I gave each other manicures and pedicures and then decided to try our hand at make-up. We weren't sure how to use much of it, but we did our best and made up each other's faces. We were trying for a glamorous look, but when we viewed ourselves in the mirror we found that we looked much more like circus clowns than the glamour girls that we had expected. Pink circles drawn on our cheeks, red lipstick smeared around our mouths and blue and brown smudges on our eyelids and brows. We both giggled and laughed until our tummies hurt.

We soon realized that we had beautified each other as much as we could and we didn't want the fun to end, so we prowled the house looking for our next victim. Certain that Linda Lou's older brothers wouldn't submit to treatment we shanghaied the family dog, Rex. Rex was an old hound dog and didn't have much interest in anything but hunting, but he was a good sport and tolerated us while we brushed and perfumed him, and then painted his toenails. The finishing touch was a little fancy hat that we had taken off of a doll and tied around his head. I don't know if Rex actually liked the hat, or if he thought that he had to wear it, but he didn't take it off. He was the perfect addition to our newly forming circus act.

Linda Lou and I had planned to stay up until midnight, just for the fun of it, but we didn't succeed. Once we had finished beautifying Rex, we fell asleep on the rag rug in Linda Lou's room. Uncle Slim came in later and picked us up and put us into bed.

We had been sleeping for several hours, when suddenly, we were startled awake by the sound of a loud siren wailing through the valley. Something was wrong! But what? We were frightened and Linda Lou and I ran from the bedroom to find Aunt Bessie and Uncle Slim. The door to their bedroom was closed and we frantically knocked. "You girls go on back to bed," Uncle Slim shouted.

Lou and I couldn't go back to bed; we just had to know what was going on. We didn't move from the door and stood quietly listening, trying to figure out what was wrong.

"Slim you can't go," Aunt Bessie said, "you've been having heart flutters all day! The doctor told you to relax and get plenty of rest."

"I took an oath to defend this valley," Uncle Slim answered, "and as long as there's breath in me that's exactly what I'm going to do! Out of my way, woman!"

We heard the sound of Uncle Slims' big boots heading toward the bedroom door and we quickly scrambled and hid before we were discovered. He headed out to the front of the house where he was joined by my father and Uncle Lee.

Lou and I ran to the window and watched their Cadillac drive away. It was night, but the sky wasn't dark, it was brightly lit … the valley was on fire!! Flames covered the surrounding hills and pastures, and the crops were burning! Linda Lou and I looked at each other in terror and wrapped our arms tightly around one another. We both knew what the other was thinking… the sheepherders were taking revenge, they were burning us out!

Lou and I helplessly watched from the window as the huge fire devoured the land. God hadn't heard our prayers.

A short time later, we saw the Cadillac coming back up the driveway, the men were already returning. Uncle Slim came stomping back into the house, "Bessie, get the boys up, I'm gonna have to take them out with us. The fire's raging at the north end of the valley, Harper's barn's on fire and his girl is trapped inside. My other brothers and the volunteer fire department are fighting to save her and get the fire under control. It's up to us to defend this end of the valley!"

Linda Lou and I rushed out of her bedroom, "Uncle Slim we want to fight the fire too!" I announced.

"You girls just stay out of the way," he kindly demanded.

But Linda Lou boldly argued our case, "Jack and Travis are only two and three years older than us. If they can fight the fire we can too!"

Uncle Slim merely patted us both on the head with his big heavy hand and then walked out the backdoor. "Back the flatbed up to the pump house!" he ordered.

Lou and I watched the men back the truck up and then pick up a big metal water-trough and load it on the bed of the truck. "Lee, get the other end of this rope," Uncle Slim said, and he and Uncle Lee tied the big water-trough to the bed of the flatbed truck. Dad positioned the hose to fill the trough with water, and then he loaded some red tanks from the Cadillac onto the truck and some gunny sacks.

When the trough was full, they placed plywood on top to keep the water from splashing out. "We're ready to roll! Load up!" Uncle Slim shouted and Dad and Uncle Lee climbed into the cab with him. "And you boys sit on the trough and hold down that plywood!" he added.

Jack and Travis climbed up on the back of the truck and Lou and I watched the truck start on its way down the driveway toward the front of the house. Suddenly, I felt emotion well up inside me, "Lou, I have to help fight the fire, the whole thing is my fault!"

"Okay," Lou answered, "let's go, but we have to hurry, we don't have time to change."

We rushed into the bedroom and quickly slipped on our cowboy boots, then ran full speed out of the house after the truck. The wooden screen door slammed with a bang behind us, and Rex raced out ahead still wearing the funny hat. Lou and I had on our new pajamas and robes, but we didn't care, we just had to get on the truck and fight the fire! "Stop! Stop!" we shouted as we tried to catch up. We were running fast in the dark and fell and skinned our knees; we were hurt and had ripped holes in our new pajamas, but we still didn't give up. We scrambled to our feet and just kept on running and running as fast as we possibly could.

Rex caught up and leaped into the back of the truck with the boys. "Go back girls, go back," Jack yelled, "you'll never catch up!"

But somehow we did catch up and the boys reached down and pulled us up on the truck. Lou and I sat on the plywood catching our breath, and the bumpy ride began. Uncle Slim drove the truck off the road, through a field and then began to climb a hill. The hill was steep, almost straight up, the engine of the old truck was straining, and black smoke was pouring out the back. We were rolling backward and I could smell the brakes burning! Then Uncle Slim shifted gears, we lurched ahead and began to slowly climb the steep grade.

All of us kids stayed on top of the trough clinging to the ropes that held it to the truck. We were struggling not to fall off as the truck bounced into holes and over rocks and mounds and jerked back and forth. It was a rough and dangerous ride.

The ropes were strong, but they were worn and under a lot of strain. I was wondering if they would hold when one of them broke loose; the trough shifted, but it didn't fall off. We were lucky; no one had gotten their fingers caught.

We kept hanging on, hoping that we would reach the top of the hill before the heavy trough slid off the truck. The truck lurched forward one more time, and I felt the trough begin to slide under me. Lou and I jumped forward, toward the cab, and clung to a chain that was hanging there. If anyone were in the way of the trough when it hit the ground they would be crushed. Travis jumped off the truck and rolled a ways down the slope. I watched the trough hit the ground with a crash and a boom as it flipped and rolled violently down the hill.

I quickly looked for Rex and the boys, was everyone okay? I spotted Travis, but I couldn't see Jack, "Jack, Jack!" I frantically screamed.

Then from under the truck bed I saw a hand reach up and grab hold of the side. "I'm here." It was Jack; he wasn't hurt and Rex was barking and running back to the truck.

The men managed to stop the truck and they got out, "You blasted kids, we told you to sit on the trough!"

"The rope broke!" Jack said in our defense.

"Well get back on the truck, now we've got to pick the thing up and refill it."

We drove back down the hill, with the truck brakes burning and smoking all the way. We picked up the trough and refilled it at the Avalar Ranch. No one said anything about Linda Lou and me being there and we were happy that they didn't take us back home.

To reach the worst of the fire, we still had to get over the hill, but this time Uncle Slim didn't get in such a hurry, instead of trying to go straight over the top, he drove at more of an angle and we made it.

When we had crested the hill, I found myself right in midst of the wildfire, in the choking smoke, scorching heat and searing flames.

We jumped off the truck and waited for orders. Uncle Lee took hold of one of the red tanks; it had a hose at the bottom with a spray nozzle on it. He strapped it on his back, "You boys fill the other tanks and let's get to fighting this fire!"

"Let's go! Let's kill this fire!" all of us kids shouted in response.

Linda Lou and I grabbed one of the filled tanks and tried to strap it on;

41

it was unbelievably heavy.

"Oh no you don't," Uncle Lee scolded, and he handed us two gunny sacks. "You girls have the most important job of all," he said.

I looked at the pathetic gunny sack that I was holding, and wondered what he could have possibly meant, "the most important job of all," but I waited patiently to hear my assignment.

Uncle Slim helped the boys strap on the heavy red tanks. The boys weren't much bigger than us girls, but they muscled up and carried the tanks on their backs like the men.

"Now you kids listen," Uncle Slim instructed. "We have to use as little water as possible. You boys make the first pass and knock the flames down low with the water. Then you girls follow with the gunny sacks and pound the flames out the rest of the way. Now girls, be sure that the fire is completely dead, leave no hidden spark or it will start burning again, that's very important!"

"Yes sir!" we answered, and we started firefighting.

Lou and I followed behind the boys, we swung the sacks over our heads and smack, smack; we pounded the flames out just like Uncle Slim had told us to do.

Suddenly, the men were hollering at each other; they had gotten a call on the radio and started running. "You kids stay here," they ordered as they ran out of sight. I don't know where they were going, but they were sure in a hurry to get there.

Linda Lou and I stayed behind with the boys and we were working hard. Those sheepherders weren't going to burn us out, we wouldn't let them! We kept swinging those gunny sacks over and over again, stomping out the flames. The smoke was choking us, our eyes were irritated and pieces of burning debris and hot ash scorched our skin, but nothing would stop us from defending our homes.

Jack and Travis moved ahead, out of sight and into a canyon, and Rex went with them. Linda Lou and I moved at a slower pace, working steadily.

Later, we saw Rex returning, he was running fast and frantically barking. "The boys must be in trouble, that's Rex's danger bark!" Lou said with alarm. "Where are the boys, Rex?" Rex signaled with his head for us to follow and we ran after him. He led us straight to the boys; they were boxed in the canyon, completely surrounded by the ominous fire.

"Boys, can you hear us?" we shouted through the flames.

"Get Dad, there's no way out!"

"Okay, we'll get help!"

"Hurry, the flames are almost on us and we're completely out of water, we can barely breathe!" they said, gasping for air and coughing with every word.

Lou and I took off like jets, we ran in the direction that we had seen the men go, screaming and crying, for our fathers and Uncle Lee, but there was no sign of them.

"Penelope, it's hopeless we'll never find them in time and the boys will die if we don't do something!"

"You're right Lou; we'll have to save them ourselves!"

Linda Lou and I made a dash for the truck; we had to run all the way back in the opposite direction and time was running out. The fire was growing taller and taller, consuming everything in its path. We were both in a panic. Would the boys be burned alive? Lou and I were running hard and out of breath, but we couldn't stop. We had to keep pushing ahead, Jack and Travis were in desperate trouble; their lives were on the line.

Finally, I could see the truck in the distance. "Just a little further Lou." I could hardly get the breath to speak.

When we reached the truck, Linda Lou and I jumped up on the bed and threw all the gunny sacks into the water trough and then we jumped in ourselves. Once we were completely soaked we gathered all the heavy wet sacks and began running again to where the boys were trapped in the flaming tomb. When we got to the entrance of the canyon, we cloaked our bodies with some of the wet gunny sacks. Linda Lou and I looked at the menacing wall of flames and then at each other.

"Boys," Linda Lou called to her brothers, "we're coming in to get ya!" But there was no reply.

We quickly tore holes for our eyes and pulled wet sacks over our heads, this was it!

"Lou, just keep on running until we reach the boys! We've got to get them out now!" I said, wondering if we were already too late.

We stood side by side and leapt directly into the towering wall of fire. I can't explain the intensity of the heat and smoke, the bottom of my boots were melting and felt hot like coals. Lou and I fought our way through the fire and reached the boys, they were on the ground and they weren't moving. Were they still alive? I reached over and touched Jack; he jumped to his feet and so did Travis, "Girls, thank God you're here!"

We were all coughing and struggling to breathe. The smoke was unbearable and choking us, we had to move fast; if the flames didn't kill us, the smoke soon would.

Linda Lou and I, gave the boys wet gunny sacks and as they wrapped up in them, I wondered if we could make it back out. We held hands and all jumped into the searing flames together. Scorched and burned, we made it through to the other side and fell to the ground coughing and trying to catch our breath.

We were all in pain, but soon had our bearings and started jogging back toward the truck, removing the gunny sacks as we went; there was still a job to be done. When we reached the truck, the boys re-filled their tanks and strapped them on their backs. Then, we started fighting the fire once again.

It didn't take long before the boys were ahead of us and out of sight again. "I hope that they're more careful this time," Linda Lou worried.

Lou and I kept beating out the flames with the gunny sacks, making sure that that fire would never re-start in any of the area that we had worked. We concentrated on what we were doing. We had to pay attention; it was dangerous, the air was bad, and we were continually getting burned.

Hours passed. Slap, slap, slap, slap, over and over again, the sound of the gunny sacks hitting the ground. I stood up to stretch my back and noticed something in the distance moving toward us. "What was it?" I questioned. When I looked closer, I could see that it was an old lady in a motorized wheelchair! "Lou look, a lady, she must be in trouble!"

Linda Lou and I ran to meet the old lady; it was true, she was in trouble. "Help me, please help me, my house is about to catch fire!" the old lady hollered.

"Okay lady we'll help you!" Linda Lou and I bravely offered.

The old lady didn't ask us if there were men nearby who were stronger and more capable. She didn't underestimate our abilities, or make light of our offer because we were "just little girls."

"Thank you girls," she said confidently, "I could really use your help. Climb onboard and ride with me, it's quite a ways and I don't want you tuckered out before we even get there."

Lou and I climbed on the wheelchair, the lady pushed the control lever forward and we were off. That wheelchair must have had a supercharged motor because we were really moving fast, racing wildly over the burnt crusty ground. Linda Lou and I in our dirty ash-ridden pajamas, our faces still adorned by the clown-like makeup, now smeared and running down our cheeks. Half of our hair was in sponge rollers, and the other half loose and partially burnt. The three of us rolled on, hair flying, riding on the old lady's hotrod wheelchair. I didn't know what to expect next.

"I'm Penelope," I introduced myself, "and this is my cousin Linda

44

Lou."

"Pleased to meet ya girls; folks just call me Granny."

The wheelchair hit a bump and Lou and I almost fell off, so we held on tighter. The old lady chuckled, "Having a hard time keeping up with ol' Granny, are ya youngins?"

"Don't worry Granny, we're okay." Linda Lou and I smiled at the tough old granny.

Granny went up and over a hill, and she headed south into sheepherder territory. "Are you sure that you know where you're going Granny?"

"Yes a course I do, my spread is on the other side of this here hill."

Linda Lou and I grimly realized that Granny was a sheepherder. "Were we being led into a trap?"

Granny took no notice of our concern, "Yeah," she went on to say, "one a the first fires started on the other side of that there crik. The men folk thought that they had put it out and left me alone to go and help them people over yonder; had their house catch fire. After they left me, the dang fire started up again and jumped the crik. I been here a-fightin' it by myself, wetting the shingles and the brush around the house and I was doin' pretty good too, 'til the dang power went out and the pump house shut down. I filled the bathtub and all my pots when the trouble first started, glad I did too, at least I got ya some drinkin' water; that is, if the house don't go up in smoke before we get there."

Linda Lou and I realized that if the fire had started here in sheepherder territory, it was clear that the sheepherders hadn't started it, and we breathed a sigh of relief. We liked Granny, she was a tough old gal and sheepherder or not, we were determined to do whatever we could to help the charming old lady.

Granny pulled the wheelchair up in front of her house. The sheep were in a corral close by and the flames were coming near. The sheep were in a panic, jumping and bleating, trying to leap over the fence to escape. The smoke was blowing right into their corral and I realized that the poor sheep were probably having a hard time breathing and I felt sorry for them. I walked over to the corral and a tiny little lamb pushed its head through the fence rails and baaed to me. I reached down and patted it; it was the first time that I had ever been close to a sheep. "Don't worry little lamb, I'll save you," I said. And I meant it!

We had to move fast if we were going to save Granny's house. The bushes near the house were ablaze. The flames were high and shooting sparks that were landing on the roof; it could ignite and go up at any minute.

45

The fire was extremely hot, and the flames so high, that Lou and I couldn't get close enough to beat them out with the gunny sacks. So, we had to take another approach. We dipped the sacks in the sheep's water trough and ran with them straight for the fire. We crouched down low and threw the wet sack on the base of the flames, then we quickly retreated before we caught fire ourselves.

Time and time again, Lou and I dipped the gunny sacks and ran and threw them on the hellish flames. When they got low enough we beat them out, but the fire was just too big and no matter how hard we worked we were merely holding it at bay. I could only hope that help would come before it was too late.

Linda Lou and I had been up since well before dawn, and had been going nonstop ever since. I didn't know how we were still on our feet, but somehow we kept moving. If we stopped, the sheep would have to be turned loose to fend for themselves, and Granny's house would burn down.

After a few more hours, Lou and I both reached a state of exhaustion. When we ran ahead to throw the wet sacks on the base of the flames our legs would collapse, and we began crawling away from the fire each time.

Just when I thought that we couldn't go on, I heard a big truck approaching. It was a fire truck! Granny was saved! The fire truck made a pass down the fires' trail and sprayed it with the big hose. When they had put out the fire the firemen just kept on going, waving as they drove away.

Linda Lou and I stumbled to Granny and fell on the wheelchair with her; it was over! She wrapped her arms around us and held us tight. "Never underestimate the power of a child," she said and she kissed us both on the foreheads.

Minutes later, we saw Uncle Slims' truck barreling around the hill. It was loaded with cattlemen and sheepmen alike. "We saw the smoke and the fire truck, is everybody okay?"

The men jumped off the truck and with them, the cute boy and his father that I had encountered the day before.

"Yes, everything's fine here, thanks to these two brave girls," Granny answered. Granny reached out to shake Dad's hand, "Just call me Granny," she said with a smile.

"Yes Granny, they are brave girls and you've got quite a son and grandson here too. They've been fighting the fire with us, shoulder to shoulder, every step of the way."

"Any news of the Harper girl?" Lou and I asked the men.

"She's fine," Uncle Lee told us. "I've seen her, and she's in much better shape than the two of you!"

Lou and I were happy that the Harper girl was okay. Then we looked at each other, covered in soot and ash and we understood exactly what Uncle Lee meant. Our hair was crispy and charred and we were covered with burns and blisters. Our eyes were so irritated that they were blood red and our eyelashes and brows were singed.

"Looking better than us today isn't saying much," Lou croaked. Her throat was so irritated that she spoke in a funny raspy voice that sounded like a frog and we all laughed.

Granny invited everyone into the house and she wheeled Linda Lou and me in with her in the chair. "Well fellas with the power off, can't do much cookin' I'm afraid that the best I can offer ya is cold beans and cornbread."

We all ate together, cattlemen and sheepmen sitting at the same table. The men made an agreement that day to work together. The cattle would graze the open land first and then the sheep would follow; sheep that bite the grass off all the way down to the ground. There would never be another wildfire again.

That night, when I climbed into bed, I realized that God had heard me after all. He had put an end to the feud once and for all and I thanked him for answering my prayer. God works in mysterious ways.

One day, not long after the fire, I was riding Dynamite in the hills between cattle and sheep territory. Now that the feud was truly over, I was free to explore the new range. I reached the top of a hill and stopped to look over the sheepherder land. I could see the sheepherder boy in the distance with his sheep and herding dogs. It was incredible watching the clever dogs working the sheep; I had never seen anything like it before. I watched the dogs run the sheep from one end of the pasture to the other, separate them into groups and then bring them back together again.

I wondered why the boy was running the sheep around the pasture and I rode down the hill to have a closer look. "Hey, sheepherder," I called.

The boy looked up and saw Dynamite and me making our way toward him. "Come on now Penelope, you know my name is Skip."

"Yeah, I know your name alright, it's just gonna take me a little time to get used to it. What in the world are you doing, herding those sheep all over the place? You're gonna run all the weight off of 'em."

"It's a lesson, the older dog is showing his son how to herd and I'm teaching him to respond to different whistles than his father does. That way, when they're working together, I can give separate commands to each of them."

Skip whistled to the two dogs to demonstrate and they circled around and herded the sheep right to us.

Dynamite was high strung, she didn't like the baaing noisy sheep, so I dismounted and held her.

"Nice horse," Skip commented.

"Yeah, she's a beauty alright." I stroked Dynamite's face and she calmed down and closed her eyes, enjoying the attention.

"I've got a horse now too," Skip told me. "I'm going riding with my friends as soon as I put the sheep away. Would you like to come along?"

"Sure, sounds great." I was excited; none of my cousins enjoyed horseback riding as much as I did and I usually ended up riding alone, so a little company was a welcome treat.

Skip whistled to the dogs and they herded the sheep toward the house and into the corral. Then Skip and I walked to the barn and saddled up his new horse.

"Nice looking animal," I told him. "Strong rear end, looks like a quarter horse. Dynamite's a Thoroughbred; see how deep her chest is? Big heart and lungs to get the oxygen to her body when she's running long and hard." I proudly patted Dynamite on her sturdy chest.

"My friends will be interested to meet you, Penelope, they've never met a cattlemen's daughter before."

I was a little tense, I wasn't sure if Skip's friends would accept me and when we rode down the dusty lane; they were already on their horses waiting for us.

I, of course, was wearing my special cowboy hat and one of the boys noticed right away. "I like that rattlesnake band. How much will ya take for it?"

I was happy that the kid was being friendly, but I wasn't about to part with my special hatband. "Thanks, but it's not for sale, killed the rattler myself."

"Cool," they all commented, and we were on our way.

"This is kind of a miracle," I thought as we plodded along, "me, riding with sheepherders." It was something that I had never thought possible.

The four of us rode our horses all afternoon, across the creek and through the hills. It was great; I had found friends who enjoyed horseback riding as much as I did.

Skip and his two friends were adventurous and daring and they raced and challenged me. Dynamite, true to form, was always in the lead.

"Let's show Penelope Devil's Drop," Skip suggested.

"It's pretty scary, Penelope, but would you like to see it?"

"I've never even heard of it, sure, let's go."

The boys headed further south and we climbed higher and higher into jagged rocky mountains. We were riding single file on a very narrow trail, carved into the side of a steep rock bluff. On our right, the rock cliff towered above us, and on our left, a perilous drop to the death.

"You're not a sissy like most girls," the boys told me, "you're actually a lot of fun."

"We'll see who the sissies are around here," I snapped back, "just try and follow me, sissy boys!"

"Yah! Let's go girl!" I shouted to my trusty steed, and Dynamite charged straight up the rock cliff. Sparks flashed from her metal horseshoes as her hooves slipped and scrambled, striking the surface of the hard boulders. If Dynamite fell, it would mean our death, but I knew my horse, she was as sure-footed as she was beautiful.

We made it to the top and I gloated, "The views great from up here. Come on chickens, if you can. What's the matter, can't keep up with a little sissy girl?"

"You're crazy, girl!" the boys shouted back at me. Then they shouted again, "Yee Ha!" and charged up the cliff after me.

The four of us stood at the top of the dangerous craggy peak, the wind whipped through our hair and adrenalin pulsed through our bodies. We looked down at the long perilous drop to the canyon below, and I wondered if I really was crazy.

After that, the boys called me Wildcat Wells and I called Skip's friends, the two brothers, Rowdy and Rascal. I never did know what their real names were.

We headed back down the mountains and the four of us rode our horses into town and got ice cream cones. It was getting late and after I finished my ice cream, I said good-bye and headed for home. The sheepherders were respectable exciting boys, and I liked them very much. Somehow I knew that I had made some true and lasting friends.

After that day, Rowdy, Rascal, Skip and I met every chance we could. We rode our horses together and I was simply one of the boys.

Months passed, it was a Saturday afternoon and we were riding in a rich green meadow. We all got off of our horses to let them drink from the stream and munch on the wild oats growing there.

The sky was full of fluffy white clouds and the four of us laid down on our backs in the soft green grass and watched them slowly float by.

"That one looks like a bear," Skip said as he pointed upward.

49

Rascal disagreed, "No, I think that it looks more like a hippopotamus, Skip, see how big the muzzle is?"

"Yeah, you're definitely right Rascal," I commented, "it looks more like a hippo to me too."

"What about that one over there on the right? Does it look like a jackrabbit to you Rowdy?"

Rowdy didn't seem interested in looking at the clouds, "You know what?" he said. "I'm tired of riding in the same old places every day, it's getting boring."

"Yeah, you're right," Skip agreed, "I wish we were old enough to drive. If we could drive, we could pull the horse trailer and ride in a new place every weekend."

"Yeah, that would be great," Rowdy chimed in, "getting away from here and going someplace new, yep, that would definitely be great."

"None of us even know how to drive, Skip," Rascal said.

"I know how to drive," I proudly stated. "Uncle Henry has old cars out in the field and when we can get gas, we drive 'em. I've been driving since I was five years old."

"Five years old? Aw, you're lying; at five you can't even reach the pedals."

"Yeah, you're right; we were too little to reach the pedals. One of us steered, on our knees in the seat, while the other one laid on the floor and pushed the pedals. We took turns, the one who was steering yelled stop, or go slow, or go fast. It wasn't any fun being the one on the floor, but we did learn how to drive."

"Does your Uncle still have the old cars?"

"Sure he does, but it doesn't matter, we can never get any gas. We used to siphon it out of the tractor, but it made us feel funny and see things. We tried not to breathe in the fumes, but we couldn't help it and we usually ended up laying on the ground watching colors spin around. My Aunt Helen says that we probably all have brain damage cuz of it. We got caught when my cousin Travis swallowed a mouthful of gas and he almost died. After that, we quit trying to siphon and we never get any more gas for the cars. "

"I know where there's some gas," Rascal informed us.

"If we have to siphon it, I'm not doing it, I already have enough brain damage," I told them.

"No, no siphoning," he assured me.

"Well then, what are we waiting for, let's go!"

We all hopped on our horses and rode to Rowdy and Rascals place.

Behind the barn was a shed, and in it, were cans full of gasoline and oil. We grabbed a couple of gas cans and rode over the hills and through the fields to Uncle Henry's place.

"Wait here guys; let me see if my cousin Cupcake is at home."

Sure enough Cupcake was there, and when I told her that we had gasoline… "Ma, I'm going out to play with Penelope," she shouted to her mother, and quickly ran out the door.

"This is my cousin Cupcake," I told the boys. "And Cupcake, these are my friends, Rowdy, Rascal and Skip."

"Put your horses in the corral and follow me," she ordered.

After we put the horses away, we all went to the back pasture where Uncle Henry had the old cars stored. We chose the two cars that we wanted to drive and put the gas in them. We had old phone books that we used to belly us up to the steering wheel, and with a little coaxing the old cars actually started.

Cupcake and I were in one car; the three boys in the other, and we all took turns driving. It was a thrill, just driving around the field in a big circle, one car going one direction and the other car going in the other direction.

I drove first and each time we passed by the boys we all waved and smiled at each other. But when it was Cupcake's turn to drive she wanted more excitement. "Have you ever played chicken, cousin?" she asked me. "Just watch, because you're about to!"

The next time that the boys came around the circle facing us, she turned directly in front of them and pushed the gas pedal to the floor.

"Cupcake, what are you doing?" I asked with alarm as the car raced forward.

"I told you, we're playing chicken."

Cupcake had a determined look on her face; she bit her lip and kept bearing straight for a head-on collision.

The boys must have known about playing chicken too, because they didn't veer away, they kept heading straight for us.

A second before we were about to crash, "Cupcake!" I hollered. "Veer off!"

Cupcake veered to the right, but it was too late, we clipped fenders and both cars spun around.

When we came to a halt, Cupcake was angry, "No sheepherder's going to make a monkey out of me," she grunted and then headed straight for the boys.

The car that the boys were driving had stalled and they were trying to

51

turn the motor over… reer, reer, reer.

"They're sitting ducks," Cupcake laughed. BAM! We crashed into the back fender of the car and kept pushing them around in a circle. The tires were spinning and rubber burning. Cupcake yelled out the window, "Demolition derby suckers!"

The boys were up for the challenge; they got their car started and came after us in a counterattack. "Cupcake! Get out of the way!" I screamed. BAM! They hit us head on, and steam billowed from our crushed radiator as the boys pushed us backward. "Come on Cupcake, get us out of here!"

Cupcake shifted into reverse and hit the gas pedal, the tires spun and the dust flew as we broke away.

By now, I was getting into the spirit of things, "Get 'em Cupcake, turn left, turn left!" Cupcake turned and crashed into the backend of the boy's car, BAM! "Alright Cupcake!" I shouted. "Got ya!" I taunted the boys.

And that's the way it went, CRASH! BOOM! BANG! We smashed and crashed and screamed and hollered. We were having the time of our lives. The dust was thick and the air smelled of burnt rubber and dirt, gasoline and coolant. We had crashed the cars on every side, but the sturdy old vehicles just kept right on running.

Cupcake and I were headed for the boys and the boys were trying to spin around and come back after us, when I smelled smoke! "Cupcake, I smell smoke! We're on fire! Bail out!"

"We're not on fire," she said mockingly, "it's just radiator steam."

Cupcake wasn't detoured, she stepped on the gas pedal to pick up speed and BAM! We slammed into the boys! Our car went out of control and flipped over and Cupcake and I were upside down inside the crushed metal. I was hoping that I was wrong about the fire, but that hope didn't last, not even for a second. There was a swooshing sound and flames shot from the engine, now above us, the bottom of the car was ablaze!

"Bail out! Bail out Cupcake!" I shouted. I wiggled my way out the tiny opening of the crushed window and looked back; Cupcake was still inside, and she wasn't moving. Was my cousin dead? I heard a boom and the swoosh sound again; the fire jumped higher and hotter and it scorched my eyebrows and lashes.

I quickly dove back into the flaming car; I had to save my cousin. I got a hold of Cupcake's ankle and started trying to pull her out through the tiny window opening.

The boys jumped out of their car, "Wildcat, get out of there, it's going to blow up!" Then, they saw that Cupcake was still inside.

"I've got Cupcake by the ankle," I shouted back, gasping and coughing.

"Hold on to her, Wildcat!"

The boys grabbed my legs and as they were pulling me out of the wreck, Cupcake began to regain consciousness. She was disoriented and she started to fight me, kicking me in the arms and head. I kept holding on while the boys pulled my legs. "Stop it Cupcake, it's me! I'm trying to get you out of here, hold still!"

The three boys frantically pulled me, desperately trying to get us all to safety. Finally, I was out and they started to pull on Cupcake's legs, but the window opening was small and Cupcake was a big girl. We got her half way through and she was stuck around the belly.

Cupcake was lucid by this time, "Penelope, get me out of here!" she screamed.

All of us tugged and tugged, but we couldn't get Cupcake through the small opening. I reached inside and put my hands around her waist, it was her belt, it had a big sturdy buckle and it was wedged in the chrome trim that framed the window. Dad had given me a knife, I pulled it from my pocket and cut through the leather belt, we whipped it off and pulled Cupcake from the burning wreck.

KABOOM!!! The car exploded and our clothes caught fire. It hadn't been that long since the boys and I had fought the wild fire, so we didn't panic and rolled on the ground to put out the flames; we were all safe.

Aunt Helen came running out to see what was going on. The field was so ripped up that there wasn't much else that could ignite, and by this time, it was already dying down.

We didn't say much because we were afraid of getting into trouble, but it seems that the only one in trouble was Uncle Henry. My Aunt was furious, "I told Henry to get rid of these old cars, just wait until I get my hands him. Hen...ry!" she shouted as she stomped back toward the house. "Get out here and see the trouble that your daughter got into because you didn't get rid of those junker cars like I asked you too! First Travis almost kills himself trying to siphon gas so he can drive one, and now Cupcake crashes and blows the thing up!"

We had gotten lucky, neither Aunt Helen or Uncle Henry ever said anything to our parents about the explosion. In retrospect, I think that maybe they were concerned that our parents would blame them for the incident.

Anyway, the boys all learned to drive that day... Wells style.

After the "driving lesson," Dynamite and I spent most of our time in the hills. Being in the hills could sometimes be dangerous; there were always rattlesnakes to worry about,(that goes without saying), but at that time there was a mountain lion that had moved into the territory and a pack of wild dogs. They had been known to take down a horse and rider. Dad never told me to stay out of the hills, like I expect most fathers would, instead; he bought me a .38 Special and a gun belt with bullets all around.

"Make sure you always wear your gun when you're riding," Dad instructed me.

Now I carried a pack of matches, pocket knife and my .38 Special, just in case of an emergency.

I loved that gun, it was sleek and beautiful with a walnut handle and a nice long barrel. Dad had sighted it in for me so it was very accurate. Every chance I got, I was out with my horse and my gun. I practiced my quick draw, shooting like a gun fighter. I set up cans, BANG, BANG… BANG, BANG, BANG, BANG. Dynamite let me shoot from her back; we ran passes in front of the cans and I shot 'em off a fence rail. We got pretty good at it too. If something was coming after me, I was going to be ready for it.

I didn't get to practice as much as I wanted to; it seemed as though I had merely blinked my eyes and winter was upon us. I didn't weather Dynamite like the highfaluting people do, blanketed and in a stall. I wasn't trying to impress anyone by keeping Dynamite's coat sleek and smooth, I let her be natural and run the pasture. She could go inside her stall any time that she wanted to, but Dynamite preferred to weather the cold winter storms outside, with her rear end to the wind. Her mane and coat got long and thick and scruffy; she looked like an old plug, but Dynamite was happy, she ran fast and kicked and kept herself in great shape.

We were still deep in the winter months, but the weather had broken temporarily, the sun came out, and the temperature climbed. I was up early that Saturday morning; I strapped on my holster, saddled up Dynamite and went out to shoot my gun.

Dynamite and I rode out by the big boulders and I set up the cans, BAM… BAM… BAM… BAM… BAM… BAM. "Whoa howdy! We got 'em all Dynamite, and in record time!"

I had dismounted to reload and started setting up the cans again when I heard someone calling me. It was the boys. "Wildcat, come on, and bring Dynamite, we have something to show you."

I followed them back to the road and to my surprise; they had a truck and four-horse trailer with their horses already inside.

"Load up Dynamite; we're going to the beach!"

I didn't hesitate, we loaded Dynamite and the four of us pulled out onto the road, headed for the ocean!

"How'd you get the rig?" I asked.

"Our parents are gone for the weekend," Rowdy answered. "I saw the chance for us to go riding someplace new, and I took Dad's truck and trailer."

Rascal was twelve, the oldest of the two brothers, and he was doing the driving. "Yeah, I knew that we could pull it off," he said, "now that we've all had a driving lesson."

"Yeah, that was some driving lesson alright," Skip added, and we all laughed.

It was exciting riding along the highway in the big truck with my friends, but we hadn't gone far when a police car started following close behind us. "Rascal, there's a cop behind us!" Skip said with alarm.

"Try and sit up tall so he doesn't know that you're a kid!" I suggested.

When the cop car pulled along-side us, I thought that we were done for, but Rascal tipped his hat, gave a friendly smile and the policeman passed us by. We were all relieved and we laughed and sang silly songs as we traveled along.

A long time passed, and there was still no sign of the ocean, "Do you guys even know the way to the beach?" I asked.

Skip answered me, "I know a great spot. There's a big parking lot and trails that lead right down to the water. It's a long hike to reach the beach, so not many people go there. It's not much farther, just sit tight."

I was impressed, Skip knew what he was talking about, "Sounds perfect," I replied.

Rascal drove us all the way there and when we arrived at the parking lot we all got out to help him maneuver the big truck and trailer. When he got parked, we all applauded, "Great job!" Rascal was turning out to be an excellent driver.

We soon had the horses unloaded and saddled and started the long trek. It was an incredibly scenic ride through the dunes and down the cliffs to the sandy beach. The ocean roared and waves crashed on the shore, but Dynamite didn't mind at all, she walked right into the surf.

This was a special day and we all knew that we might end up in jail before it was over, so we made the very most of it. The boys and I ran and raced each other for hours and hours up and down the rugged cliffs and through the cold surf. Further and further we galloped down the jagged coastline. At the end of the day, we were worn out and decided that it was time to start heading back. Dynamite was dragging; of the four horses she had run the furthest and the hardest all day, she was hot and foamed up and so tired and winded that she hung her head and slowly plodded along.

"Hey look up ahead," Rowdy said alarmed, "here come some horses, and the riders look like they're dressed in uniforms. I hope it's not the sheriff hunting us down, if it is, we're in big trouble!"

We all decided that it would give us away if we ran, so we just kept slowly walking, closer and closer toward the approaching horses. "Try to ride casual, don't act like there's anything wrong," Skip meekly suggested.

The minutes slowly crept by and when we were close enough to see more clearly, we were relieved that it wasn't the sheriff. There were four riders, boys much older than us; their horses slicked out, trimmed up and shiny, and they arrogantly pranced along with their heads held high. The young men rode with English saddles; they wore sophisticated riding outfits, with polished fancy, leather boots and distinguished riding helmets.

When we passed by, I raised my hand and said a friendly hello.

"Randolph," one of the young men said, "did you hear that hayseed speak to me?"

"Yes I did," his friend answered.

Then the snob addressed me, "If you know what's good for you, you'll stay in your place you dirty little hick."

Infuriated, Rowdy shouted back at them, "You're the one who better stay in your place, fancy pants!"

"Listen hayseeds, it's obvious that you don't know who you're talking to, so let me fill you in. I, am Randolph Lancaster the IV, son of Randolph Lancaster III and this is my horse, Militant Melody. Now out of the way with you and your inferior animals." He then shooed us, as if we were flies.

My father always watched the news, every news program that was on television. I had heard the reports, over and over again about Randolph Lancaster III and his unbeatable horse, Militant Melody. Militant Melody had never lost a race, but Lancaster was thought to be connected to organized crime, and he and his horse had been barred from professional racing for illegal activities.

I took a closer look at the fine animal; he had the distinct star, stripe and snip markings that I had seen in clips of Militant Melody on the news broadcasts. It was true; we were in the presence of the mighty Militant Melody.

Skip had heard of Militant Melody too, we all had. "If that's really Militant Melody, prove it," he said.

"Why should I bother to prove anything to you, hayseed?" the arrogant snob answered.

"Because I'm challenging you to a race."

Lancaster threw his head back and laughed. "You…are challenging me? Why that's the funniest thing I've ever heard," he said. Then all of his friends began to laugh and mock us. "No horse can beat Militant Melody, why you're obviously out of your simple little minds."

"This one can," Skip answered, and then he pointed to Dynamite.

Dynamite was standing there hanging her head and she looked pathetic. She was the smallest, the scruffiest looking, and by far the dirtiest one of the bunch.

The snobs really laughed it up then, "That ugly little thing?" they taunted.

"Skip," I whispered, "what are you doing? Look at Dynamite, she's done in, and Militant Melody has never been beat!"

"Don't worry Wildcat, Dynamite can take 'im."

When the snobs finally quit laughing one of them spoke up, "Oh go ahead and race the hayseed Randolph, just for laughs, it'll be funny. As a matter of fact, let's all race the hayseed."

Rowdy got off of his horse, he picked up a piece of driftwood and drew a line in the sand, "Start here," he said. Then he pointed down the beach, "The rock wall at the end of the beach will be the finish line."

When Dynamite saw the other horses lining up, she knew that it was a race; her head rose up and a spark flashed in her eyes. Dynamite bowed her neck and pranced with excitement, her nostrils flared as she began to breathe in deeply, taking in oxygen to prepare for the race. I gave my gun to Rascal, and Dynamite and I took our place in line.

BANG! The gun shot! The race was on! Dynamite took her powerful lunge ahead, like she always did, she was so fast at the break that the other horses were immediately left behind. "Go! Dynamite go!" I heard my friends screaming in wild jubilation.

Dynamite kept up the pace at a full gallop and stayed in the lead. I could hear Lancaster whipping his horse; they were picking up speed and catching up to us.

Militant Melody was well rested and fresh and Dynamite had been tired out, well before the race had even begun. I didn't know how she could possibly have the stamina to go the distance and win the race against a powerful competitor like Militant Melody.

Militant Melody ran faster and faster and caught up to us, we were side by side galloping at an incredible speed. Our opponent, Militant Melody, was a highly trained, professional racehorse; Dynamite had never been challenged to this degree before.

"Give it up hick, you're all washed up," Randolph sneered at me. He took his riding crop, and with a fiendish look he fiercely tried to whip me across the face with it.

I grabbed hold of the riding crop and yanked it from his hand. "Come on Dynamite, let's get out of here girl!" I urged her on.

Dynamite should have had nothing left to give me, but she had the heart of a champion. She looked Militant Melody square in the eye, as if to tell him something, then, on nothing but sheer willpower and guts Dynamite dug in and poured it on. She ran faster than she had ever run before, it felt as though her feet had left the ground. I didn't think it possible for and animal to reach such an incredible speed, it actually felt like we were flying.

We left Militant Melody and Randolph Lancaster IV behind us in a cloud of dusty sand. When we reached the rock wall Dynamite jumped clean over it, she reared up and whinnied in victorious elation! I waved my cowboy hat in the air and yelled, thrilled at our incredible triumph! There was no question who had won the race; Dynamite was superior, she was truly The Champion!"

The Lancaster bunch was furious at the defeat of Militant Melody. They were shady characters, much bigger and older than us and we knew that they could be dangerous if we allowed them the opportunity. So the boys and I got the heck out of there. We ran the horses down the beach and looped back around to the trailer. We quickly loaded up and made it all the way home without being caught.

We never got the chance to take the truck and trailer out again. Rascal and Rowdy's father suspected that it had been moved, and locked it up, real good.

That left the boys and me plodding along, still riding in the same old places, but I had other plans. "Have you guys ever been to The Horse Center?" I asked.

"Of course we haven't, that place is just for highfaluters."

"We can go there anytime we want to, my Uncle Glen owns the place. We can't ride the horses on the highway, but I've been thinking about it, and I'm sure we can make it if we take the side roads and then cut across to Old Gold Miner's Trail."

The Horse Center was in the next town, and Old Gold Miner's Trail was a winding narrow and very busy road. But the boys were always up for an adventure, and the four of us started off on our quest to The Horse Center.

We rode on the side of the road, being as careful as we could. It was difficult for me to control Dynamite, as usual, she always wanted to go fast and be first. I used the bridle that Uncle Glen had given me with the long braided reins and the strap at the end. I slapped her with the strap to get her attention when she tried to gallop away with me…crack, "No girl! Walk!" She'd jump around a bit, but then knock it down a notch or two.

It was a very tense ride, and dealing with the cars on the road wasn't easy either. Some of the drivers would honk their horns and wave to us, thinking that they were being friendly. It amazed me how ignorant people were, honking and waving at horses; it spooked them and made the trip that much more dangerous.

We had been riding for several hours, when we crossed the highway and were finally on the last leg of the trip, Old Gold Miner's Trail. There was a stretch of the winding two lane road that had a very small shoulder and we were forced to ride partially on the pavement. We rode in single file and stayed to the side as far as we could, but even so, the cars were forced to follow behind us until they had an opportunity to safely pass.

We hadn't gone far on the treacherous road when I heard the sound of a raging engine in the distance. A car was approaching and it sounded to me as if it was going much too fast to maneuver the hazardous curves and twists. Suddenly, a fancy sports car came screeching around the corner behind us, when the driver saw the horses on the road he didn't slow down, but swerved into the other lane in an attempt to pass us. I was alarmed when I saw another car coming around the bend in the opposite direction. Both drivers slammed on their brakes and swerved to avoid the collision. Tires screeched and the horses bolted throwing up dirt and gravel, barely dodging the reckless driver.

My friends and I ran, looking for a place where we could get off of the road. Skip spotted an empty lot just past a gas station, and we stopped there to settle down a bit. The horses were shook up and so were we.

We all stayed in the lot except for Skip. He left his horse with us and walked to a vending machine at the gas station to get us all something to drink.

Suddenly, I heard the loud raging engine of the sports car again. The driver spotted Skip and turned into the gas station; he screeched to a stop and got out of his car. He pointed to a chip in his windshield, "You good-for-nothing kids chipped my windshield!" he screamed at the top of his lungs. His eyes were wild looking; he grabbed hold of Skip's arm and lifted him from the ground. Skip screamed and kicked, "Let go of me!"

When the three of us saw what was happening, we quickly rode over to help our friend.

The man who worked at the gas station saw what was happening and came out. "Put that kid down, mister!" he shouted.

"I'm not releasing this boy until he pays for my windshield! I'll take it out of his hide; I'll kill him if I have to, but he's going to pay!"

Dynamite and I were first on the scene, "Let him go!" I screamed at the crazed violent man. The man was in a fit of rage and when he didn't let loose of Skip, I started beating him with the strap at the end of my reins. Crack! Crack! I hit him hard, over and over again, but he still wouldn't let go.

Skip was putting up a good fight, thrashing and kicking, but the man was insane and had superhuman strength. "Ahhh, you're breaking my arm!" I heard Skip screech in pain.

Dynamite heard it too, and she knew that the man was hurting her friend. She reared up and whinnied wildly as she kicked her front legs and started to come down on top of the enraged maniac. When the man saw that the horse was about to stomp him down, he dropped Skip and jumped aside.

He then ran to the gas station attendant, "Did you see that horse? It tried to kill me!" he angrily shouted as he grabbed the gas station attendant by the shirt. He screamed in his face with blaring eyes, "You're my witness!"

The gas station attendant shoved the man in the chest, "Get away from me!"

By this time, Skip was on his horse again and we were all riding together down the street, trying to escape the crazed maniac. "Turn on this little side street!" Rowdy shouted, and we all ran down a tiny lane.

We were riding on high alert, ready for anything, nervously looking around. But after about an hour of walking through the maze of winding lanes we hadn't seen any sign of the sports car, and we all began to relax a bit.

"We must have lost him," Skip presumed, and we all agreed that we were finally safe.

I settled down and noticed that we were in a very pretty neighborhood. Lining the quaint tiny lane were houses that looked much like gingerbread. The four of us started to ride side by side and began to talk about what had happened. "I think that the guy must have escaped from the nut house," Rascal said, and we all agreed. Yep, we had met up with a real live lunatic.

Skip was riding beside me and I noticed him favoring his arm. "How's your arm Skip?" I asked.

"It's a little sore, but it'll be okay in a few days, it's not broken. I'm more worried about finding our way out of here. Where in the world are we?"

Rascal and Rowdy had a good sense of direction and had begun to navigate the way out when I heard the racing car engine again. I gasped when I saw the expensive sports car waiting for us in ambush, just a few short yards ahead.

The man had big red welts across his face and neck, where I had whipped him. He screamed out the window, "You're not getting away this time!" The tires screeched and the car headed straight for us. We all tried to get out of the way, but there wasn't enough time, or enough room, on the tiny lane.

Certain that he was invincible in his car and that no harm could come to him, the man tried to hit Dynamite. When I saw that there was no escape and that my horse and I were about to be hit, I screamed and prepared for the blow. But Dynamite had a different idea. She jumped on top of the car and landed on the hood caving it in; she crashed through the windshield with her front hooves and then ran right over the roof and leapt from the back. Dynamite hit the ground running. All of the horses were frantic, and the four of us went galloping through the streets once again.

When we were far enough away, we rode into an alley to check Dynamite and see if she was hurt. I looked her over and ran my hands down her legs; there wasn't a mark on her.

Then we heard sirens coming in our direction, "No need to worry about that idiot," Rowdy said, "sounds like help's on the way."

"Or it's the cops after us!" Rascal exclaimed.

"We must be close to The Horse Center by now, let's make a run for it!" Skip shouted. We jumped back on the horses and made a dash for the safety of The Horse Center.

As luck would have it, we managed to find our way and arrived safely at The Horse Center. The Horse Center was always bustling with excitement, and when the four of us rode in through the gate no one paid us much attention.

"Follow me and try to blend in," I said, and we rode down the lane to a trail and turned the horses loose in a pasture after putting our saddles and bridles in a tack room.

When we started walking back toward Uncle Glen's office, we heard the sound of a police radio and we ran for the hay. It was a huge stack and we climbed from bale to bale up to the very top. From our position, we could hear and see everything that was happening.

The crazy man was on the property with the police and he was all banged up. He had bandages on his face and head, his arm was in a sling and he was even walking with a limp.

"Wow," Skip exclaimed, "Dynamite really messed him up good!"

"Right on Dynamite!" we all chimed in together.

"I'll bet that idiot wouldn't even go to the hospital, just so he could come after us," Rowdy said with disgust.

"I bet you're right," I agreed.

The man was shouting at the police, "I saw those hooligans run in this direction and I know that they're here! I want to press charges, I tell you! Creatures like that are dangerous and they should be caged and not allowed to be free with the rest of us!"

"Calm down now sir, we'll do everything we can," the officer said in a soothing voice, trying to calm him.

Uncle Glen noticed the commotion, "What's going on here?" he asked in a loud authoritative manner.

"This gentleman was attacked by a girl on a horse and he thinks that she came in here," the policeman told Uncle Glen.

"It was a girl with a long red ponytail, riding a little black horse!" the man shouted. Then the horrible man started shouting and cursing at Uncle Glen with his shoulders and head twitching and jerking about.

Uncle Glen could tell right away that the guy was a nut, he also knew that they were looking for me and he was curious, "What exactly happened?" he asked with a grin.

"I was driving along, minding my own business when suddenly, out of nowhere, a girl forced her horse to jump on top of my car! My Ferrari has been destroyed, and I was nearly killed myself!"

"So, you say that she jumped on your Ferrari for no reason at all, huh?" Uncle Glen thought about his scrappy little niece and Dynamite jumping on a Ferrari; he couldn't keep a straight face and he began to chuckle.

"Quit laughing at me! Quit laughing at me!" the man screamed, practically going into a convulsion. "I'm going to find that girl and make her pay!"

"I'm sure that the kid gave you exactly you deserved, you crackpot," Uncle Glen shouted back at the crazed man. "Now get the hell out of here!"

"You can't tell me to get out of here, I know my rights! I know you're hiding her and you're going to jail!" The man yelled at Uncle Glen jerking and waving his arm around.

Then he pointed his finger at a group of people riding their horses nearby. "You people should know who you're associating with, this man is aiding a fugitive and you're all going to jail as accessories! Officer, shut this business down! Arrest this man! He's obviously hiding her! I'll prosecute you to the fullest extent of the law!"

Uncle Glen wasn't fazed by the man's theatrics, and he wasn't concerned about looking bad in front of his clients either, he just chuckled again and it infuriated the man even more.

"I'm not afraid of you!" the man screamed at the top of his lungs, challenging Uncle Glen.

Uncle Glen wasn't intimidated in the least, and when the enraged man took a swing at him, he merely blocked the blow.

At that point, the policemen were finally fed up with the unruly man, "Would you like to press charges Mr. Wells?"

"No, just get this nut off my property."

The officers asked the man to get in the car to leave, and when he realized that they weren't doing what he wanted them to, he began to shout curses at them. "You work for me, I'm a taxpaying citizen, you arrest that man or I'll kill you!"

"Terrorist threat against an officer, you're going to jail."

The policemen tried to put the man in handcuffs, but he put up a defiant fight. Things quickly escalated as the man went into a violent fit, he hissed and spit, and bit one of the policemen.

"Look at him!" Rowdy said. We could hardly believe our eyes.

After the man was finally tackled, hog tied and gagged, he was thrown in the back of the police car.

We heard the police radio as they drove away, "Be advised, suspect escapee from Lunatic Asylum, handle with caution, considered dangerous."

"Well, looks like I was right, the guy really was a lunatic and he was trying to kill us!" Rascal stated.

"Duh, he tried to run us down!" Rowdy retorted.

Uncle Glen walked out to the hay where he knew we were hiding. "Come on down now kids, that crackpot won't be giving you anymore trouble."

We climbed down from the hay. "Thanks Uncle Glen," I said.

"Now you kids don't get into any more trouble riding on the road. Leave your horses here and enjoy the place; just let Little Pacheco know when you're ready, and he'll trailer your horses home for you. Stay as long as you want, go and ride the trails, take some lessons and enjoy yourselves. But first head on down to the Chuck Wagon and have Cookie rustle you up some grub. You better get something in your bellies."

Uncle Glen walked away, "Rory," he hollered to one of the workers, "I want to go over the plans for the next rodeo, meet me in my office."

My friends and I headed for the Chuck Wagon and they asked, "Wildcat, does he mean it? Does he mean that we can come out here whenever we want to, just like highfaluters?"

"Sure he does, and if you want a lesson, just tell the teachers that Uncle Glen said so, and they'll give you one."

After we had lunch, I showed the boys around the place. We walked down the main drive and I pointed to the bleachers, "That big arena over there is where they hold the rodeos." Then we walked a little further and I explained more, "The bulls and broncs are kept in the corrals at the back."

When we went around back to have a closer look, the vicious bulls pawed the ground and charged the fence at us…BAM! "Whoa!" the boys exclaimed as they jumped back, "Good thing that's a sturdy fence!"

"Yeah, we better move on," I suggested, "we don't want to get them all riled up. Let's go to the bunkhouse where the cowboys stay."

The boys wanted to meet a real cowboy and were pleased to find that there were two on the front porch; one sitting in the rocking chair playing his harmonica, and the other cleaning his saddle.

One of the cowboys recognized me, "Howdy, Miss Penelope."

I said hello and introduced my friends.

"Do you ride bulls?" Rowdy asked them.

"Why sure we do."

"What about steer roping, do you know how to rope a steer?"

"A good cowboy knows how to do it all. Might be somebody out back a-practicing right now. Why don't you kids go and have a look."

We went behind the bunkhouse and sure enough, there was a young man practicing with a lasso. The boys and I sat down and quietly watched him throw the lasso around a post, over and over again. "I'm just learning myself," he told us. "Would you boys like to give it a try?"

The boys were excited and they all took turns throwing the lasso. When the young cowboy saw how enthusiastic they were, he went inside and got lassos for all three of them. "These lassos have seen better days," he apologized. "Nobody uses them anymore; you can keep 'em."

The boys were elated and would have stayed there all day, learning and practicing, but I wanted to move on and show them the rest of The Horse Center. "Come on now boys, there's a lot more to see, let's get going."

We waved good-bye, said thank you, and walked off together headed toward the big barn. On the way, we saw a riding lesson in progress and stopped to watch. A cute little girl was afraid of the horse and wouldn't even mount, so we quickly got bored and moved on.

I pointed further down the lane. "The barns here at the south end are full of horses that are boarded here; none of them belong to Uncle Glen." We walked down the rows and rows of stalls looking at the fine animals and then walked back outside.

"Beyond the fence line, down there on the east side, are the riding trails," I explained. "We'll go riding there later. But come on over here, I want to show you something special, and be very quiet."

My friends and I walked a little further down the road. "The pasture and stables over here are for broodmares and foals," I informed them. "There's a special setup inside the barn for birthing. Midwives and a vet are on the premises at all times to care for them."

The boys and I leaned on the pasture fence and watched the cute little foals running on their long wobbly legs. When they ventured too far from their mama's, the mares whinnied and their babies came running back. "Reminds me of you Rowdy, always running to Mama," Rascal teased his younger brother.

I interrupted, "I've seen a lot of foals born, they're running animals, and they get up just a few minutes after they been dropped."

The tiny foals were so cute and entertaining that we ended up watching them for nearly an hour. "We better get going if you want to see the rest of the place before dark," I said. "Come on, I want to show you the racetrack."

"Wow," Rascal exclaimed, "I can hardly believe it, there's even a racetrack! Wildcat, your Uncle Glen thought of everything."

"Yeah, everything that has to do with horses; that's for sure. The racetrack is down this road here." When we turned the corner it soon came into view. "Oh wow! Hurry! Come on," I said excitedly. "Looks like they're training racehorses right now!"

We quickly ran down the road and climbed the fence surrounding the track. The four of us watched excitedly as the sleek long-legged horses raced by us, it was thrilling.

After we watched for a while and had seen several horses run, Rowdy spoke up, "I bet there ain't a horse here could take Dynamite."

"Aw, come on now Rowdy, you really think that Dynamite's that fast?" I asked.

"Absolutely I do, she beat Militant Melody didn't she?"

"Yep, she surely did," I agreed, "but Militant Melody was probably out of shape. And maybe he didn't know how to run in sand or something, or maybe he lost because idiot Lancaster didn't know how to ride. There could be a hundred reasons why Dynamite beat him."

"Nope," Rowdy said, "don't be so humble, Dynamite beat Militant Melody because she's the better horse."

I closely watched the racehorses run by, and as they did I wondered, "Was Dynamite really faster? Was she as fast as my friends thought she was?" It stuck deeply in my mind.

Eventually, the horses finished running and the track was cleared. "Come on boys," I said, "we're not done with the tour yet, the best is yet to come; I'm going to show you my Uncle Glen's prize stud."

We went into the office and told Uncle Glen that we wanted to see Chief. He called security and told them to allow us entry, then we headed to the special barn where Uncle Glen had the famous horse and went inside. "This boys, is The Grand National Champion; the greatest horse in the country!"

The boys were breathless as they admired the stunning colored animal. "He's an Appaloosa," I proudly told them.

"We don't know much about Appaloosas Wildcat, can you tell us anything about him?"

"Well boys, over in Uncle Glen's office are magazines about the horse, and postcards and photos of him, but I'll tell you the whole story myself. You see, being The Grand National Champion was a victory a long hard time coming for the Appaloosa breed."

"It all started one day when I was a very little girl. I was riding in the car with Uncle Glen when he pointed to a horse standing in a field. "See the beautiful colored coat on that horse over there?" he asked me.

I glanced at the pathetic looking animal; it was a big cumbersome plow horse, with a large jug head and a bare meat tail, with sparse little sprigs of hair for a mane. Even though he had pointed out the horses beautiful colored coat, that wasn't at all what I saw. "You mean that old plug?" I commented.

"That old plug, Penelope, has a very noble history, it's an Appaloosa."

A noble history, this surprised me; I knew that the horse was an Appaloosa, and I also knew that the Appaloosa was looked down on by most horsemen and considered an inferior breed. "What do you mean, Uncle Glen?" I asked him.

Then Uncle Glen began to tell me about the Appaloosa. "Here is the story, as it was told to me," he said, "told to me by an old Nez Perce Indian, a direct descendant of the great Chief Joseph himself. The old

66

Indian had deep grooved wrinkles in his weathered face, his lower lip dropped on one side and his voice was raspy and cracked as he spoke. He said that his throat had been slashed by the claws of a grizzly bear. The ancient Indian had pain in his eyes as he began to tell me about the horse of his people, The Appaloosa.

It all began when the country was young and the Native Americans ruled the range. There was a tribe of Indians called the Nez Perce whose leader was the noble and brave Chief Joseph. The Nez Perce bred a horse that was superior to other horses in every way. Chief Joseph's horses were strong and surefooted as mountain goats and they could climb any terrain. The beautiful spotted coat of the animals blended with the landscape and acted as camouflage, making it nearly impossible for an enemy to spot them and it gave Chief Joseph an important advantage. The Appaloosa could reach incredible speeds, and run at a full gallop all day long and never grow tired. No horse could compete with Chief Joseph's magnificent Appaloosa.

Later, during the settling of the country, the Calvary was commissioned to capture Chief Joseph and his tribe. They set out on their gallant steeds, armed with superior weapons, determined to bring down the renegade Indian tribe and force them to surrender. When the Calvary found the Nez Perce, they were not prepared for what they were to encounter... the Appaloosa.

When Chief Joseph and his band realized that the enemy was upon them, they mounted their magical horses and disappeared. The highly-trained rugged men of the Calvary were unable to capture even the women and small children of the Indian tribe.

As time went on, Chief Joseph was found to be a formidable adversary; he outwitted and outmaneuvered the Calvary at every turn. The fast-running sturdy Appaloosa was always out of reach.

Time and time again, in hot pursuit, the Calvary was left behind, as the swift Appaloosa horses raced out of their grasp. They failed at mission after mission to capture the renegade Indians and were forced to suffer the shame of defeat each time they reported to their superiors that Chief Joseph had escaped once again.

The Appaloosa was too difficult to detect, too sure-footed to follow and most of all, just too fast for the Calvary horses to keep up with, let alone catch.

The Calvary had been defeated by the superior breeding of the Indian horse. Each time the Calvary saw the spotted rumps of the powerful unstoppable horses leaving them behind, it taunted them, and the men of the Calvary began to hate the Appaloosa. The hatred grew and grew with each defeat, as Chief Joseph and his horses made fools of them all.

The Calvary relentlessly pursued Chief Joseph and he headed for the treacherous mountains of Montana, knowing that the Calvary horses would be unable to follow him through the rough terrain. Tired hungry and many of them sick, Chief Joseph and his tribe of warriors, women, and children crossed the craggy rock-faced mountains on the sturdy sure-footed Appaloosa. The Calvary horses couldn't begin to maneuver the rugged terrain and the wily Chief left them behind him, defeated once again.

Chief Joseph and his band would have surely made it to safety, but there was something that he was unaware of; the telegraph. Telegraph wires had been strung up, and the Calvary wired a message ahead. Fresh troops were waiting in ambush for the unknowing Chief and his weary band.

Chief Joseph and his tribe, had crossed thirteen hundred miles of harsh terrain, but in the end, he was forced to surrender, and the destruction of the magnificent Appaloosa began.

The Calvary drove the Appaloosas off cliffs where they fell to their deaths, one struggling broken body on top of another. The remaining horses throats were slit from side to side and the gurgling gasping sounds of the valiant animals struggling to breathe through the gashes in their necks horrified the people residing in the area. It was said that the blood from the pitiless brutal slaughter ran in rivers from the horrific scene.

As time went by and more Appaloosas were discovered, they were bred to heavy-boned, jug-headed plow horses with bare meat tails and sparse manes to diminish the breed."

"And that's the story of that old plug standing out there in the field," Uncle Glen concluded. Then he went on to tell me something exciting, "Today, I've decided to bring the Appaloosa back to its original glory."

"And boys, that's exactly what my Uncle Glen did. He accomplished his dream and this horse standing here in front of you is due to his determination and hard work. The Appaloosa truly has returned to its original glory.

"Wow Wildcat, what a great story!"

The boys were in awe, and we sat quietly admiring the magnificent horse as he stood before us in all his splendor, as valiant and proud as the original Appaloosa.

I hope that Chief Joseph, where ever he is, knows that his horse has returned from the slaughter.

At the end of the day, Uncle Glen gave my friends and me a ride home

68

and then he headed out to his place. He didn't live in the valley with the rest of us. Uncle Glen had become the biggest horse breeder in the state and moved to a huge ranch in the hills where he had the room to breathe in deep and spread out.

After his young Appaloosas were weaned, they were turned loose to graze and play in the hills until they were old enough to be saddle broke. It was always a thrill when I was lucky enough to catch a glimpse of the whole herd, hundreds of young magnificent colored horses running together through the hills, each one a stunning beauty.

Every year, there was a roundup at Uncle Glen's ranch. It was a big event, branding the cattle and breaking the young horses. This year, Uncle Glen brought me up to the ranch a few days before the roundup, so that I could spend time with his daughter, my cousin, Laurel.

Uncle Glen's two children went to The Little Red Schoolhouse. There weren't many children who lived up there in the hills, and grades K through eight were all taught by one teacher, in a single room. The ranches in the area were spread so far apart that my cousins, Laurel and her younger brother Lester, didn't have any friends to play with. Even though they only had each other, they fought like cats and dogs and rarely played together. Uncle Glen made it a point to bring his nieces and nephews to spend time with his children whenever he could.

I enjoyed the ranch, it was a lovely place and with all of the horses living there, I was in heaven. The ranch house was big and rustic with tall open beam ceilings and a huge fireplace built from rocks collected on the surrounding countryside. Uncle Glen had a grizzly bear skin on the floor in front of the fireplace; a trophy from one of his hunting trips. The bear's head was posed in a fierce growl, displaying its huge teeth. Every baby born to the clan was drawn to it, they growled and wrestled the fierce beast, pretending to make the kill, then they sat on its head and pulled at the menacing teeth with their tiny little hands.

Uncle Glen's wife, Maureen, or Aunt Mo as we called her, was a ravishing Irish beauty; she had dark hair, fair skin and violet eyes.

Back then if you were a millionaire, you were considered filthy rich, and Uncle Glen, building his empire from the ground up, had become a millionaire before he was thirty years old. He lavished Aunt Mo, his beautiful glamorous wife, with furs and diamond jewelry. She wore designer clothes, and had her shoes custom made by a shoemaker in Italy that she and Uncle Glen had met while vacationing there.

But, Uncle Glen was a risk-taker and as quickly as he had made the money, he lost it. They say that Aunt Mo had a nervous breakdown when

Uncle Glen went broke. Losing all of her material possessions was too much for her to take, and when she saw her lavish furs coat go out the door, she cracked up.

Even though the financial crisis was long over, Aunt Mo never pulled out of her personal crisis. I had heard the grownups speak about her taking pills and drinking. While it was true that Aunt Mo was a little strange, she was always nice to me and I didn't care what I had heard said about her.

It was fun staying at Aunt Mo's; she would call the country store and have everything delivered, corn chips and potato chips with dips, pizza, hot dogs, every kind of soda pop and sugary breakfast cereal, frosted cupcakes and candy. It was a real treat because there was never any junk food at our house. My father wouldn't stand for it; chips and soda pop were taboo, but at Aunt Mo's that was all there was, a true childhood smorgasbord.

I enjoyed nearly everything about the ranch, but there was one thing that I didn't like, Duke the Doberman. I liked Dobermans, in fact I had owned one myself, but this dog was mean and it would viciously attack, without provocation, anyone who wasn't in the immediate family and had to be locked up whenever people came to visit.

One Thanksgiving, when my sister, Pat, was just a baby, we had the family celebration at Uncle Glen and Aunt Mo's ranch. That was the day that little Pat took her very first steps for Uncle Glen. He excitedly praised the incredible feat and made his adorable tiny niece feel like she had conquered the world.

Locked in the next room, the neurotic Doberman could hear what was going on and was crazy with jealousy, pawing and leaping at the door. Somehow the demented dog broke out of the room and lunged at my tiny baby sister. He knocked Pat down and went for her throat. Uncle Glen was fast on the draw and grabbed the dog before it tore into the innocent baby. He threw it back into the room with a kick, and secured the door. "Maureen you've got to get rid of that dog, it's going to seriously hurt somebody one of these days!"

"Glen, you know that I'm up here isolated and alone with the children nearly all the time, and Duke is a great comfort to me. I need a mean dog for protection and Duke won't trust anyone who comes around here, even if he knows them, I won't give him up."

After that incident, Uncle Glen, brought new dogs up to the ranch from time to time, hoping that Aunt Mo would like them and get rid of the Doberman, but so far, she hadn't.

Uncle Glen and I made the long winding drive to the ranch that day, and when we arrived, a regal German Shepherd ran up to greet us, "This is Prince, Penelope."

I petted the hearty friendly dog. "He's beautiful, Uncle Glen, I really like him, I sure hope that Aunt Mo will get rid of Duke now."

"We'll see, we'll see," he said hopefully.

Before we entered the house, Uncle Glen, called to Aunt Mo, "Maureen, do you have that crazy dog of yours' locked up? I've got Penelope here with me." Aunt Mo locked up the dog and then we went inside.

Uncle Glen didn't stay for long, since he had pressing business to attend to back in the city. "See you in a few days for the roundup," then he said good-bye and dashed off.

It was lunchtime when I arrived, and Laurel suggested going on a picnic. "Sounds good to me," I agreed, and we packed a basket full of delicious junk food and set out to find a good place to have, what we considered, a lavish meal. Prince came along and politely trotted ahead of us down the lane.

Laurel and I ended up going by the stream and spreading a blanket near the water. We ate so much junk that we thought our stomachs would burst. "I can't eat another bite," Laurel said as she patted her belly.

"One more cupcake, Laurel," I laughed. "I dare you to eat just one more." I playfully smeared a touch of icing on her nose.

"Oh no," Laurel exclaimed, "I'm going to be sick!" She ran for the house and Prince followed her.

"Why don't you just throw up in the stream," I shouted to her as she ran away, "and feed the fish."

"Eeewww, it's not that kind of sick."

"My poor cousin," I said to myself, shaking my head.

I patiently sat looking at the road, waiting for Laurel and wondered if she was coming back at all. How sick was she? Then I saw something that horrified me, the big Doberman running down the lane toward the stream. Duke was loose!

After the dog spotted me, I started screaming, "Duke is loose! Duke is loose!" But the house was so far away, I doubted if anyone could hear me hollering. What was I going to do? When Duke was out of sight momentarily behind a tree, I pulled out my pocket knife and ran up under the bridge; that was where I decided to make my stand. Even though I knew it was senseless, I still hoped that he wouldn't find me hiding there.

Duke ran to the edge of the bridge and looked down, right at me. I tried to avoid him and I moved to the other side, but then he went to that side of the bridge and jumped down. The demented Doberman was growling, showing me his fierce teeth and walking slowly toward me.

I held tightly to my pocket knife. "Duke is loose!" I shouted one more time in desperation.

Then from out of nowhere Prince appeared, he jumped down from the bridge between us and stood there growling and looking Duke square in the eyes. I was hoping that Duke would back down and return to the house, but I knew that the chances of that happening were slim, because Prince was challenging him.

Then I heard my cousin Lester, "Duke...Duke...come here boy." The Doberman turned and went back to the house. What a relief, I wrapped my arms around Prince and stroked him. "Thanks for protecting me boy." He panted and smiled and gave me a sloppy slobbery kiss.

Finally, Laurel came back out. "Duke was loose and he came after me," I told her.

"Don't worry, he won't get out again," Laurel promised. But somehow I couldn't believe it.

Uncle Glen had brought Laurel a new game that day, and she wanted to play it with me, so we packed up the rest of the food and the two of us headed back to the house. Prince walked along at my side, he didn't leave me. Even when we got in the house and started playing the game, he laid close by and kept a watchful eye. Prince knew that Duke was after me and he also knew that he was just in the next room.

There was a lot of bending and twisting to play this game and my pocket knife was digging into my leg, so I pulled out the knife and my matches and laid them on the coffee table.

Unfortunately, Aunt Mo didn't share the same beliefs as my father did, and when she saw that I was carrying a knife and matches she freaked out. "Oh no Penelope, we don't play with matches and carry knives around here, it's very dangerous and you might get hurt." She clumsily reached down and took my knife and matches. Aunt Mo rarely noticed much of anything, and of all things, why did it have to be my special knife?

"Aunt Mo, please don't worry about it, I even carry a gun when I'm in the hills at home, the knife and matches are no big deal. My dad wants me to carry them in case of an emergency."

"I'm sorry to hear that your father allows you to do such a dangerous thing. You can have the knife back when you go home." Then she stumbled into her bedroom and closed the door behind her, and that was the end of it. We all knew that we wouldn't see her again until sometime the next afternoon.

After Aunt Mo had taken my knife, I felt naked as I always had my knife with me. I knew that she thought that she was protecting me, but I was still upset and didn't feel like playing the game anymore. "Let's go outside, Laurel," I said, and I picked up the game. Laurel agreed and we went outside. Prince followed us and we all sat in the gazebo. I was petting Prince while Laurel and I talked about what we wanted to do next. We had only been out there for a few minutes when Prince noticed something. "Laurel look," I said quietly, "a little domestic rabbit. I wonder how he got here?"

"I don't know, let's try to catch it. Come here little rabbit," she called.

"Laurel, go in the house and get some lettuce, rabbits love lettuce."

"Okay," she agreed, "and I better lock Prince up too, he'll scare it away. Here boy, come on Prince."

Laurel quickly came back outside with the lettuce and the two of us tried to catch the fuzzy little bunny. The bunny was a tease, he wiggled his cute little nose and acted like he was going to come to us, then he would give a few quick hops and stay just out of our reach.

Laurel and I followed the adorable little creature through the barn, into the pasture and kept on going. That little bunny was sure giving us the runaround; further and further we followed him into the hills and without realizing it, we had traveled far from the ranch and into the wild.

I noticed that the sun was starting to go down, "Laurel we better give up, that bunny isn't going to let us catch him and it's starting to get dark."

Knowing that the sun sets in the west; meant that the house was east. Laurel and I headed east and that's when we realized just how far we had actually gone ….we would never make it back in time!

We both knew that being caught out after dark meant that we would soon become part of the food chain, prey for the wild animals that lived there. We began to run, trying to beat the darkness, but sadly we didn't make it. When the sun went down, a thick heavy blackness covered the hills; there was no moon or stars to light the sky that night, just total and complete utter darkness. Laurel and I were terrified; we couldn't even see our hands just inches in front of our faces. It was hopeless; we couldn't find our way back to the house until the sun rose again the next morning! Dreadfully, we would have to spend the night outside with the predators.

Laurel and I stood together silently holding hands, the darkness clinging to our minds, cloaking our senses in a shroud of blindness hopelessness and fear. Would we be alive to see the sun rise the next morning?

Laurel broke the silence, "I saw a story on T.V. about getting lost. They said that you shouldn't keep walking around because it makes it harder for the rescuers to find you. Let's just stay right here and wait for help to come."

Laurel knew that she was just kidding herself and so did I; there would be no one searching for us. Aunt Mo was passed out and Lester was just a little kid who was engrossed in a project, I doubted if he even noticed that we were gone. Just the same, Laurel's idea sounded as good as any since in the dark there was no way to see where we were going. I was afraid that we might step on a snake or fall off a cliff or something, so staying in one spot did seem like our best option.

My dad had given me the pocket knife and told me to carry matches for an emergency just like this. If I had had my matches I could have started a fire and it would have given us light and warmth and kept the wild animals away. And on the off chance that there was a rescue team looking for us, it would have been a signal fire. The small book of matches would have insured our survival.

At that time of year, it was warm during the day, but in the hills, the temperature dropped dramatically at night. Laurel and I were in shorts and sleeveless shirts, huddled together, shivering and trying to keep warm.

Laurel started to whimper a little. "Laurel stop, there's bears and coyotes out here, they'll hear you," I scolded.

I had no weapon; Aunt Mo had taken my pocket knife. I groped around on the ground trying to find a rock for protection, but all of the rocks that I could feel were too big, or buried too deep in the ground for me to pick up.

We sat quietly, listening and hoping that we would make it through somehow. How much longer until sunrise? Laurel and I waited and waited, listening and hearing nothing for the longest time. Perhaps this wasn't the end, perhaps we wouldn't be eaten. Then suddenly, the deafening cry of the coyote's eerie voices echoed through the hills, yipping yowling and howling wildly.

Laurel and I clenched each other tightly, "Shhh…maybe we're downwind of 'em, be quiet and they might not find us," I whispered very softly.

We waited, shivering, our teeth chattering, still trying not to make a sound. Then I heard the heavy rapid panting of a large animal and hurried footsteps drawing near. This was it, we were about to be attacked by a pack of hungry coyotes! Laurel and I stood up to prepare for the attack.

"Laurel, kick and fight with everything you've got, it's our only chance!"

BAM! A beast slammed into me and knocked me down. Laurel was left standing, screaming in terror, she couldn't see, she couldn't do anything else. I fought the menacing animal alone, kicking and punching in a fight for my life. I never imagined myself dying this way, dismembered, my body ripped apart as food for the wild beasts.

In the struggle, I got my hands around the animal's neck … it was wearing a collar! It was Duke and he was trying to kill me! "Laurel, it's Duke! Call him off!" Laurel screamed and tried everything to stop the crazed pet, but no matter what she did the dog wouldn't end the attack. I was no match for the powerful fierce dog, with my blood in his mouth, he was completely crazed!

Suddenly, a strong force rammed into Duke and knocked him off of me. Had Laurel finally been able to do something? No! It was another animal, another animal had knocked Duke off and they were fighting. I heard snarls and growls, what was going on? I knew that coyotes saw dogs as competition; had the coyotes attacked Duke?

"It's the coyotes!" Laurel screamed in terror.

I was closer to the fighting. "Laurel, I think there's only one, it might be Prince!"

It was Prince and he was fighting Duke, protecting me from the demonic dog once again!

In the darkness, there was no way of knowing what was happening as we listened to the fury of growls and crushing bites. Which dog would win? I could only stand by and hope that Prince would be the victor.

Duke and Prince were both strong dogs, Prince, on the side of good, and Duke, the embodiment of evil. If Duke won the fight, I thought that he would try to kill me again. I pawed the ground trying to find a rock to defend myself with, but again, to no avail.

The vicious fight came to a fever pitch, Laurel and I held hands when we heard the loud wailing scream of a dog in mortal pain and then we heard nothing but panting, relentless rapid panting. One of the dogs was dead, but Laurel and I had no way of knowing which one it was.

Suddenly, I felt a rub against my leg, it was Prince! "Oh Prince, Prince, thank you boy!" I held him in my arms and gently stroked him, "I love you, I love you! Thank you!"

The coyotes in the area smelled the blood, "Yip, yip, yahoooo, yaaoowww!" they yowled in an excited frenzy.

The coyotes were getting closer and all three of us were bloody; Prince and I from fighting Duke, and it had rubbed off on Laurel as well. "Laurel we've got to get out of here before the yotes come, we've got to get as far away from here as we can!"

Laurel was on one side of Prince and me on the other, holding his collar, "Go home boy, go home!" Prince was a smart dog, he knew that the coyotes were coming and that we were in danger, he put his nose to the ground and started off in a valiant effort to lead us to safety. Laurel and I held tightly to Prince's collar, it was the only thing between us and death.

I hoped that the coyotes wouldn't catch us; Prince would never be able to fight off the whole pack. We were walking uphill, up and up it seemed as though it would never end. Laurel and I were winded and when we stopped for a second to catch our breath, we heard the growling snarling, feeding frenzy of the coyotes as they tore the flesh from the bones of the downed evil dog.

The sounds terrified us. It was a blood fest, like the soundtrack of a horror show playing to us in the pitch blackness. But it was a comfort just the same, the coyotes finding the dead dog had bought us time, and maybe they would get enough to eat and wouldn't come after us.

"Go Prince, go! Get us out of here!" We held on to Prince and when we made it to the top of the hill, we could see a light swinging back and forth in the distance, a flashlight, it was Lester! "Lau…rel, Lau…rel," he called.

"It's my stupid brother! Oh thank God we're almost home!"

We got down the hill, through the pasture and into the yard. "Oh Lester, thank you! You're wonderful!" I praised as I hugged my younger cousin.

"You're still a creepy weirdo," Laurel told her brother, "but I love you anyway." Then she gave him a hug too.

Duke had had all of his shots, so I didn't have to worry about rabies and other things, that I would have if I had I been bitten by a wild animal. I did have a few big bites, but nothing that needed stitches, we just put on some iodine and pulled the skin together with butterfly bandages and I was fine. Prince was okay too, he had a few gashes and tears, but Laurel and I doctored him up as well.

It was a horrifying experience that we had been through, but on the bright side, we were finally rid of the vicious troublesome dog.

Laurel and I had barely recovered from our harrowing experience and it was time for the roundup. During the first phase of roundup, we rode out into the hills on our fastest horses and cut the two-year-old horses from the herd. We then drove them down closer to the house and into the north pasture for training.

Once all the horses had been at least green-broke. (ridden once with a saddle and bridle), we headed back into the hills and rounded up the newly acquired cattle and the calves, and then the branding began.

That morning, our family members and the cowboys began arriving at the ranch, loud and excited. The roundup was a big event full of wild action, fierce competition and lots of fabulous food. Every year, Uncle Glen roasted a huge pig over a hickory fire on the rotisserie. As the smoke filled the air, the near-intoxicating aroma was akin to a torture that lasted until it was finally time to eat.

Early that morning, Laurel and I were working in the barn, mucking stalls. Laurel stopped for a moment and leaned on her rake, "Penelope, do you remember out first roundup? I mean the first time that we helped with the branding."

"I sure do," I answered, "we must have been about five or six that first time."

"We were six and I thought that we were so grown up, but now when I look at our six year old cousins, they look so tiny to me. It's hard to imagine that they'll be working the branding this year like we did."

During the roundup everyone had a job to do, even the littlest children took turns turning the rotisserie.

The first time that I worked the branding, Laurel and I were a team. We stood on the wooden fence rails, one of us on each side of the narrow cattle chute. We both had sticks in our hands and we held back the cattle and let one through at a time as the men branded them.

I'll never forget the first calf that Laurel and I let through the chute. The men lassoed it, tied its feet together and then removed the hot branding iron from the fire and pressed our brand on the steer's hip. We could smell the burning hair and flesh and the animals eyes rolled back into its head.

"Stop it, stop it!" Laurel and I cried, "You're hurting it!"

"We're not hurting it!" Uncle Slim shouted back at us as he loosed his lasso from the calf's legs. The calf jumped to its feet and was released into the pasture where he ran out of sight. "See, he's fine. We don't have time for this nonsense, now do your job, quit whining and let another steer through!"

And we did, even though we didn't fully believe that branding didn't hurt the cattle, we knew that they had to be branded. People weren't above cattle rustling, so Laurel and I toughened up and got with the program.

We did our job well that day with only one slipup, two steer managed to push their way past us and into the ring at the same time. When we saw that two had made it through, Laurel and I were scared that we were in

77

trouble. The men lassoed, tied and branded the first steer while the other stood aside and watched; it didn't attack or anything. After they had finished and released the first steer, they branded the second one. We were both relieved that there hadn't been an incident, but made certain that it never happened again, unsure of what the penalty might be.

Standing on the fence rail was a precarious situation. While the fence did keep the cattle inside, there was nothing preventing them from goring us from between the rails. We had to be on guard every second dodging the sharp horns. The cattle would ram the fence, sometimes knocking us off. They tried to jump over and our fingers would get smashed under their hooves if we didn't move our hands out of the way fast enough.

If we stretched and reached too far over the fence, we would lose our balance and start to fall, face first, into the herd, where we would be crushed and trampled. Always aware of the impending danger, and ready to take action whenever this happened, we used our sticks to knock each other back up on the fence. Each time the saving act was met with a, "Thanks cousin, you saved my life." A flippant remark, but true just the same.

The cattle crowded ahead, pressing together, trying to force their way through the chute, and there was nothing stopping them, but two little, six year old girls with sticks in their hands who smacked them back and kept them under control.

I worked the chute for a few years, but as soon as my legs were long enough to get a grip around a horse, I was breaking 'em. I learned at an early age that when you get bucked off, no matter how hard you hit the ground, you shake it off and get back on.

That year, Uncle Henry had bought a new horse and he trailered him up to Uncle Glen's place to show him off, and I think to get some help breaking him. They called the horse Lucifer, he was a real beauty, but he was a mean one and nobody wanted to ride him.

While I worked in the barn, I could hear the cowboys talking, "No, partner, I ain't a-goin' in thar with that crazy animal. They don't call him Lucifer for nothin'!"

I wanted to see what all of the excitement was about, so I walked over to the corral. I leaned on the fence and watched as the regal animal pranced around the ring tossing his head, snorting and whinnying. Then suddenly, he reared up and charged the fence at me. I jumped back, "Whoa! I wasn't ready for that! That horse nearly knocked my head off!"

"Yeah we know, he's a rowdy one alright, just like the devil!" the cowboys laughed. "Starr's gonna ride 'im. We been takin' bets on how many times he's gonna bite the dust before he gets the job done."

My family had a habit of pushing the kids past their limits, they challenged us beyond our years and abilities, and then made fun of us if we failed. Success was merely expected.

On account of that, I wasn't surprised when mean-spirited Uncle Henry, said, "Penelope what are you doing standing around being lazy? You don't work, you don't eat." Then knowing that everyone was leery of riding his vicious horse, he taunted me further, "Get in there and ride Lucifer!" He was laughing when he said it, it was supposed to be a joke, a joke at my expense.

It really pissed me off and I decided to show him a thing or two! "Okay Uncle Henry, you want me to ride him? I'll ride your devil horse. Saddle 'im up boys," I shouted to the ranch hands.

I knew that I was in over my head, but I was too proud to let the others make fun of me if I backed down. I wasn't stocky and sturdy built, like my cousins; I didn't look strong, but I was, and twice as stubborn.

I started walking toward the gate of the corral and no one said a word. When it was clear that I had meant what I said, and that no one was trying to stop me, Starr politely stepped in front of me. He was tall and thin, a handsome man, his skin was weathered and he looked older than his years. "Miss Penelope, now you let me go on in thar and take care of this ol' bronc, I don't want to see a pretty little thing like you gettin' hurt."

"It's okay Starr, it won't be the first time I been hurt."

The cowboys lassoed the wild horse, saddled him and held his head. When I stepped into the corral, you could have cut the tension with a knife. Was this kid really going through with it?

Starr broke the silence, "Henry you gonna let this go on? This little gal's gonna get hurt."

Starr had just hired on and he didn't know what Uncle Henry was like. Uncle Henry answered exactly what I, and everyone else knew that he would, "No snot-nosed kid is going to defy me, if she gets hurt it'll teach her a lesson."

I closed the gate of the corral and looked over at the horse; he was enraged, whinnying wildly, struggling and bucking, fighting to break free. I slowly approached him and gently stroked his face to reassure him, "No one's going to hurt you," I said in a sweet soothing voice, trying to calm him down.

Suddenly, Uncle Henry grabbed me from behind, "Quit playing around, we don't have time for this nonsense." He picked me up and threw me in the saddle, then he gave that horse a hard crack on the behind, and the battle was on.

Lucifer reared up, spun around and charged Uncle Henry. I pulled back on the reins and tried to veer him away. Uncle Henry jumped the fence and the horse slammed into it. It was quite a jolt, but I was still hanging on. The cowboys were screaming, "Yee hah little gal! Ride that horse!"

Usually a horse, unlike a bull, will buck with a certain rhythm and you can anticipate its next move, but not Lucifer, he was completely unpredictable. I never had a horse throw me very often, but this one did and when I hit the ground, that crazy animal came after me and tried to stomp me! He was a killer! The cowboys quickly jumped into the corral to protect me. I shook my head, spit the dirt from my mouth, and got back on him.

It seemed like it went on forever then finally, the horse began to settle down a bit and I figured that he was getting tired and about to give up. I must have let my guard down a second, when without warning, he jumped and twisted to the side. I went flying and landed on a fencepost, I heard a crack, I had broken a rib. I fell down off the post to the ground and grabbed my side, ahhh, it hurt bad, but I had to finish the job, I had to get back on, especially since Uncle Henry was watching.

"Had enough kid? Devil got you down?" he asked in a sarcastic tone.

I didn't answer him and looked at the horse, it didn't charge me this time. The cowboys caught him again and when I got back on he went wild, spinning in a circle. The dust was flying so thick that no one could see what was going on. I held onto that horse with everything I had left in me and when the dust settled, I was still in the saddle and the horse was trotting nicely around the ring. I had won! Everyone was cheering even Uncle Henry!

At that moment, Uncle Glen arrived in his big Cadillac with a load of groceries. When he saw me on that crazy wild Lucifer he was furious and jumped out of the truck. "Henry what the hell are you doing putting that kid on that horse? What are you trying to do, kill her?"

"Shut up, I know what I'm doing. Why don't you go on back to the grocery store and leave the tough stuff to me."

BAM! Uncle Glen punched Uncle Henry and knocked him down, then he ripped open the gate and stormed into the corral. He could tell that I was hurt, he gently pulled me off the horse and put me on his shoulder. "The champ! The champ!" he chanted in his big deep voice. He paused for a moment and asked, "What's that you're little friends call you? Wildcat! Listen here boys, you're looking at Wildcat Wells, the toughest little cowgirl in the West!"

The cowboys threw their hats in the air, "Wildcat Wells, yee hah!"

From that day forward I had gained respect and was known to everyone as Wildcat, not just to my "little friends."

The roundup went off without a hitch. Everyone had a great time, but the next day I was definitely ready to go home, and Uncle Glen drove me back to the valley. It was nearly summertime and he told me that he would board Dynamite and my friend's horses at The Horse Center for the duration.

Elated at our good fortune, the boys and I found a safer route to get to The Horse Center, and we rode our bicycles there nearly every day. Being at The Horse Center was a wonderful fun time for us. We enjoyed learning from the teachers and other knowledgeable horse people and we trained our horses well. We exercised and rode hard on the mountainous trails.

After spending time with the cowboys, the boys decided that they wanted to be cowboys too, and they practiced with their horses every day.

The four of us also enjoyed the racetrack. We didn't bet on the horses, but pretended that we had, and we cheered for our favorites to win. Watching the sleek high-spirited animals give their all, and cross the finish line, was a thrill every time.

One day, when the racetrack was closed and no one was around, the boys and I decided to take Dynamite out on the track to see what she could do. The boys stood by while Dynamite and I moved into position. "Get it Wildcat, show us what that badass horse can do!"

Dynamite was excited, she couldn't wait to run, and when I shouted, "Yah!" she took off like a shot.

It wasn't often that she got the chance run wide open and she was loving it, running as hard and fast as she could. I don't believe in reincarnation, but I do believe in genetic memory, and Dynamite, coming from a long line of racehorses, found the rail and knew instinctively exactly what to do.

It was great not having to worry about rocks and potholes. Running on the smooth obstacle-free surface was a dream, there was nothing to slow us down and we blasted over the finish line!

The boys all cheered, "Wow! Dynamite looked great out there Wildcat, just like a professional! I'd bet anything that she could win a real race!"

Dynamite hadn't had enough, she was rearing up and dancing sideways, trying to keep going. "She loves it, I'm going to take her around another time."

Dynamite and I took another lap on the track and she ran as fast and

81

beautifully as she had the first time.

"That horse sure has good endurance," Rascal said, "must be from all the climbing and hard riding that we do."

"Yeah, she's in great shape all right, but I better make her stop now, I don't want to run her to death."

Uncle Glen had told me that a spirited horse, like Dynamite, will keep on running, giving you their all until their heart blows up and they drop dead at a full gallop. With some of the crazy things that I had done, I was grateful that I hadn't already killed my high-spirited horse.

"You know guys, running the track is really good exercise, let's come out here and exercise all of our horses tomorrow," I suggested.

The boys thought that it sounded like a great idea, and the next day we all took our horses out on the track to run. It was fun pretending that it was a real race, lining up the horses and dashing around the track. Dynamite was in heaven, she thrived on the racetrack.

The boys and I had accomplished our goal; our horses were in prime, physical condition and we decided that it was time for some special grooming. With all of the show horses at The Horse Center, there were plenty of people to show us how. We trimmed and polished and groomed our horses, using professional clippers and products, and soon we had them looking their very best. We couldn't have been more proud and we showed them off to everyone.

I went to Uncle Glen's office to ask him to come out and have a look, but when I got there Uncle Glen was having a serious conversation with three scary, threatening men. I sat on a bench nearby and quietly waited for them to finish. It wasn't my intention to listen to what they were saying, but it was a heated conversation, and the men were speaking harsh and loud. From what I could make of it, they were Lancaster's men, the owner of Militant Melody. He was involved with Uncle Glen somehow and was trying to strong-arm him and take over The Horse Center. Uncle Glen had to come up with a huge sum of money before the end of the month, and everything was riding on races that were to take place the next weekend.

I figured that since Lancaster had been barred from racing, he must have been trying to use The Horse Center to somehow bend the rules and get back in the game.

"I'll show you who's washed up," Uncle Glen shouted as the men headed for the door. "I've got a line-up of horses that will run yours into the ground! He shook his fist in the air, "And tell Lancaster that I've got something for him too!"

"Oh no! If Uncle Glen goes broke again Aunt Mo won't be able to take it, she'll end up in the Mental Hospital for sure!"

I wanted to do something to help, but what? I couldn't figure out how, I only had thirty seven dollars saved up and that wasn't enough to do anything. I walked away shaking my head in despair. But then it occurred to me, "My Uncle Glen isn't stupid, he knows exactly what he's doing, if he said that his horses can run Lancaster's into the ground, that's the way it is! Uncle Glen's a tough guy; he can handle that rotten ol' Lancaster. Everything will be okay."

I turned and went back to the office, "Uncle Glen, I'm sorry for eavesdropping, but I heard what those men said. Are you in trouble? Is there anything that I can do to help?"

"Oh don't worry about it Wildcat, all I have to do is win two of the three races on Saturday, and with the horses I've got running, it's already in the bag."

"Which horses are you running Uncle Glen?"

"Jumping Jeopardy, Frantic Heartbeat and The General will anchor the relay race. Those silly jokers don't know who they're messing with, they can't possibly compete with my champions. The only horse that Lancaster ever had worth its salt is Militant Melody, but that idiot Lancaster just couldn't play it straight. He had to get "creative" and now he can't race that horse at any track, under any pretext. He's finished, but he just doesn't want to admit it."

"If you're going to worry about anybody, worry about Lancaster's bunch, they're the ones that are going to walk away from here broke and crying on Saturday."

What a relief! Uncle Glen really did have it under control, and with three powerful horses running on Saturday, victory was already in the bag.

"You and your little friends don't miss the big races Saturday, you kids can sit in the seats next to me and watch your ol' Uncle Glen rake in the dough."

"Wow Uncle Glen, that's great!" I gave him a big hug and happily skipped away.

However, the following week turned out to be disastrous for Uncle Glen. It seemed as though everything that could go wrong did, and then came the hardest blow of all, his strongest and fastest racehorse, The General, got a kinked gut (a life-threatening intestinal kink). The horse was fed and exercised properly and there was no understandable reason for it to happen.

"Sometimes things like this can't be explained," the veterinarian told us.

He tried everything short of surgery to help the distressed horse, but the kink wouldn't release and there was no other option, The General would have to undergo surgery, and was out of the race.

Uncle Glen had horses die from kinked guts before and always for no good reason. "It's a curse!" he shouted as he walked away, distressed.

Things were going wrong, and Uncle Glen was starting to worry. What would the outcome of the relay race be without The General, Uncle Glen's champion? He had been counting on The General to pull the other weaker horses through in the last stretch if they fell behind. It seemed that things weren't in the bag after all.

Ready or not, it was Saturday morning, the day of the big races. Uncle Glen picked me up early and we went to The Horse Center together. There was a lot riding on the races that day, and I think that everyone must have known it; there was a tension in the air that I had never felt before. I stayed out of the way and watched Uncle Glen walk up and down the stables talking to jockeys and trainers, pointing and shouting last minute instructions. "That's okay," I heard Uncle Glen say to one of the trainers, "don't get rattled, we'll just run Frantic Heartbeat in the relay race, she's the only winner I have left."

I wondered what he meant, "She's the only winner I have left." What had happened to Jumping Jeopardy?

After my friends arrived, Uncle Glen walked with us to our seats. He didn't sit in luxury, in a fancy booth and casually watch the races through a picture window, like most owners do. Uncle Glen liked to be as close to the action as possible and we were practically sitting on the track. Uncle Glen tried to act like everything was fine, but he seemed stressed.

"What's wrong Uncle Glen?" I asked.

"It's okay Wildcat, don't you worry your pretty little head, Uncle Glen has it all under control."

One of the trainers came walking up behind us and wanted a word with Uncle Glen. "You kids say put," he told us and he went to talk to the trainer.

The trainer asked why he had changed the lineup and Uncle Glen told him, "Jumping Jeopardy came up lame this morning and I'm putting Frantic Heartbeat in to take his place in the relay."

"It's too damn much, that little gal can't run two races today!" explained the trainer.

"What do you mean it's too much for her, are you saying that her leg won't hold up? The blasted vet released her to run today!"

"Legs sturdy enough," the trainer said stroking his jaw, " but she just don't have the endurance that she usually do, she ain't trained hard enough with that dang leg injury to run two races. But Frantic 'ill still run ya one good race, she's a champ."

"Okay fine, we'll put Cassie's Crush in the relay, hopefully she's got enough left in her to win for me just one more time."

It didn't look good for Uncle Glen; with The General in surgery, Jumping Jeopardy lame, and now running Cassie's Crush in the relay race, things were quickly becoming a disaster.

The boys and I had seen Cassie's Crush run, and even we could tell that she was past her prime and slowing down. We knew it, and so did Uncle Glen; he was simply running the fastest horses that he had left and hoping for the best.

"Wildcat," Rascal whispered to me, "why don't you tell Uncle Glen about Dynamite? She's faster than Cassie's Crush, hands down."

"You're right Rascal, I'll give it a try."

"Uncle Glen, why don't you let Dynamite run the relay? She's really fast, way faster than Cassie's Crush."

"Dynamite? You mean your little horse?" Uncle Glen chuckled. "That's very sweet," he said and gave me a pat on the head, "but this is a serious race."

"I'm serious too Uncle Glen!" My voice got louder, "Dynamite is very fast and she knows what she's doing, I've been working her and running her on the track!"

"I'm sure that your little horse is very fast Wildcat, but this is serious business, now you settle down and sit quietly, Uncle Glen can still pull this off."

I knew that the only thing that would convince Uncle Glen how fast Dynamite was, was if he knew that she had beaten Militant Melody in the race at the beach. But I couldn't say anything; I couldn't break the code of silence, and risk getting my friends into trouble for stealing the truck and trailer.

Rowdy knew what was happening and he spoke up without hesitation, "Dynamite beat Militant Melody in a race at the beach!" He shouted loud and clear, his voice boomed out, and seemed to have an almost paralyzing effect on us all.

"What do you mean son? Dynamite beat Militant Melody; you mean Lancaster's horse? What in the world are you talking about?" Uncle Glen asked.

Rowdy blurted out the whole story, "We stole my father's truck and trailer and drove the horses to the beach. Randolph Lancaster the IV was

85

there and he was riding Militant Melody. We challenged him to a race and Dynamite took him, hands down!"

Uncle Glen knew that we wouldn't lie to him and he got a gleam in his eye. "Are you kids sure that it was Militant Melody?"

"Uncle Glen, I've seen that horse at least a hundred times on the news, believe me, it was Militant Melody all right, and Randolph the IV looks just like his old man."

"If this isn't poetic justice, I don't know what is," Uncle Glen said with a grin. "If Dynamite is horse enough to take Militant Melody, there's nothing that can stand in our way! You kids go get her and bring her to the track; I'll meet you in the stable."

I felt a rush of excitement; Dynamite was actually going to run in a real race! The boys and I dashed to the pasture where Dynamite was. When she heard me calling, she came trotting to me, tossing her head from side to side in greeting. "Come on girl, today is your big day!" I haltered Dynamite and we all ran to meet Uncle Glen.

When we arrived at the stable, it was buzzing with excitement; everyone was wondering what was going on. Uncle Glen took the lead rope from me and gave it to his trusted jockey, Lapishay. "There's no time to play around boys," Uncle Glen ordered. "Get this baby ready and get her out there for the relay race!"

Lapishay started to walk away with Dynamite. "Wait a minute," I shouted to him, "you need to know some things about Dynamite! Wait, wait! I have to tell you how to ride her!"

Lapishay snapped back at me, "Listen, I don't need no instruction, there ain't a horse alive that I can't ride."

Uncle Glen took me by the arm and pulled me away, "He's the best jockey I have, just leave him alone we don't want to get him rattled right before the race."

We all went back to our seats, and when the lineup was announced, all I heard was… DYNAMITE, my horses name, loudly over the speakers; the sound was like music to my ears.

Dynamite was the anchor horse and expected to pull the team through. Each horse was to run a single lap around the track and then the jockeys were to pass a baton to the next rider on their team, and then they ran a lap. There were four horses on each team.

BOOM!! The race began! The crowd screamed and cheered as I anxiously watched the other horses take their turns around the track. The first horse ran, the second, and then the third began his lap. Dynamite was the next horse to run, and Lapishay moved her into position. Dynamite

86

was a hard horse to handle, and with all of the excitement and a stranger on her back, I could tell that she was uneasy.

"I hope that that jockey is as good as he thinks he is," I said quietly, and squeezed Skip's hand.

The first three horses in the relay race were far from Uncle Glen's best stock, but they were running strong and hard and Uncle Glen's team was ahead. All Dynamite would have to do was maintain the lead.

She stood ready to take her tremendous leap, charge ahead and win the race! My heart was pounding hard as the third horse came to the end of his lap and raced up alongside of Dynamite. The jockey reached to pass the baton to Lapishay, but Lapishay missed it and the other horse ran past. The rider came back and tried again, but the jockeys fumbled around trying to recover and actually dropped the baton! I couldn't believe my eyes, this just couldn't be happening!

Hindered by the bumbling jockeys, Dynamite was rearing up and raging with frustration as the other horses passed her by... one... two... three... Soon every horse in the race had whipped past her, leaving Dynamite in last place.

At long last, Lapishay finally had the baton in his hand, he released the reins and Dynamite lunged ahead, running hard, she gave it all she had and was quickly catching up. Dynamite was still in last place when she ran out of our sight behind the hedge, but when she came back into view on the other side, she was already in second place! The crowd roared, everyone was screaming in wild excitement at this magnificent feat!

Dynamite was closing the gap, rapidly gaining on the lead horse. It was truly a miracle! Despite the baton disaster, Dynamite had recovered and was looking good to win the race! Lapishay started whipping her, but that was what I did to make Dynamite slow down!

"No! No! Don't whip her!" I screamed in frustration.

Every time that jockey whipped her, Dynamite slowed down. When he stopped whipping her, she picked up speed and when she picked up speed, he whipped her some more and she slowed down again.

"That idiot! Can't he figure it out! He's blowing the race!" The boys and I screamed, helpless to do anything, but shout uselessly at the stupid jockey.

Dynamite had made a valiant effort, but between the late start, and the jockey whipping her it was just too much, and the winner crossed the finish line ahead of her. Senselessly, the jockey had cost Uncle Glen the race.

It was horrible! With everything that was riding on the races that day, I felt like my guts had been ripped out. Standing by helplessly, watching my magnificent horse beaten, not because she wasn't fast enough, but because of the jockey's foolish mistakes.

I couldn't bear it and I collapsed forward in my seat in agony, "Ahhhhh." What would happen to The Horse Center? What would happen to Uncle Glen and Aunt Mo? Now that Uncle Glen had lost the first race, things were even more bleak than before. And poor Dynamite, what about her? She knew what had happened and she must have felt terrible too.

Skip reached over and patted me on the back, "It's okay Wildcat, Uncle Glen knows what to do."

Uncle Glen was already on his feet talking to some of his men, "We're making some changes," he told them. "Put Dynamite in the final race. And fire Lapishay! I want that man thrown off the property! No one could be that ham-handed, he must have been paid off! It explains a lot of things that have been happening around here! I've been sabotaged, betrayed by my own man!! And don't let anyone near Dynamite or Frantic Heartbeat; both of those babies have to win or I'm finished!"

Knowing the weight of the situation, I walked up to have a talk with Uncle Glen. "Uncle Glen, Dynamite is my horse and she can win if I ride her!"

Uncle Glen held me by the shoulders and intensely looked me in the eyes, "I know you can ride kid, they don't call you Wildcat for nothing. All right, call your father and get his permission, if he says it's okay, you'll ride Dynamite in the final race."

I called my dad and he was fine with it, but he was out of town and couldn't make it back in time for the race. "You and Dynamite blow 'em up Puppy!"

I looked after Dynamite and got suited up. I was putting on my cap when I noticed Lancaster III and his son Lancaster IV coming down from their seats. The son disappeared into the crowd, but Lancaster III walked into the stable with two of his henchmen and began sneering and making fun of Uncle Glen. "Getting desperate, Wells? I never thought I'd see you stoop this low. How pathetic can you be? It was bad enough entering a puny backyard pony in a race, but now I find out that your jockey is a twelve year old girl! You're embarrassing yourself, Glen. You give up now and I'll let you keep that shiny belt buckle that you're so proud of."

Lancaster and his crew began to laugh like a bunch of hyenas. I was so angry that I wanted to punch them all in the nose, but I knew that Uncle Glen could handle it himself.

"Sounds to me like you're the one who's getting nervous, Lancaster," Uncle Glen said as he chuckled and shook his head. "Maybe you should throw in the towel now, just to save yourself the humiliation of being beaten by that backyard pony and twelve year old girl. I'm only thinking of you, buddy. "

I knew that Lancaster's son had recognized me from the race at the beach, and that he must have told his father that Dynamite and I had beaten his prized champion, Militant Melody. Lancaster III was furious, he began to shout angrily at Uncle Glen, "I'm going to stop you Wells! You mark my words, you'll regret this day!" Then Lancaster III and his men went back to their seats.

I had a lot to do before the race, and it was my last chance use the restroom. I gave Dynamite to her handlers, "Here, get her ready, I'll be right back, and don't let anyone near her!"

I preferred to use the private restroom at the back of The Horse Center, so I cut behind the bull pen and walked down the lane. When I reached the restroom, I went inside, but when I tried to close the door, it was forced open by Lancaster IV and two young thugs who grabbed me by the arms.

Lancaster stepped inside and locked the door behind him. "You stupid ugly, little bitch," he said as he slapped me across the face. "Who do you think you're dealing with, some country hick?" He began to hit and punch me, again and again, working me over.

This wasn't like a scene in a movie; I didn't shout defiant insults at my captor, further enraging him. I didn't spit in his face and put up a senseless struggle that I could never win; it would only escalate the violence against me and prolong the beating, so I shut up, gritted my teeth, and took my beating, hoping that it would soon be over.

While Lancaster pounded me, he insulted and threatened to kill my family if I dared to win the race. "You're way out of your league, little girl, and you aren't going to beat me again, not this time!"

When Lancaster spoke of how Dynamite and I had beaten him, it made him crazed with anger; he began to scream so wildly that it looked as though his eyeballs were going to pop right out of their sockets. In his fit of rage, spit flew from of his mouth and I turned my head away. Lancaster gave me one last brutal blow, with his fist clenched tightly, he hit me as hard as he could in the stomach. I fell forward and his cohorts threw me down and left me lying on the floor, coughing and gasping.

They slammed the door behind them as they left the scene. "She won't be riding in any race today, ha, ha, ha, ha, ha." Their laughter faded as they walked further away.

As I laid there struggling for air, I realized how foolish I had been. "Boy was I stupid, I should have known better than to come in here alone." It hadn't occurred to me that they would come after me; I had only been concerned about Dynamite's safety. This was a lesson that I had learned the hard way.

When you get beat up, you really don't know how bad it is at first, you just feel pain all over. I waited, hoping that it would let up. After a few minutes, I managed to catch my breath. Then, I slowly tried to move each of my arms and legs to see if they still worked. I had taken a rough beating, but the thugs knew what they were doing, they were professionals and hadn't left a mark on me. I wasn't bleeding and nothing was broken.

When I realized that I could move, I reached up and took hold of the sink; it hurt like heck, but I managed to pull myself to my feet. Suddenly, I felt nauseous and I spit up some blood. I don't know what it was about seeing that blood in the sink, but when I saw it, I felt a rage welling up inside of me like I had never felt before. Lancaster couldn't even face me alone, he had to bring backup with him to beat up a little girl. I wasn't going to let these cowards get away with it! I was more determined now than ever before to beat the Lancaster's. I wiped the blood from my mouth, "It'll take more than an ass-whuppin' to stop me Lancaster!" I slammed opened the door and painfully made my way back down the lane to the track.

As I walked, I could hear the announcer blaring over the loudspeaker; the horses were lining up; the next race was about to begin. If Frantic Heartbeat lost, it was all over and I wouldn't ride. I listened closely and kept walking toward the stable.

The race was on! Frantic Heartbeat was off to a good start and despite the fact that she had recently recovered from a leg injury, she was running like the champion she was. It sounded like she was good to win! It was wonderful! It gave me the push that I needed, and I picked up my pace, there was still hope!

As I stepped into the stable ... Frantic Heartbeat crossed the finish line first, she had won the race! "Yes!" I shouted and put my fist in the air.

The race was over and my friends came running from trackside back into the stable looking for me. Everyone was excited and shouting, spirits were high, things were finally going our way! I was happy too, but in a lot of pain, and I was trying to hold it together. My stomach was hurting and I started to cough, so I stepped behind the barn to spit ... it was blood again. Skip had followed me, and when he saw the blood on the ground he looked at me alarmed. "Don't you tell anybody," I said fiercely, and walked back with the others.

The pressure was on, and now it was all up to Dynamite and me. I felt as though I had the weight of the whole world on my shoulders.

Uncle Glen was feeling the pressure too, "Are you alright kid? You don't look too good; why is your face so red? What's the matter? Are you sure that you can handle it? Don't get rattled now!"

About that time, I wished that there was someone else who could ride Dynamite, but it had to be me; there was no other choice. "Uncle Glen, I can handle it," I said, not knowing if I was telling the truth.

I stood alongside Dynamite and looked at her, admiring her magnificent beauty. She held her head high, her eyes were bright with excitement and her shiny sleek, black coat was glistening in the sunshine. "Okay girl, this is it, the big race, it's all up to you." I took a deep breath, put my foot in the stirrup and mounted my majestic steed.

Uncle Glen was beside me, "Okay kid, don't get nervous now, you can handle it."

"Uncle Glen, I'm not nervous, I'm just going to ride my horse."

Dynamite and I were led onto the track as the horses were lining up. Dynamite could smell the tension and excitement in the air; the adrenaline got the best of her, and she reared up whinnying and leaping. "Settle down girl! Take it easy!"

The race was about to begin; I was shaking badly and my heart was pounding loudly in my ears. Dynamite was ready, always strong at the break, she was breathing heavy, anxiously waiting. Those few moments seemed like an eternity, then suddenly BOOM! The race was on! Dynamite exploded! She took her tremendous mighty leap and immediately took the lead. She hugged the rail and ran at an incredibly fast and steady pace leaving the other horses further and further behind her with every stride.

This race was no contest for Dynamite, all I had to do was hang on and not fall off, but that wasn't as easy as it sounded. I was getting dizzier and more nauseous by the second. I stayed in position as long as I could, but I started to lose my balance and I laid down on Dynamite clenching her around the neck. Dynamite knew that something was wrong with me… and she stopped dead in her tracks.

"It's okay girl, keep going!" I urged her on, but she wouldn't listen, she wouldn't move ahead, not a step.

The other horses were catching up, but Dynamite still wouldn't move. She had never let me fall off of her before, and this race was no exception.

What was she to do? Let me fall on the track, leaving me behind to be trampled? Never! She was waiting until she knew that I had regained my balance before she would make another move, just as she always had.

The other horses were getting closer, they were nearly ready to pass us and I realized that I might as well get off and call it quits if I couldn't make Dynamite believe that I was okay. Dizzy or not, I pulled myself together, "Come on girl! Let's go!"

Sensing that I was better, Dynamite rocketed ahead and began to run again at a full gallop, just maintaining the lead. I focused my eyes on the top of her head, trying to keep my balance. "Come on Penelope, hold it together," I whispered to myself. I slapped myself on the cheeks trying to snap myself out of it. "You can do it, just stay on the blasted horse!" Dynamite was on her own, I couldn't direct or help her, the best I could do was not fall off.

Dynamite was pouring it on, and I listened to her hooves hitting the ground, ba, da, doomp…ba, da, doomp… ba, da, doomp, when bam, it hit! Suddenly, blood came bursting from my mouth! I bent to the side, it splattered all over Dynamite and again, she came to an abrupt stop. There was nothing that I could do, I heaved and heaved hoping that it would stop and that I could continue the race, but I wasn't sure what was happening to me. I didn't know if I was going to bleed to death right there on the racetrack.

Dynamite was beside herself, she was trying to stand still and not jar me, as one horse after another passed her up!

I couldn't pull it together and sadly, Dynamite was in last place again, just like in the relay race. Of no fault of her own, victory was being snatched away once again from the magnificent animal.

Just when I thought that all was lost, the heaving stopped and I suddenly felt better, I was no longer dizzy or nauseous; seemed that throwing up had helped. Even though things looked hopeless, I couldn't give up, "This race isn't over yet! Come on Dynamite, let's go girl! Yah!!"

Dynamite knew that I was okay, and that it was time to pour it on… KA…BOOM!! She lunged ahead once again and tried with all her might to win the high-stake race, the race that everything was riding on. But was it too late? Was The Horse Center lost? Or could the sleek and powerful Dynamite still win with the odds stacked so heavily against her?

Determined, steady and unwavering, Dynamite kept up an incredible pace and she began to gain on the other horses. She passed one, and then the next; with each stride she stretched her legs and body out so far that it felt as though her belly was glancing the ground. I was riding so low that when we passed the other horses, their riders were above my head.

We were in the final stretch; there were two horses still ahead of us. "Come on Dynamite, come on girl!" Dynamite was determined; she was taking it on, running fast and furious; she was a champion, a champion expecting to win!

I could feel each breath that she took and the steady pounding of her big strong heart, the sound of her hooves hitting the ground thrusting us forward, faster and faster and faster!

Dynamite passed the horse in second place and was pressing in on the lead, still faster and faster she went. I could see the finish line; we were quickly closing the gap, but it didn't look like she could possibly make it in time!

I was focused on the finish line when suddenly I saw a bright flash of light, and then everything seemed as though I was looking through a mysterious clouded veil. I tried to clear my vision, I blinked my eyes and shook my head, and then I blinked again. My mind couldn't believe what my eyes were seeing; Dynamite was adorned by a pair of shiny black, feathered wings! She gave her mighty wings a beat and we glided over the finish line!

We had won! Dynamite had really won the race!! The victory was sweet! I stood in my stirrups with my fists in the air! Everything seemed surreal, like it was moving in slow motion, but it was very real, Dynamite had finally tasted the victory that she so greatly deserved!

Dynamite won more than a race that day, she had not only saved The Horse Center; she had finally won her place in the world. After being underestimated from the very start of her life, misplaced and misjudged, she had made her way back to where she belonged; doing what she had been born to do, run like the wind!

Dynamite moved on to her new life as a highfaluting race horse. I didn't see her much after that, I never tried to interfere, it was her time to shine and I set her free to live it.

EDUCATION IN WAR

Being chased by bulls, bucked off horses and shot by B-B guns, were common occurrences in my young life. I had broken my nose at least twice, along with some ribs and a variety of other bones. I always had cuts, scrapes and bruises. I remembered my mother saying, (while I was digging gravel out of my knees) "Your legs are going to be scarred and ugly by the time you're a young lady."

And that's what I was thinking about, my knees, when Dad stopped the car to get gas, and abruptly ended my daydreaming. I had been daydreaming about my childhood for hours and was so deep in thought that I forgot where I was for a moment, but quickly remembered that I was in the car traveling East with my family. Yes it was true; I was leaving the country life, and everything I knew behind me. Thirteen years old, and on my way to start a new life in the big city. "Once we get there, I don't expect I'll get knocked around anymore. Mom will be happy; I'll do my best to be a sophisticated lady, and maybe my legs will look okay after all." I knew that city life would be completely different from what I was used to and I was looking forward to the adventure.

After several days of travel, we reached our destination and moved into a beautiful grand home on the beach. I ran on the white sand and played in the cold water. It was fall and the weather crisp, but I didn't let that stop me, I loved the beach. It was an exclusive area, and the neighbors were welcoming and friendly.

That Monday morning, I got up early, as it was time to get ready for school. I tied a ribbon in my hair to look nice for this big day and my long red curls fell down my back. I wore a pink wrap-around skirt with a white cotton blouse. I viewed myself in the mirror before I walked out the door, "What would the folks back home think about Wildcat Wells now, all gussied up like a sweet little, city gal?"

I went to the new Junior High a little apprehensive; being the new kid is never easy. I climbed up the stairs of the school bus and smiled shyly at the other students. There was a seat by the window behind the driver and I sat down. The bus made a sharp turn and headed inland, directly away from the beach.

The area quickly changed from the big beautiful homes with pristine landscaping, to blocks and blocks of cramped dark, apartment buildings with broken windows and screens. Letters and symbols were written on the buildings that made no sense to me, and dirty young children were running on the sidewalks and in the streets.

A shabbily dressed man stumbled in front of the bus; the driver swerved, barely missing him, then the man fell face down in the gutter. When I saw that the driver intended to do nothing, I stood up and put my hand on his shoulder, "Shouldn't we stop and help that sick man?"

"Don't worry about it kid, he's just an old drunk."

I slowly sat back down; this was something that I had never seen before,

94

and it greatly disturbed me.

Soon, the bus pulled up to the school, and before it had even stopped, the children began pushing and shoving toward the front of the bus. I waited until they had all gotten off, and then climbed down the stairs and stepped onto the sidewalk. I stopped and looked around; everything was dreary and cold, grey cement and asphalt. There were no trees or hills, no fresh green grass; even the air felt heavy and gritty and dirty.

I walked into the ominous school building and found my way to the office. The woman at the front desk was very rude. She spoke to me in a sharp tone and acted as though I was bothering her. I told her my name and she yelled in a shrill voice to someone in the other room, "Where's the schedule for the new kid?" She found it under the counter and without a word, sharply handed it to me; it read; first class geography; room; cafeteria. I left the office and ventured off to find the cafeteria. I could see numbers on the doors of the classrooms, but had no clue as to where the cafeteria would be, so I went back to the office to ask for directions. The same rude woman ignored me for the longest time, then finally looked at me annoyed, "What do you want now?" she sneered.

I asked her where the cafeteria was, and if it was the location of my geography class. "Turn right, end of the hall," she said, as she pointed her long boney finger toward the door. I kindly thanked her for her help, even though she didn't deserve it, and I started down the long hallway.

Weighing in at barely one hundred pounds, and with a lost look on my face, I might as well have been wearing a target.

The bell rang and the halls were soon full of racing young teenagers, hurrying to class. When suddenly… BAM! I felt myself slam against the tile wall by the drinking fountains. I had hit my head hard, but quickly recovered from the shock to see three, heavy-set black girls walking away. They were looking back at me over their shoulders, laughing with glee, their big hips swaggering back and forth as they congratulated one another, patting each other on the back and interlocking arms.

I felt pain surge through me, but the thing that filled me more was anger. I ran the few steps and caught up with them. "Do you have a problem with me?" I angrily shouted. I grabbed the one who had struck me and jerked her around, so I could see her, face to face. "Because if you do, let's settle it right here, right now!" I stood there, ready for her to make a move. She was twice my size and there were three of them, but I didn't care, I wasn't about to be bullied.

"We ain't got no problem wit you white girl," was what she said.

I let loose of her arm and sternly looked her in the eye, "Stay out of my way or I'll gut you like the pigs back home!" I backed away a few steps; and then they walked down the hall. They weren't laughing this time; they had met Wildcat Wells.

I went back by the drinking fountains. I had a big knot on my head and I splashed some water on my face, picked up my notebook and went on to class.

By the time I got there, class had already begun. I went to the teacher and told him who I was. When the teacher announced that I was the new girl, the boys wolf whistled and the class applauded in welcome. No one had ever whistled at me before. "I guess I must have done a good job fixing myself up," I proudly thought.

Finally, I was in a comfortable place. As I walked to my seat, I wondered why no one seemed to take notice of what had happened to me earlier in the hall. It wasn't more than twenty minutes later when I found out why. Suddenly, without warning...CRASH! CRASH! CRASH! I jumped to my feet! Were we being bombed?! I looked in the direction of the uproar, and saw a barrage of bricks crashing through the cafeteria windows. The windows were at least twenty feet high. We scattered to get out of the way of the flying bricks and glass. We burst through the cafeteria doors and into the hall; it was the only exit or way of escape.

When we reached the hallway, bombs exploded and the air quickly filled with suffocating gas. We were all choking and gasping for breath, it felt like needles were poking me in the throat and lungs. My eyes were watering and burning and I could only make out shadows. I tried to find my way out of the dense fog, but I didn't know my way around this school and I didn't know a single soul! What was I going to do? I wondered how much longer I could last without air. Was this poison that we were inhaling? Were we all going to drop dead?

"Here, this way!" I heard a voice say; it was a girl from my class. She pushed open some doors and I saw the blue sky; other kids quickly pressed behind us, desperately running out into the air. We were all coughing and gasping for breath, rubbing our eyes and trying to clear our vision. I heard someone say that it was a Mace bomb. Mace was sure miserable, but at least I knew that it wasn't fatal.

I glanced around me and noticed something strange, everyone with us was white. "What happened to all the black kids?" I asked the girl.

"There," she said in a grave voice as she slowly raised her arm and pointed across the schoolyard. I looked in that direction, and saw a huge group of black kids slowly walking towards us, each one opening a bigger knife than the last.

The school doors closed behind us and puffs of gas billowed out as they locked shut. At this point I knew it was an ambush; I was in a war, we were greatly outnumbered, there was no escape, and I had no weapon. I remembered the giant golden, safety pin on the flap of my skirt. It was just a decoration, but I pulled it off and it fit perfectly in my hand. "Better than nothing."

The color of my skin determined which side I was fighting on; right or wrong, there were no choices. It was a horrible battle, over what I never knew, but I fought for my life back to back with the girl from my class.

In the heat of the attack I was struck on the side of the head; I felt the shock, then everything went black. When I came to, I was on the ground, and someone was kicking me in the stomach. It must have been the girl who had pushed me by the drinking fountains because I heard her say, "You the pig now, white bitch."

I rolled over on my right side, away from her, then she started kicking me in the back and ribs; hard, sharp blows. She mercilessly pounded me, one kick after another! "Ahhh," I couldn't get up, but still clenched in my fist was the safety pin. It was sharp and strong as an ice pick. I swung around and savagely rammed the pin deep into her thigh until I felt it hit the bone. I held tight to my weapon and pulled it back out. She stopped kicking me and grabbed her leg as she limped away screaming and crying.

I shook my head and was starting to stand up when someone grabbed me from behind. He was tall and strong and had me firmly by the neck with his left forearm. He held my right wrist with his other hand, tight like a vise; I was still holding the pin and he made sure not to get stuck with it. He tightened his arm around my throat and lifted my feet from the ground, while he strangled me. I pulled on his forearm with my left hand; I was kicking, thrashing and trying to get free, but I couldn't break away, he had such a strong hold on me.

Then I saw someone running toward me, her eyes were crazy looking, foam was oozing from the corners of her mouth and her black hair stuck straight out in clumps. She was holding a dagger above her head and screaming, "You stabbed my sister, white bitch, you gonna die!"

I had one chance to survive the attack, even though I was being strangled, I still had to stop her. When she got closer, I bent both of my knees to my chest, kicked out and hit her square in the face. The heels of my shoes were heavy and she hit the ground hard, knocked out cold.

The guy was still holding me, but the jolt of the kick had changed my position. I got his forearm in my teeth and bit him hard until he let go. He released me, leaving a trail of blood streaming from his arm as he ran from the scene.

I fell to my knees, choking and gasping for air, but I couldn't catch my breath, there was something in my mouth. I realized that I had bitten off a chunk of his arm! I spit out the flesh and took in a deep breath of air.

My head was down, my hair tangled and hanging in my face; I slowly rose to my feet and tossed back my head, blood spattered from the ends of my long curls as they flung back, and blood was dripping from my mouth. My pretty outfit now stained red from the battle; I stood looking over the schoolyard at a sea of students lying injured on the ground. It was over, there was no one left to fight. I raised my fists to the sky and let out a long loud, victory scream to the heavens... I had survived!

I tried to walk away, but the blood was slippery under my feet and it was hard to keep my balance. I slowly made my way to the girl from class. She too was still standing, and we threw our arms around each other. Those who could walk away, did.

The girl and I went into the restroom arm in arm, steadying each other as we walked. When we got inside we washed the blood from our hands and faces and I looked at her in the big mirror, "I'm Penelope."

With a smirky grin she said, "Kate." At that moment, I knew that Kate was my best friend.

Later that day, when the school released us, I climbed slowly up the steps onto the school bus. As I sat in the seat the bus pulled away from the school. I could tell that some of my ribs were broken and at least one of my toes. "And I expected that city life would be easier. It's a good thing that I have a hard head."

When I got home, I never said a word about what had happened; I simply accepted it; this was the way that my life was now.

I knew from experience that the doctor couldn't do anything about broken ribs or toes, so I wrapped my ribs in an ace bandage and taped my broken toe to the one next to it. I climbed into bed and somehow found a comfortable position and started drifting off to sleep. "I don't like my new school," I said to myself out loud.

When I returned to school, I found that I already had a bit of a reputation. It seemed that the new girl didn't back down and had fought with a safety pin in a knife fight. I was befriended by the tough kids; they hung out by the tree at the back left side of the schoolyard and smoked cigarettes; and they offered me one. I had never smoked a cigarette before; no one in my family smoked. "No thank you," I answered.

"Don't you want to be cool like us?" they teased.

These people were my new friends and my only protection in this school of depravity. "I don't want to offend them," I thought, "maybe I should have a cigarette." Still I hesitated; it seemed like a serious decision. "I'll let you know on Monday," I answered. It was Friday and I figured that I would have the weekend to investigate. My answer satisfied my new friends, and we went on talking about other things, like how we would survive the next attack.

Back then, smoking didn't carry the stigma that it does today; it was openly accepted and smokers smoked wherever they pleased. I don't know if it's true or not, but it seemed to me that the smokers outnumbered the non-smokers.

What was the attraction? What did people get out of this nasty habit that yellowed their teeth and blackened their lungs? I was going to find out.

That Saturday and Sunday, I happened to come in contact with several adult smokers, and I studied them. I watched them smoke and I asked them what they had to say about it. Every one of the adult smokers, without exception, wanted to quit and wished that they had never started. They were no longer smoking because they wanted to, or because it was cool, they were now driven to smoke and the cigarettes controlled them. I didn't want anything controlling me, and I decided then and there that I would never smoke. Why should I start something that everyone wanted to quit, and couldn't?

At school on Monday, while I was out by the tree with my friends, they offered me another cigarette and I told them that I had decided not to smoke. When they asked me why, I simply told them that I could find no good reason to start. After that, no one ever asked me again. Though it was never said, I think that they respected me for it.

I never did smoke a cigarette, and as the years passed and people became more aware of the dangers, I was grateful for the decision that I had made back in Junior High School.

I hung out with my friends by the tree every day. We had fun laughing and flirting, and playing teenage games. It was there that I received my first gift from a boy; a special boy that I liked very much, his name was Bucky. Bucky shyly handed me a burgundy velvet, gift bag. I opened it up, reached inside, and to my surprise, pulled out brass knuckles. It was a shame that an appropriate gift for Bucky to give his sweetheart were brass knuckles, but I was happy to have them and I put them in my pocket.

Bucky and I lived far apart, and as both of us were too young to drive, the only time that we could see one another was at school, during lunch break, in the "war zone."

In a place like that, you can't be alone, and I welcomed the friendship and protection of my newfound friends, all seasoned warriors at thirteen years old. The first lesson they taught me; never pull out a weapon unless you intend to use it, a lesson I live by to this day.

The school was akin to a prison; the code to survival...respect the color line, regardless of your individual belief. I wasn't a racist, nor would I ever become a racist, but I was hated because I was white. There are realities that demand a response, and in a violent institution you have to find a way to protect yourself and survive. Survival for me was my gang.

Over time, I became very close to the kids in my gang; we clung to each other and protected and trusted one another. It was unspoken, but we were all devoted to one another, and had a strong bond and a love between us. We knew that our survival depended on the gang watching our backs, and we appreciated it. We fought and risked our lives for each other, knowing full well that when we were the one in danger, our friends would be there to back us up.

Things were different back then, than they are now. We never used guns; not because we couldn't get them, but because you were considered weak, and a coward if you weren't strong enough to fight your enemy face to face. It takes no courage to simply pull a trigger and gun someone down; at no risk to yourself. We fought hand to hand, toe to toe, eyeball to eyeball.

I stayed close to Bucky when we had to go back into the school building from the yard. Tightly grouped together in the hallway with other people pressing against us, was when we were in the most danger of being stabbed. It was easy for someone to get close, stick you and then move away into the crowd. We kept a sharp watch on the hands and eyes of the enemy, trying to judge who they might target; ready to jump into action and fight instantly if someone made a move against one of us. Even though we took every precaution we could, sometimes we would still get shanked.

The tension was too much for some of the kids to handle and they got involved in drugs and alcohol to ease the pain and tension. As for myself, I never wanted to be in a vulnerable state. I figured that I needed every bit of my wit and coordination to survive and I wasn't going to handicap myself voluntarily.

The kids in the gang lived by a set of rules; the most important of them all was never, never, go anywhere alone, not the halls and especially not the restroom, it was by far the most dangerous and vulnerable place to be.

Tack bombs were thrown into the restrooms; they exploded so quickly that there could be no escape. They were homemade bombs that exploded tacks when they blew up. Being hit by one was painful and dangerous, tacks stuck all over your face and body.

When we went to the restroom, one of us had to guard outside the door to watch for bombers and at least two of us inside in case of an ambush. Having to use the toilet was a dangerous undertaking, but unavoidable.

I had survived the seventh and eighth grade, and was half way into the ninth. I battled my way through the winter months, just trying to graduate from Junior High. While children in normal schools could enjoy their education; learning new things, sports, clubs and other activities; I just hoped to make it out alive. I prayed that no one would scar my face, tear my hair out or gang rape me before it was over.

Through it all, my friends and I stood together and they never let me down. It may seem strange to say, but I enjoyed a closeness and camaraderie at that time of my life that I would never experience again.

In the spring, before the end of the school year, my wild cousin Peggy came to live with us. I had only seen her once in my life when her family was passing through town. We were small children at the time, and I didn't remember her very well, only that she was older than me. I guess that we were related in some way through my mother's, mother's first husband. I was never sure exactly what the connection really was. In any event I didn't know her in the slightest.

Peggy had run away from home and hitchhiked across the country. When her parents got her back, they couldn't handle her and my parents graciously, although foolishly, took her into our home. Was I the one who was supposed to rehabilitate her? I didn't understand it. Peggy insisted that I share my bedroom with her, all of my belongings, and most importantly, be sworn to secrecy.

One day, Peggy decided that she and I were going to take a walk down the beach. My parents didn't object, after all, exercise is good for you and they naturally assumed that we would be walking in the sand and surf. But that wasn't the way that it went, Peggy wanted to walk down the street. When we got away from the house, she unbuttoned her blouse all the way down and tied it in a knot under her breasts, then she had me shorten her bra straps for her. This girl was stacked, with a walk to match, long red hair, blue eyes and cute little freckles across her nose. She lit up a cigarette and swaggered down the street.

Needless to say, it didn't take long for her to get attention. Two greasy haired guys on Harley Davidsons roared ahead of us and stopped across our path. One of the guys was talking to Peggy; I shied back, but to my surprise, the other guy started talking to me! I thought he was incredible, strong and rugged looking. "They call me Chainsaw Charlie, what's your name, sweetheart?" I wouldn't tell him. "That's alright," he said, "I'll just call you Angel, that's what you look like, an Angel."

I didn't want any part of the whole thing. I tried to get Peggy to go back home, but there was no stopping her. She hopped on the back of the hog and the greasy haired guy revved the engine. They were smiling while Chainsaw Charlie circled around me on his bike, asking me to get on. Peggy started calling me a sissy and making fun of me. No kid wants to be called a sissy, especially not me. After all, I was supposed to keep an eye on Peggy, so I climbed on the back of the huge motorcycle. Chainsaw Charlie told me to put my arms around him and lean with the road, then we roared off.

As we rode along, it started to rain a little and I buried my face in Chainsaw's neck; he smelled like leather; his hair and neck were wet and greasy and dirty.

We were going up a steep hill with a sharp turn and Chainsaw told me to hang on. "I don't want you falling off darlin'," he said as he turned his head to the side. The wind was blowing his hair and he smiled at me. It was then that I felt his strong heavy hand, cloaked in that big black, leather glove cover my hands tightly, to hold me safe. He gunned the engine, the powerful bike roared, and off we raced.

I didn't know it at the time, but I was now hooked on the bad boys.

Peggy and I rode with the bikers for about an hour and then we headed back toward the house. They dropped us off a few blocks away and Peggy gave them our phone number. As I watched the loud motorcycles drive away, I wondered if I would ever see Chainsaw Charlie again.

The next day, it was back to school and nothing had changed. I was still suffering through the same dangerous situations that I had faced from the very first day. Nothing had been done to ease the racial tension and violence. We openly carried knives and weapons right into the school. Kids were being attacked, beaten, stabbed and raped. The principal, police and parents of the children did nothing and simply blamed the gang wars on bussing. Bussing was meant to transport the less fortunate students living in bad areas, to good schools to receive a better education. Obviously not true in my case.

Some of the teachers were actually contributing to the violence. I saw one of the teachers slam a young boy against the lockers and have a fist fight with him. The teacher came back to school the next day as if nothing had happened and there was never anything said about the incident. It was complete chaos.

One day, I had to go into the restroom alone, I had no choice. Sure enough, while I was in the stall, I heard someone being knocked around. I peeked out the door and saw three black girls, beating on one little white, nerd girl. One of them held the girl against the wall, pressing her forearm against her throat while the other two kicked and punched her, shaking her down for money.

I stood up on the john and grasped the bar that ran across the top of the stall with both hands. Then I pushed off of the back wall and kicked open the metal door. It slammed hard, BAM! With the acoustics in the restroom it sounded like a bomb had exploded. I jumped into the middle of the room, ready for a fight.

The black girls stopped what they were doing and looked in my direction. They were rattled; I took advantage of it and quickly told them to back off. They shuffled around a little, muttered a few things under their breath, and then left.

I bent down and picked up the girls books for her and asked if she was okay. She screamed at me, "Leave me alone!" Then she ripped her books from my hands and ran out. I stood there stunned; what was this? I had made a big mistake.

Because of this incident I was then targeted; word came to my friends through a reliable source that the largest, most vicious, black gang in the school was after me. They said that I had interfered with their business. They intended to cut my hair to teach me a lesson and if anyone tried to help me, they would get the same. This was a threat that we all took seriously.

This gang was notoriously cruel and known for committing heinous acts. One of their favorite atrocities was to rip out the long blonde ponytails of young girls, scalp and all, and then beat and gang rape her. This gang was so cruel that even the other black gangs disapproved of their tactics and steered clear of them.

During this perilous time, my friends stood by me. It was decided that I could not be alone, not even for a moment, and my faithful friend Kate never left my side.

Three days after we had gotten news of the threat, we were all gathered by the tree having lunch when here they came, the most vicious black gang in school. The whole gang, every one of them made a showing that day, trying to intimidate us with their vast number. Ever so slowly they walked across the schoolyard, hoping to instill us with fear.

We rose to our feet to meet them in battle. Once again we were greatly outnumbered, and once again I saw the knives, but this time my friends pulled out their knives too, we were ready for them. When they got closer, the enemy stopped and stared us down, then the leader began to speak. I wasn't surprised to hear him say, "Give us da red-headed bitch, dat's all we want. Den we leave de rest a-you alone."

Bucky stepped in front of me and pushed me behind him. "We ain't afraid of you, you fuckin' ugly baboons! Bring it on!"

With that, the enemy began to walk toward us again, still moving slowly. They were sneering and flashing their blades in the sunlight while they viciously described the different ways that they were going to mutilate us.

My friends pulled me further and further back passing me from one to the next, each pushing me behind themselves. "They'll never get through me," each of them promised; until I was standing behind them all.

Kate was beside me, she threw her arm around my shoulders, "Don't worry Palsy, I won't let 'em get ya."

I stood ready to fight, knife clenched in one hand, brass knuckles in the other. This was it; I was the target of every one of the enemies' menacing weapons. I was hoping that my friends could hold them off, while I drove the thought from my mind of what would happen to me if they couldn't.

At that moment, from the tall grass, in the field behind us, our backup men stood up. One at a time, each revealed himself and took his place beside us. The backup men were the drop-out boyfriends of the girls in our gang; we had smuggled them into the schoolyard earlier that day.

This evened the odds a bit; the enemy didn't want any part of it and they turned and went back toward the school building. We had backed them down, at least for now. It was a temporary relief, but we all knew that it was far from over. The stakes were merely higher now; they would wait for a more opportune time for their attack, a time when I was vulnerable.

I made it through the day and headed home on the school bus. As surprising as it may be, I still had to do school work in this hell hole of a school and try to make good grades. I had a report due and I needed to go to the library that night. My cousin Peggy saw this as the perfect opportunity to meet Chainsaw Charlie's friend Bill, so she went with me. When we arrived at the library, Peggy waited in front for Bill and I went inside to start my homework.

I was writing at a table when I heard the sound of chains jingling. I looked up and saw Chainsaw Charlie in his leathers and big boots, strutting through the library looking for me. When he saw me, he nodded

104

hello, and as he sat down next to me. He gently took my face in his hands and gave me a sweet tender kiss on the forehead. "Hello Angel" he said in his smooth sexy voice.

I quickly finished my report and we went outside and sat on a bench in front of the library and he asked me what was going on at school. I was hesitant to tell him at first, but I think he must have known something because he pressed for more details.

Finally, I spilled the whole story, "Chainsaw I've got a big problem; the toughest black gang in the school is after me. They've threatened to cut my hair, and I know what that means; catch me alone, rip my hair out by the roots and then beat me and gang rape me. They've already done it to some of the other girls."

Just as I finished telling Chainsaw Charlie my harrowing story, Bill and Peggy came back from their ride and pulled up on the sidewalk in front of the library. Before they could get off the bike, Chainsaw jumped up from the bench and rushed toward Bill. "We're picking the Angel up from school tomorrow, she's having some trouble." Chainsaw Charlie was waving his arms and screaming as he told Bill what was going on.

Bill was furious, "You be out in front of the school at three o'clock tomorrow Angel."

Peggy wanted to go, but Bill said, "No, no girls, there might be trouble."

"But Penelope's going to be there," Peggy foolishly whined.

"Yes, but she's already in the middle of this thing," then, he put his head in his hands and sighed.

The next day after school, I went out front to meet Bill and Chainsaw Charlie. I could hear a low roar in the distance and it came closer and louder. Like thunder, a hundred Harleys or more roared into the school parking lot. They had guns strapped to their thighs, swords on their backs and knives clenched in their teeth. Some even had old medieval, mace-like weapons, swinging them in the air above their heads. They were yelling and sticking out their tongues, spinning the bikes in circles, burning rubber and making smoke. The air smelled of gas fumes and exhaust and was thick with burning rubber smoke. It was wild!

"And I thought that I was just getting a ride home from school!"

Then Chainsaw Charlie pulled up and stopped in front of me, "Come on Angel," he called. Without a second thought, I left Bucky behind. Chainsaw picked me up and put me on the front of the bike facing him. I wrapped my legs around his waist and gave him a big kiss on the mouth. His dark greasy hair hung down on his forehead and into his eyes; he tossed his head, "Don't you worry Angel, Chainsaw's taken care of everything," then he flashed me a cocky grin. Chainsaw Charlie had a wild untamed look in his eye and he was watching everything. We drove slowly into the middle of the other bikes and they closed rank around us.

Snake and some of the other bikers lunged up on the sidewalk in front of the school and the crowd quickly scattered to get out of the way of the roaring raging machines. Snake put his hand on the big gun strapped to his thigh and screamed a wild crazy scream, "Don't fuck with the Angel!" Then he stuck out his long tongue, threw his head back and let out an ear-piercing war cry. With that, the other bikers joined in, shouting wildly, they gunned their engines and flew off the curb and we all roared off together.

Bill was President of the motorcycle club.

The next day at school, everyone wanted to be my friend. I could walk down the halls without fear and no one gave me any more trouble. Chainsaw Charlie really had taken care of everything, that is, everything but Bucky, he now hated me. I tried to explain to him that Chainsaw and I were just friends, but he didn't believe me. "You disrespected me in front of my friends," he said, "and don't think that I don't know what those guys are like. Chainsaw Charlie wouldn't waste his time with you if you weren't puttin' out!"

He, like everyone else, thought that he knew all about bikers, but he couldn't have been more wrong. But Bucky wasn't wrong about one thing, I had disrespected him and we couldn't get past it.

At first I was deeply upset and hurt and felt myself plummeting downward, but then I snapped myself out of it, "Hey, wait a minute I'm just a kid, I have my whole life ahead of me!" There was no doubt; I would find love and happiness with someone else. Yep, that's what I told myself, and I cowboyed up and swallowed the pain and heartbreak of losing my first boyfriend, Bucky.

It was true, Bucky hated me, but I still had the friendship of Chainsaw Charlie. With the devilish tattoos on his chest, arms and neck he was the typical stereotype biker. But, there was one thing that you wouldn't expect from a fierce young man like this, the fact that Chainsaw Charlie always dated a beautiful classy girlfriend from the wealthy part of town. The sophisticated feminine creatures riding on the back of Chainsaw's roaring wicked motorcycle always seemed out of place. But somehow the girls managed to struggle through the discomfort, just to have a piece of him. Chainsaw Charlie wasn't particularly handsome, but there was something very special about him that all the girls loved, and they continually battled for his affection.

Chainsaw's girlfriends always hated me, but there really wasn't a reason for them to. He considered me off limits in that regard, but for some reason he had assumed the responsibility of protecting me from harm. And that was all it ever was, a close and caring friendship.

Chainsaw Charlie was always careful where he took me, and who he allowed to come near me. He didn't like it much, but I always wanted to ride with him and the other club members. When he was certain that there would be no trouble, he would sometimes take me along on afternoon runs with the guys. I loved roaring down the streets with all the dirty bikers, and I always dressed for the occasion. Even though I was just a slip of a girl, I tried my best to look the part of the big bad, biker bitch. I wore my tightest Levis', a thick black belt with an eagle buckle, and pulled on heavy motorcycle boots. I had a tight top that slung over one shoulder, and on my left arm I tied a leather strap. I put grease in my hair and pulled it back in a braid, then rolled up a bandana and used it as a headband.

When I met up with Chainsaw, I was always excited to see him; I would run into his arms and give him a big hug. "How's my Angel?" he would say. Then I would swing my leg over the bike and sit on the seat behind him.

Chainsaw pushed the foot pegs down while the bike engine slowly sputtered, then he would grab my ankles one at a time, with his big black gloves and place each of my feet firmly on the pegs. His leather jacket squeaked with every move he made. Once he knew that my feet were secure, he pulled my arms tightly around him, and then squeezed my hands. "Hold tight Angel," he would always say as he gave me a pat on the thigh. Then he revved the thunderous engine and we rocketed off. As we thrust forward the sound and vibration pulsed through me, it was a rush every time.

When we met up with the other club members the excitement would build. There were no electric starters back then, (at least I had never seen one) and I loved to watch the guys jump-start their bikes. They cussed and screamed when the bike wouldn't turn over, but one by one each boisterous beast ferociously came to life and the roar grew louder and louder. The excitement; the sound; when we were ready to roll, as a hundred motorcycles thundered down the streets together.

When we passed through a town, our presence demanded a reaction from everyone. I watched curtains open as people ran to their windows to look out to see what the commotion was. Others stopped what they were doing to stand on the street corners and wave as each bike passed by. But sometimes, people ran away in fear acting as though it was an invasion, and in a way, I guess it was.

I was just a kid having a fun exciting time, but I'm certain that being seen with these untamed ferocious barbarians may have hurt my reputation. But, at the same time, because of that reputation I was protected.

It was the protection of Chainsaw Charlie and his friends that got me safely through the blood-ridden Junior High, but now I was moving on to High School. It was scary, wondering what new horrors awaited me there. I didn't have much hope of improvement; the students were older now, hardened, stronger, and more experienced which made them even more dangerous than before. How could things possibly be any better? I figured that the racial line would be even more distinct and I was expecting higher stakes and more pain in the new High School.

On the first day, I sadly discovered that I was correct in my assumption, the racial hatred and tension was predominant at the High School as well.

I was shaken when I learned that none of the members of my gang were attending the same school as me. They were spread out among the other school districts; we had been divided, scattered throughout the huge city.

I tried to make myself small and unnoticeable until I could get my footing. I had to find a way to survive without the protection of my gang. But walking down the halls, I found it impossible to remain unnoticed. Everyone knew who I was and they all knew my name; seems that my reputation had preceded me. I found that I had come through the most cutthroat school in the city and that my gang was among the toughest and most respected. I learned that the people in the High School knew of the goings on at the Junior High, they knew the players and because of it, I was shown respect and given a wide berth.

I managed to get through the morning without incident, but after lunch the principal called me into his office. I wondered why he wanted to see me and as soon as I entered, I found out that he intended to straighten me out; and I had done nothing to deserve it.

"This will be your first and only warning," he sternly told me waving his finger in my face. "Let it be known that I will not tolerate any violent behavior in my school. Even if you just happen to be in the general area, when violence breaks out, I will consider you responsible and you will suffer severe consequences!"

I was taken-back by the principal's heavy-handed theatrics; it was an extreme position that he was taking against me and he was completely wrong. Since when had I become the bad guy? All that I had ever done was defend myself from unwarranted attack! It certainly wasn't my fault that the administration had lost control of the Junior High School, yet here he was blaming me for the violence!

If this principal was making an effort to try and get control of his school, he was definitely barking up the wrong tree; I was on his side, but he would have never believed it. This man didn't make an attempt to find out what kind of a person I was; he didn't even care about the truth, or what had really happened at the Junior High. He asked me no questions and wrongfully believed that he already had all of the answers.

I didn't speak to the principal that day, I considered him an ignorant fool. I sat in defiant silence while he badgered me. While sitting there, I wondered what he would have done had he attended my Junior High. Could he have survived? What would he do if a knife was pulled on him, or if he was attacked, three against one? I looked up into his face and I saw right through him; I had seen it before, a coward trying to act tough. At the first sign of trouble, I pictured him curled up in a ball on the floor, crying and whimpering.

This man was completely out of touch with the students and didn't have a clue as to what he should be doing. He was incapable of understanding something that he had hadn't come close to experiencing himself. He had obviously never been called on to prove what he was made of, and lucky for him, because I knew that there was nothing there but a whimpering coward. I wondered if God protected people like him; or were they simply killed the first time that violence struck?

I realized that by fighting and defending myself, I had been mistaken for a violent person by people with no experience or understanding. Come out the victor and you're a vicious troublemaker. I also knew that if I hadn't fought, I would have fallen victim and ended up badly scarred, brain damaged or crippled like many of the other students had. If that had been my fate, would everyone have had pity on me and thought me a wonderful peaceful person? Is that what it takes to get sympathy or understanding? Didn't anyone realize that the victor also suffers?

I had made the right choice at the time, the only one that I could have made; I had bravely fought for myself and my friends and I was proud. I had endured a hellish environment and not only survived, but had gained the respect of my peers. I wasn't a cowering victim, I was a warrior, worthy of praise and admiration, and I considered myself above reproach. This small-minded man didn't have a clue, and had ignorantly placed me in the same category as a criminal. I stood and marched from his office, I would not accept his warped evaluation of me; he couldn't have been more wrong.

When I got out into the hall I grinned; it seemed that maybe the principal was a little afraid of me himself. He had probably heard about the day that Chainsaw Charlie and the guys picked me up from school. I chuckled and shook my head as I walked to my next class.

Later that same day, I was approached by an extreme white-supremacist group. They didn't waste any time trying to recruit me, guess they figured that I would be full of hatred by now and that I was ready for them.

I don't know why, but I wasn't; it just didn't make sense to me to blame a whole race of people for the actions of a few. My enemies were responsible for what they had done, them and no one else. I had been attacked and hated because I was white; I knew what it felt like and I had the scars to prove it. I wasn't going to do the same thing to someone else, and attack and hate them simply because they weren't white. Joining this group was a lifetime commitment, and even though I needed the protection, I decided not to join.

I was counting on my reputation to continue to protect me, trying my best to stay on my own and not affiliate myself with anyone. I was hoping not to be singled out and attacked; it was difficult and scary at times, but it also had its perks. Without the gang dictating my behavior I was free to do as I pleased, free to be friends with whomever I wanted, and I liked it.

As time went on, I ended up with an unusual group of friends, none of whom liked one another. I assumed that it was because they were all so different from each other. Like my chubby brainy friend, Chris, who studied my handwriting and did all of my schoolwork for me, and the wealthy voluptuous Marcia who all the boys wanted, and of whom all the girls were jealous. I was fortunate to have many wonderful friends, but the one that was the most controversial, was my black friend Cherry. Cherry was a gifted artist who sat next to me in art class; we were assigned a project together, so I got to know her well. One day, we made plans for her to come to my house to complete our project; but tensions built when her friends found out that Cherry had plans to go to a white girl's home. To avoid trouble Cherry and I found it best to respect the color line and we never socialized outside of the classroom, but she was still very much my friend.

Cherry was concerned about the racial problems and she formed a committee and planned "A Dance for Peace," in an effort for us all to socialize and have fun together. She invited all of the schools in the city to participate.

Marcia and I went to support Cherry and to meet some boys from another school. After we arrived, we found the boys and before we separated, we agreed to meet at the front door at ten o'clock; the time when Marcia's father was planning to pick us up. I soon got lost in the crowd with the boy that I liked, and I didn't see Marcia again for the rest of the evening.

I was having a fun time, dancing and playing around and before I knew it, it was almost ten o'clock. I said good-bye to my boy and started searching for Marcia.

I was standing at the top of the bleachers looking over the vast crowd when I spotted her. She was being forced into the center of a circle of white girls, who were mocking her and shoving her around.

The game had just begun and I knew how it was played; as the excitement of the violence built, the punching and kicking increased in intensity. The game wasn't over until the victim was finished; unconscious or so badly beaten that they could no longer move or make a sound. I had to hurry, if I didn't get to Marcia in time, she would be badly hurt. I started running down the tall bleachers as fast as I could.

When I was nearly to the bottom, I saw a girl kick Marcia hard in the shin; it knocked her off of her feet and she lay on the gym floor crying. Now that she was down, all of the assailants began to kick her.

Marcia was a gentle cultured girl, she had no violence in her and didn't know how to defend herself. She was completely helpless against these vicious bullies who derived a sick pleasure out of hurting her, for no reason. Each time that they struck a blow, the vicious girls laughed loudly with big smiles on their cruel ugly faces.

By the time I got there, Marcia had taken a blow to the face, her lip was split, and her mouth was bleeding. I thought that they may have knocked out some of her teeth. I was enraged and I shoved two of the tormentors aside, knocking them down. Then I stepped into the center of the circle and stood over my injured friend.

All of the girls engaging in the game attended another school accept for one, Susan; she was the ringleader and had a reputation for preying on the weak. She was the one who knew that Marcia was easy prey and I blamed her for the incident.

In a low rumbling voice I spoke to Susan, "You wanna show off how tough you are? Try kicking me, you ugly sick bitch." I was so angry that I could have killed her.

After I had spoken, it was silent. There were at least fifteen girls that I was up against and I didn't know what would happen next, but I did know that whatever it was, I was on my own.

Seconds later, they all backed down and slowly walked away hanging their heads. It almost looked as though they were ashamed, I wondered if maybe they were, and I hoped that that would be the end of it.

Lucky for Marcia I had gotten there in time and she only suffered a few bruises and the split lip. Her teeth were a little loose, but they were all saved.

The next Monday, I was at school standing by my locker when I heard my brainy friend Chris loudly calling my name from down the hall. "Penelope, Penelope!" she shouted. I looked up and saw her clumsily running toward me juggling her books, trying not to drop them. Chris was definitely no athlete, and it was cute. I smiled, thinking that she probably wanted to tell me about a pop quiz or remind me to turn in my homework assignment.

"Chris, slow down," I shouted back to her. I was afraid that she would fall on the hard cement floor. "It's okay, I'm right here."

"Susan's after you!" she shouted out of breath, "she's telling everyone that she's going to kick your ass today!"

"Good luck with that," I grinned and whispered under my breath.

When Chris got closer she went on, "Susan's friends from Central High are coming here, the ones from the dance that hurt Marcia. They're all going to jump you in the alley by the bus after school!"

"Thanks for the warning Chris, but how do you know about this? Are you sure that it isn't just gossip?"

"I heard her say it myself! I have English with Susan and she's been bragging about it to everyone all day!"

"Do you know where her locker is?" I asked. It was the end of the day and I figured that I would catch her there and take care of her before she could meet up with her friends.

"Yes I do, it's in the other building."

"Show me." I put my hand in my pocket and felt my knife, just in case. "Let's go."

"What are you going to do?" Chris asked.

"Don't worry about it, you just show me where her locker is, and get out of the way."

Chris and I quickly walked down the hall and I started braiding my hair in a single braid down my back. There was no choice or question in the matter. I knew what I had to do; confront Susan and get it settled right away. Yes, I could have avoided the bus stop that day, but it would only prolong the inevitable. I couldn't wait for Susan to catch me alone and

112

jump me in her chosen place, at her chosen time, overpowering me with all of her friends. I knew the only reason that I had been able to back them all down at the dance, was because of the element of surprise. They didn't know who was there to back me up, or if I had a dangerous weapon. This time, they had a plan and they were ready; I wouldn't stand a chance.

When we turned the corner I saw Susan standing at her locker turning the combination. I walked up and casually leaned on the locker next to hers. "My friend tells me that you're after me." I spoke quietly with a smirk on my face.

"No, I'm not after you." She denied it; she didn't want to fight me, one on one, in a fair fight. She wanted to wait and follow through with her evil plan, a cowardly plan, where there was no risk to her; a plan where I didn't stand a chance and would be given a brutal beating.

I pressed her, "You sure about that?"

"Yes I'm sure about that," she answered sharply.

I raised my voice, "Well then it sounds to me like you're calling my friend a liar." At that moment she opened her locker and I slammed it shut with my fist.

Chris realized that it was going down right then, and being the good student, she was concerned about me being expelled. "No Penelope, not in school!" she grabbed my arm and determinedly tried to pull me away.

When Chris pulled my arm, she knocked me off balance, my head turned and I was off guard for a split second. Susan saw her opportunity; she took a swipe with her cat-like claws across my face and scratched both of my eyeballs. I saw a white flash and then darkness... I was blind!!!

I couldn't let the terror of losing my eyesight immobilize me, I had to take care of the problem at hand and I began to fight Susan by touch.

I didn't know if I would ever see again, but I did the best I could; fighting blind. I didn't have any idea where I was hitting her, but I could feel Susan under my fist each time that I threw a punch. It was one of the longest fights that I had ever been in. Not being able to see was tough, it was difficult to block punches and I couldn't judge accurately enough to hit her in the right spot to knock her out.

A crowd quickly gathered in the hall and surrounded us. Students were racing down the stairwells and pushing in to watch the fight, I could feel them pressing near and shouting.

After a while my left eye began to clear a little and I could faintly see the kids jumping up and down with excitement, black and white blurred images cheering, "Get her Penelope! Get her!" I was shocked; I didn't know that so many people liked me. "Or maybe they just dislike Susan," I

113

wondered.

Now that I could see a bit through one eye, I was ready to take the bitch out, but before I could, Susan was grabbed from behind and pulled backward into the crowd, where she disappeared.

I heard someone shout, "The cops are here!" Uniformed officers pressed through the crowd trying to find me. Some big black girls closed in around to hide me and Chris straightened my hair and clothes, while I dried the tears from my watering damaged eyes.

"Who's been fighting?" the officers asked. "No one," they all said; black and white students together; all covering for me.

Shortly after that, an ambulance pulled up in front of the school. Susan had been found in the restroom, unconscious, beaten and thrown over the john. Seems that her plan had backfired; what she had schemed and plotted for me, had happened to her. She was the one who had been outnumbered and crushed.

Many of the students witnessed what Susan and her friends had done to Marcia at the dance, and then heard her bragging about her plan to dog-pack me with her friends. Susan had put her hands on the wrong person this time, and it was all over for her.

As for myself, I had a long gouge along my jaw and slices cut from the whites of my eyes. I was lucky though and my vision returned completely. If my eyes hadn't been at the angle they were, Susan could have blinded me for life. I was happy to have my sight, but I did have a red scar on my face that ran the length of my jaw line that didn't fade for the next ten years.

As far as Susan goes, I heard that she recovered from the beating, but she never returned to school and I never saw her again.

After that day, things at school were different. It was strange, but my fight with Susan had a profound effect on all of us. It seems that a common enemy had somehow brought us all together.

The racial problems weren't completely solved, of course, but we had definitely crossed the color line. It was now blurred and soon more of us began to cross over. From that day on, we were on the upswing and things at school began to get better. I give much of the credit to Cherry; I'm certain that she had a lot to do with why the black girls protected me from the police.

Looking back on my education, I had always said that the only useful things that I learned in school were how to type and how to street fight. But now, after telling this story, I can honestly say that I learned a great deal more.

School was finally over and Kate and I had graduated. The flowers were in bloom, it was summertime, and we were enjoying every minute of it. We spent most of our time with my brother Pete and his best friend Mike, four best friends together.

My brother has always been very special to me, from the day that mother brought him home from the hospital. Mom told me that he was my baby to avoid sibling rivalry, and I'm happy to report that her plan worked beautifully and from that point on he was my real living doll.

As time went on, I found that I wasn't the only one who thought that Pete was a living doll. With silky blonde hair, like threads of spun gold, aqua blue eyes, and a muscular flawless build, Pete had every girl in town after him.

In his early teens, he was dating two beautiful blonde, identical twins at the same time. When I asked him what in the world he was doing, he just told me that he couldn't figure out which one he liked better and that he wasn't able to tell them apart anyway. As long as the girls didn't mind, I guess it didn't really matter; they were all having fun. Innocent kid stuff, I guess.

The strong silent type and fearless to a fault. I never saw my brother back down from any physical challenge. I once pulled into the mall parking lot to find Pete fighting three guys at the same time. He moved so fast that it looked as though his feet never touched the ground. His enemies decided that they didn't want any part of this Tasmanian Devil and ran from Pete as fast as their legs would carry them.

When it was over, I motioned for Pete to come over to me. "Wow Pete, you were incredible! I never saw anything like it in my life, those guys never even hit you!"

Pete didn't care to hear it; he waved his hand at me and started to walk away. "Don't tell mom I was fighting," he said, and that was the last time that it was ever mentioned. I never did know what the fight was about.

Pete had learned to fight, not in self-defense class, but in self-defense.

One day, when Kate and I were at the beach, she told me that she liked my brother. The news didn't surprise me as everyone liked Pete. But, that wasn't what she was really trying to say, and months later I found out that she had been having sex with my younger brother, behind my back. Kate was older, more experienced, and much more sophisticated than Pete. She tried to explain to me that she was in love with him and that the relationship was serious. But I was angry that she had kept such a secret from me, and believed that she had seduced and taken advantage of him. We had a horrible argument and out of respect, she stayed away. I missed

115

her very much, but felt that my best friend, who I had believed told me everything, had betrayed me. I loved Kate dearly and my heart was broken. I had lost my dearest friend.

After losing Kate, I started hanging around with a new girl, named Janet. I never considered her a close friend, and I couldn't trust her very far, but she was fun and pretty and I enjoyed chasing the boys with her. One hot summer afternoon, Janet and I were shopping at the mall. We had been invited to several parties that night and wanted to buy new clothes for the occasion. We hadn't been there long when we saw an incredible looking guy. We were both dying to know who he was, but before either one of us could get up the nerve to talk to him, he was gone. I was disappointed and thought that I would never see him again.

During the warm summer months, my friends and I would go to the beach during the day, and after dinner we hung out together in the park. When I arrived at the park that evening, who should I see there, but the incredible guy. I couldn't believe it; I was actually going to get another chance to meet him! I didn't waste any time and struck up a conversation with him right away. His name was Timmy, he was as charming as he was good looking and I really liked him. Timmy had just moved to the city from out of state to join his family, and come to find out he was the older brother of my brother's friend, Mike. What an incredible coincidence! I invited him to join my friends and me for the parties that night, and he accepted the invitation.

Timmy and I really hit it off, even thought I had just met him; it seemed as though I had known him for years. Before we even left the first party, we had already nicknamed each other Babycakes.

When it was time to leave that party and go on to the next, Babycakes and I walked out into the driveway and sat on the trunk of Janet's mustang. Janet started the car and warmed up the engine while we waited for the other kids, who were riding with us.

The night was warm and there wasn't a cloud in the sky; Babycakes and I held hands and leaned back on the rear window to admire the stars. He was so gentle and sweet that I thought I was falling in love. Babycakes was just about to kiss me, when jealous Janet gunned the engine, the car jumped ahead and we were thrown off onto the ground. There was a rough edge on the trunk that caught the seat of my jeans and ripped a hole in them; it was a big flap that flopped open downward. I couldn't go home to change or I wouldn't be allowed to go back out again. I was having way too much fun for it to end, so I decided to stay out. No one could really see anything anyway, just my hot pink panties.

On we went with our night of fun, Babycakes and I danced and played and had a great time. He appointed himself in charge of guarding my panties from curious onlookers. Every time that he would notice someone looking at my unmentionable, he would cover my bottom with his hand. He never took it too far and I was totally comfortable with him. That was unusual for me; he was indeed a very special person.

A few short months later, Timmy's family moved away. His father was in the military and they moved quite often. Timmy stayed behind to be with me and his other new friends. We met every day at the beach; we played hard and lay in the warm summer sun. In the evenings, we relaxed at the park and visited with our friends. Timmy was everything that I had ever dreamed of, he was sexy and fun and so easy to be with that we never fought ever, not about anything. Babycakes wasn't rough and tough, he didn't carry a gun or knife, and he didn't have a drinking or drug problem. He was a respectful kind person and I could have easily seen myself with him for the rest of my life. I couldn't believe it, I actually had a nice sweet boyfriend.

One night in the park, Babycakes and I were sitting on the grass talking; he was resting his head in my lap while I ran my fingers through his long luxurious hair. Suddenly, we heard a loud crash, it startled us and we looked up to see the Gumm brothers. They lived in the back woods and were known as drunken rowdies and everyone always steered clear of them. The Gumm brothers were breaking beer bottles against the big fountain in the park, looking at us and saying over and over, "Should we do it? Should we do it?"

I couldn't imagine what they were talking about, but it obviously had something to do with us. There were plenty of people at the park that night, so I didn't feel that we were in danger as long as we stayed with our friends.

I looked closer and noticed who the Gumm brothers were with, and driving the car was Klay Kerby. Klay had been in prison, and nobody was sure exactly what for, we just knew that he had committed a violent crime.

Since his release, I kept seeing him nearly every time I went out. When I left my house, he would drive slowly by me and stare. When I arrived at my destination he would stop his car and watch me. When I came back out he would still be there, waiting. He never said a word to me nor I to him, he just stared, a stare that went right through me. It was strange and scary and I didn't know what he wanted or why he was doing it. Back then, it wasn't considered serious, but now I know the name for it, stalking. I tried to ignore him, but he looked like the devil. He had a dark goatee that pointed at the end and a sinister look in his eye. I never told anyone about what he had been doing; after all, he hadn't really done anything but watch me. I didn't want to borrow trouble but still, I knew that he was waiting for an opportunity to do something. But what? It was hard for me to believe that he was harmless.

I told Babybcakes to stay away from Klay Kerby and the Gumm brothers, that they meant trouble. I wanted him to leave the park when I did, but he wouldn't. I had to be home by eleven o'clock and he wanted to stay out later. I was certain that he thought that I was just making a big deal out of nothing.

I reluctantly went home and after I left, Klay Kerby called Timmy over to his car. When Timmy went to see what he wanted, the Gumm brothers pushed him inside and jumped on top of him. Klay took off and drove deep into the woods. Timmy had been kidnapped!

When they finally stopped, they forced Timmy out of the car and into an old shack. There was another Gumm brother waiting for them there, Otis, the big fat one. They all attacked Timmy, beat him and threw him to the floor. Otis sat on top of him with a knife to his throat while the other brothers took their knives and began to hack off Timmy's long beautiful hair, one chunk at a time. They chopped it off right at the scalp, cutting Timmy's face and head. They didn't stop until there wasn't any hair left.

Beaten, bald, cut and bleeding, they dumped him in a ditch on the side of the road. There was my Babycakes in the middle of nowhere, lost and badly hurt.

Luckily someone came by and gave Timmy a ride out of the woods. From there he walked to my family's home. It was in the wee hours of the morning when Timmy arrived and he didn't want to disturb anyone so he got in a van that we had parked on the property. He climbed into the back seat and collapsed.

When I got up that morning my dog, Suzy, took me out to the van, she knew that he was in trouble. There was Babycakes, covered with dried blood, bruised and muddy. He sat up when he heard me call to him. He was bald and cut up, my God, what a shock! I jumped into the van to help him, I wanted to take him to the hospital, but he wouldn't go, he wouldn't even let me bandage his wounds. All he wanted was a shower. Babycakes had taken quite a beating, but he was okay. I will never know everything that happened to Timmy that night, but I'm certain that the terror of it devastated him.

A few weeks later, the carnival was in town and Babycakes and I went together. I didn't know it then, but it would be the last time that I would ever see him. He showed me a nice time and when the carnival left, Timmy went with it. He called me from some little town in the south; he was heading back to where he had come from. I didn't blame him for not sticking around, but I would have at least liked to say good-bye. When I asked him why he didn't tell me that he was leaving, he said, "I don't like good-bye's," then he hung up the phone.

I had lost more than Timmy that day, it was the day that I realized that I couldn't be with someone who was kind and gentle. Look what happened to him! Was it my fault in some obscure way? Why was I ever foolish enough to think that I could have a gentle sweet boyfriend in my rotten violent world? I should have known better. I vowed that I would never let it happen again to another kind and trusting soul like my precious Babycakes. I had to live the life that fate had dealt me and from now on the only guys that I would be around would be the biggest and the baddest.

I felt emotionally desperate and I needed Chainsaw Charlie. I called him on the phone and good ol' Chainsaw came to get me. I climbed on the bike and Chainsaw and I headed out of town to a country road surrounded by open pastures and wildflowers. The air was clean and fresh from the morning rain and the wind was blowing through my hair. Soon, I was feeling better and I asked Chainsaw to pull over on the side of the road. When he did, I jumped off the back of the bike and then slipped back on, in front of him. "Slide back Chainsaw, I want to take this baby for a ride!" I expected Chainsaw to object, but he didn't, instead he showed me how to shift the gears and then he slid back in the passenger seat.

"Okay, you little badass," Chainsaw said in a gruff voice, "let's give it a try, but remember, I just spent a fortune on this paint job." Chainsaw was leaning over me with his hands on my thighs, carefully watching. He didn't admit it, but I knew that he was apprehensive.

I firmly took hold of the handlebars and shifted into first gear; the bike was very heavy and when I gave it gas, it was hard for me to hold the handlebars straight, until I got it rolling. Things were going well, but the road wasn't in the best of shape, it was bumpy and there were big dark patches where huge holes had been filled in. I could feel Chainsaw bouncing behind me, each time that I hit one, but even so, I was still beginning to get the hang of it. After a few miles, I was confident and thoroughly enjoying myself, I felt incredibly free, as though I didn't have a care in the world!

I began to feel daring and I turned the throttle, the bike jumped ahead and I felt a burst of energy course through my veins, "Hey Chainsaw," I shouted to him, "I LOVE IT!" Just then, I hit a big dark spot on road. I thought that it was just another patch, but it wasn't, it was a huge muddy hole! We went flying from the pavement and when we hit the mud the bike immediately started to slide sideways, leaning only inches from the ground! Seconds later, the tires hit the broken edge of the pavement, on the other side. When I felt the strike, I gunned the engine and the bike came back up. I straightened her out, and Chainsaw and I were quickly sailing back down the road without a scratch!

Chainsaw was laughing in disbelief, "I thought that we going down for sure!" he exclaimed. "How'd you know what to do?"

"Just instinct, I guess."

"I couldn't have done better myself," Chainsaw admitted, "and the next time that we go riding with the guys, I'm gonna let you drive. They'll get a kick out of it, a little bitty thing like you, with me on the back. (And that's exactly what we did, and I became an excellent rider.)

After the slide, I drove for a little longer, but had Chainsaw take over when we got near the city. We were both thirsty and stopped to get something to drink at a convenience store. Chainsaw parked and went into the store, while I waited outside to keep an eye on the bike. And guess who pulled up? That's right, Klay Kerby, he parked his car and sat there and stared at me with his devilish stare, as usual. After what had happened to Babycakes, I would have been terrified if I hadn't been with Chainsaw.

Then, out of the store came Chainsaw Charlie, looking like a barbarian in a movie. Chainsaw was always aware of everything around him, he spotted Klay Kerby and didn't take his eyes off of him. "What's that crazy doing here? I don't like the way he's looking at you." He handed me the drinks, "Cover my license plate and get ready to go," he instructed, then Chainsaw started walking toward Klay.

When Klay saw Chainsaw Charlie headed his way, he had a look of alarm on his face and reached to start his car. Chainsaw saw what he was doing; he made a quick dash and got there just as the motor started up. Before Klay could shift the car into gear, Chainsaw reached through the window and grabbed hold of him. He pulled Klay halfway out the car window and slammed his head down as he drove his knee into Klay's face. I heard a loud crack, like a baseball bat hitting the ball. I'll never forget that sound, it made me cringe.

Chainsaw left Klay hanging out the window with the car engine still running and ran back toward me. I covered the license plate with a sweatshirt that I had tied to the sissy bar, then Chainsaw kick-started the bike and we were gone, flying down the freeway. I wrapped my arms around him and leaned my head on his back. It was over, I knew that I would never see Klay Kerby again. Chainsaw Charlie was the perfect man, the answer to all of my problems.

I later asked Chainsaw how he knew that Klay had been bothering me. "I didn't," he said, "let's just say that I know why that freak show was in prison."

"Why was he in prison Chainsaw?"

"Now that's something that you don't ever need to know, it might give you nightmares."

One day, I happened to be near Chainsaw's house. He lived in a beautiful area on the beach. The white sand went right up to the doorway, it was a lovely setting. I decided to drop in and say hello and I knocked on the door.

Someone, whom I couldn't see, pulled back a heavy dark drape in the window next to the door, and peered out at me. I stood there waiting for the door to open, wondering what the holdup was. Finally, I heard rustling and the sound of the lock being unbolted. There was a girl standing there looking through the crack in the door with one eye, and I asked for Chainsaw Charlie.

She answered me in a raspy low voice, "Oh yeah, right, you're the Angel, I'm sure he'd love to see you, especially today, come on in." The girl opened the door and I stepped inside, I could hear her muttering to herself, "This is perfect, her showing up right now." I wondered what she meant by it and I followed her down a dark hallway; she walked funny. I thought that I recognized her from school, but she looked so much older.

A gloomy feeling came over me, the house smelled dank and dirty. Why didn't anyone open the windows to let in some air? There was a curtain hanging across the doorway at the end of the hall; the girl pulled it aside and stepped into the smoke-filled room. Chainsaw Charlie was sitting slumped over in a chair. His friends were on the sofa and other chairs surrounding an extra-large coffee table.

"Hey Chainsaw," she yelled loudly, "there's someone here to see you." She started laughing and then coughing, that hard smoker cough. When she smiled, I could see that she was missing some of her teeth. Chainsaw barely stirred. "It's your An - gel," she chimed in a sarcastic tone.

When he heard that it was his Angel, Chainsaw slowly raised his head, he had a long cut on his cheek and his knuckles were scraped and bloody.

Bill was there and he yelled at the girl, "Brenda, you know better than to bring her in here!"

Chainsaw interrupted, "No Bill, that's okay, I'd love to see my Angel." His speech was slurred and he struggled to get to his feet. He walked clumsily across the room and put his arm around me; he was heavy and awkward and I tried to steady him. Even in the state he was in, Chainsaw was still sweet and considerate and he tried to make me feel comfortable.

I glanced around the room; there were needles on the little table next to Chainsaw's chair. I saw pipes, pills, bottles and the lid to one of those big aluminum trash cans full of butts on the coffee table.

Bill got up and tried to intervene, but Chainsaw waved him off, "No Bill, I want to tell these assholes something." He looked at me and slurred, "I'm sorry Angel, I didn't mean to curse." Then he went on, "Don't any of you pricks," he looked at me again, "Is it okay to say prick?"

"Don't worry about it Chainsaw."

"Don't any of you pricks get any ideas about this little girl right here; not one of you is good enough for her and you're not going to touch her. She never lies or does anything wrong; she really is an Angel."

Then he singled out one of the guys in the room, "Kickstand... I know what you're thinking, you back off or I'll kick your ass again."

Kickstand was a good looking guy, with dark dreamy eyes and a cleft chin. He was the Romeo of the bunch and from his knick-name, I can guess why. He was always smiling at me, but I never thought much of it.

When Kickstand heard what Chainsaw had said, he snapped back, "She ain't your ol' lady, you got no right Chainsaw! I'll take what I want!" And then he slowly got up, but he was having a hard time standing too. When I looked closer, I noticed that his eye was bruised and I realized that he must have been the one who Chainsaw had been fighting with earlier.

Bill could see it coming and he pulled me from under Chainsaw's arm. Chainsaw lunged at Kickstand; they both fell down fighting and hit the coffee table. The table collapsed and ashes went flying, the beer spilled, and everyone was scrambling to get out of the way. Things were banging and crashing, Chainsaw Charlie and Kickstand were hitting each other and wrestling on the floor. They were both so messed up, that the fight was like slow motion. Chainsaw got the best of Kickstand, he was on top of him, pounding him in the face when Snake pulled him off and started dragging him back to his seat. Kickstand just laid there on the floor; he was done, passed out or knocked out, I don't know which.

I tried to go to Chainsaw to make sure that he was all right, but Bill wouldn't let me; he was holding my arm. "Never mind about Chainsaw, he's fine, you've already caused enough trouble." He walked me to the door, "You know Penelope, you really shouldn't be here, there are things going on that I don't want you involved with. Now go home, I'll have Chainsaw call you tomorrow."

I hadn't meant to cause trouble, but somehow I had. I knew that Bill was right, I didn't belong there. But where did I belong? I needed to move on; but how? I wanted to date nice boys but I couldn't, they couldn't protect me. I didn't want to fight, but I had to, fight or die. I wanted to be a nice kid, but my world just wouldn't permit it.

TRANSITIONS

The next spring, my father decided to move the family back to where we had come from. I was going home! I couldn't believe it! Home to a place where I could walk down the street and not be afraid. Home; where I could be friends with whomever I wanted. This was my chance for a fresh start; a whole new life awaited me. The violence and fear would soon be behind me. I was being released from a prison of sorts, a prison where I had done time, but had committed no crime. It was over and I was ready to go.

I made a serious promise to myself that day; I determined that when I got back home I would find a nice man. This was my opportunity for a fresh start and a chance to be the person that I really wanted to be. I couldn't be careless and waste what might be the only break that I would ever get.

It wasn't long before we were in the car headed home. Fortunately, the trip passed by quickly, and as soon as I hit town I went straight to see my favorite cousin, Linda Lou. We were so excited to see each other that we held hands and jumped up and down like we were little kids again. We talked non-stop, catching up on all the latest news. Lou, like all of my cousins, had been married while I was away, and I had never met her husband. When I arrived that day, he was still at work, but she told me that he would be home soon and that he was bringing a friend with him to meet me. The men had plans to take us out that night and celebrate my return.

"Sounds terrific," I said. I was excited to meet someone new and go out with my cousin and her husband. What a wonderful way to start my first day back!

Soon, the guys arrived, Linda Lou's husband Jason, and his friend Parker. Jason was a handsome man, but his conceit exceeded his looks. I didn't care too much for him, but his friend Parker was wonderful, he was outgoing, friendly and fun to be with. Parker was as big as a bull and twice as strong, he was free-spirited and spoke in a loud booming voice. I enjoyed every minute that I was with him.

About mid-way through the date, Parker decided that he was in love with me and asked me to marry him. I thought that it was just his over-done way of making me feel welcome and didn't think much of it at the time.

The next few nights after work, Parker came home with Jason and we all went out and had fun. I was enjoying my first week back, I couldn't have asked for more. I sincerely liked Parker and was crazy about going out with him. He was a blast, generous and considerate. Wherever we went he made sure that everyone knew that he was with the sexiest most beautiful girl in the world. It embarrassed me of course, but I enjoyed the overzealous attention.

Parker rarely let me walk he always liked to carry me. We would be walking along and he would suddenly reach over and pick me up. He was so strong that I never felt shaky or fearful that he would ever drop me; I completely trusted him. Parker was powerful and would have been scary had he not had such a sweet disposition. But, he had one flaw, he let people take advantage of him, he was too helpful and giving, both of his time and money. If someone needed his help he gave it, expecting nothing in return, whether the person deserved it or not, and people tended to take advantage of him.

I hadn't taken Parker's marriage proposal seriously and yet, he continued to ask me over and over again. Every day he proposed, and every day I told him that we didn't know each other well enough yet. After all, wasn't that the logical answer?

I acted as though I thought that Parker was just being silly, but inside I wanted to believe him. Even though I didn't admit it at the time, I had fallen deeply in love. I wanted to melt safely into Parker's big muscular arms. But he was impulsive, too wild and unrestrained, and it was highly possible that he wasn't sincere. Or maybe he was fickle and his feelings would soon pass. I was afraid that he would be "in love" with someone else the next week and it would crush me. How could we be in true and lasting love so quickly? I thought it impossible.

Parker began to get more and more desperate to push me into marriage. He said that if he didn't marry me right away, he was afraid that I would have time to meet someone else and leave him. Everything was out of control, including me; I was beginning to weaken and fall under his spell and I was tempted to accept Parker's marriage proposal. But would I be making a mistake? I didn't know him well enough to make such a serious decision and I had pledged to myself to find a nice man. I kept reminding myself that I was getting a second chance for a good life, and after what I had been through, I couldn't afford to blow it now. Parker wasn't at all what I had in mind when I made the promise to myself; as a matter of fact he was exactly the opposite. My life had been a string of violent episodes, one after the other and I wanted peace and a reasonable calm man. Should I fight my emotions, stick to my guns and wait for someone that fit better into my plan? My mind was telling me one thing and my heart something different. It was all happening too fast, I needed time to sort it all out, and Parker made it clear that he wasn't going to give me any.

I had to get alone so I could think things through; this was a big decision and I had to be sure. I decided to go back to where I had just come from, the far-away big city. I planned to stay at the house on the beach; it was still vacant and Parker would never find me there. I quickly packed my bags and caught the next flight out of town.

I never thought that I would ever go back to that stinkin' city, especially not so soon, but I knew that I could be alone at the beach house and have the time and space to clear my head. I decided that I would keep to myself and not let anyone know that I was back, but things didn't work out that way. After my flight, I got off the plane and caught the first shuttle and as I climbed inside, to my surprise there were three girls from my Junior High gang sitting in the back seats. When we saw each other, we all screamed with delight, we hadn't been together in years. The girls were just the same as they had always been, loud and foul-mouthed, wearing heavy make-up and gaudy jewelry.

During the ride from the airport, we talked and laughed about old times, and before I knew it they had made plans for us every day for the coming week. I was happy to see the girls and I couldn't hurt their feelings by refusing to spend time with them; after all that we had been through together, turning them down was completely out of the question and I decided to ride it out.

The girls and I went out every night and met dozens of interesting men. I was going along, trying to have a good time, but all I could think about was Parker, I really missed him. No one else could compare to Parker. Being with him was magical, and I realized that just because it had happened fast didn't automatically make it a mistake, and I hoped that he

125

still wanted me.

The next morning, after one of my escapades with the girls, I called back home and caught my brother Pete on the phone. I found out that he and Parker had been spending a lot of time together since I had been gone. Pete told me that Parker was broken hearted about me leaving and that he knew that he had made a mistake by coming on too strong. He said that he had decided that when I came back home he would be more patient and less pushy.

That was all I needed to hear; Parker still wanted me and he planned to be more considerate of my feelings. I was ready to go back and marry my big cuddly bear. I told my brother to tell Parker that I would be home the next day.

I let the girls know that I was leaving in the morning and that I planned to marry Parker and I invited them over to the beach house for the last hurrah.

The girls showed up with big smiles and a beautifully wrapped gift, silk lingerie for my honeymoon. We ordered pizza and had fun talking and laughing.

The time passed much too quickly, and before we realized it had gotten very late, so I invited them to stay over and we all went to bed in the wee hours of the morning.

We hadn't been asleep long when the phone started ringing, and whoever was calling just wouldn't hang up. It wasn't even dawn yet, and I didn't feel like answering, so I tried to ignore it and go back to sleep.

"Isn't anyone going to answer the damn phone?" someone sleepily complained.

"Answer it yourself," I moaned. After that, I didn't hear the phone ringing anymore and I tried to go back to sleep.

A few minutes later, I heard the girls coming into my bedroom, "What now?" I turned and looked to see what they wanted.

Their faces were solemn, "Penelope you better talk, it's your cousin," they said and handed me the phone.

It was Linda Lou, she didn't sound right, and I could tell that she had been crying. "Penelope, something horrible has happened," she said. "Parker went out with a buddy and his wife to the neighborhood bar last night. After they got inside, his friend realized that he had left his wallet in the car and went back out to get it. His wife went to the ladies room and some drunk grabbed her ass. She went running to Parker, crying and making a big deal out of it… Oh why didn't the bitch just tell her husband what happened? Why did she have to get Parker involved?" Lou started

126

crying uncontrollably.

"Lou, Lou! Pull yourself together! What happened?! Tell me what happened!"

"Parker walked over to ask the guy to apologize to his friend's wife and when he saw Parker coming, I guess he must have panicked, you know how big and scary looking Parker is," then she started crying again.

"Lou! Lou!" I screamed.

"He hit Parker in the neck with a beer bottle. There was no warning, nothing, it was horrible!"

"Lou, is Parker okay? Is he hurt?"

"HE'S DEAD!!! PARKER'S DEAD! The bottle cut his jugular vein and before help could arrive, he bled to death on the floor. That bitch! That stupid bitch! She's the one who killed him!"

When I heard the news I was devastated; if I had been there this would have never happened. If only I hadn't left! My God, what had I done? I was sick inside; there would be no second chance for Parker and me.

Later, I heard that Parker's killer was an off duty cop and that nothing ever happened to him as a result of the killing. The whole town was in an uproar because of it. As far I was concerned, I agreed with Linda Lou that it was the woman's fault. She had pitted the two men against each other and was completely responsible for what had happened. Did it make her feel good that she had the power to have a big scary man do her bidding? What right did she have to involve him in her trivial little problem? Because of her bad judgment and self-centeredness, my Parker was dead.

I was having trouble coping and decided to stay on at the beach house for a while longer; I didn't have the courage to go back and face what had happened. People were protesting against the police department and the news teams were camping at my parent's house, looking to interview me, the girl that Parker loved. Parker had a lot of friends and I guess that the protesting was their way of avenging him.

It was hard to believe that going back home hadn't freed me from the violence; in fact, it had followed close behind me.

I didn't want my friends to see me fall apart, so I told them that I wanted to be by myself. I stayed inside the beach house and closed all the curtains. I unplugged the phone and holed up all alone in the big lonely house. I grieved and I grieved, I couldn't eat or sleep and I didn't get out of bed. It was a shocking horrible thing that had happened. Parker was so young, so handsome and full of life and he hadn't even had the chance to live before he was senselessly killed. For days I cried and struggled to pull myself together, but it was no use, I just couldn't seem to find a way to climb out of the dark, depressing, bottomless pit that I was trapped in.

After three days of this agony, I heard the doorbell ringing and whoever it was wouldn't go away. I forced myself to get up and staggered to the door and when I opened it, I couldn't believe my eyes… it was Bucky, he had finally forgiven me! I was so happy to see him that I fell into his arms, "Oh Bucky!"

Bucky picked me up and carried me to the sofa. Holding me tightly, he sat down with me in his lap and didn't let go. I sat quietly with Bucky; he held me close to his chest and the only sound that I heard was his loving, beating heart. We didn't speak, we didn't need to, his presence alone spoke loudly and communicated everything that hadn't been said between us for all those many years.

When things finally became calm, Bucky asked me how long it had been since I had eaten. It had been three days, ever since I had heard the news about Parker. I couldn't keep anything down so I had given up trying.

"Well, I think I can take care of that." Bucky called the deli and had them send over some chicken soup. After it arrived he sat next to me and patiently fed me one spoonful at a time. Bucky never got impatient, bit by bit, he kept feeding me until it was gone. After I had eaten the soup my strength returned and I felt much better.

With his support and friendship, Bucky had helped me to pull out of the crisis, and by the time he left, I felt like I could cope again. I knew that my girlfriends must have told him what had happened, and I was grateful to them for sending my Bucky back to me.

The next night, the doorbell rang again and I peeked out the window to see who it was; I was happy when I saw Bucky standing there. I started to rush to open the door, but paused for a moment. Suddenly, I realized that he was no longer the Junior High boy who had given me the brass knuckles; he was a man now and he still cared for me. A flood of emotion ran over me; my mind raced back to Junior High and to all of the violence and terror that Bucky and I had faced together. He was always there protecting me, holding my hand and now, here he was again comforting me in a time of crisis and I suddenly felt an overwhelming love for him.

What was wrong with me? I had to get hold of myself! This was crazy latching on to Bucky so quickly after Parkers death! Was I merely doing this to ease the pain of losing Parker, or did I really love Bucky? Had it been Bucky all along, or was I on the rebound? Fact was; I had good reason to love him, after all, it wasn't as though he was a stranger; we knew each other well and had a history together.

The proper thing to do after Parker's death was to let some time pass before getting involved with another man, but if I waited to tell Bucky how I felt, maybe something would happen to him too! What should I do? I was a bundle of confusion, but despite my fears I decided to do what I thought was best and wait until I could be more sure of my feelings. I couldn't risk hurting Bucky, not again.

Even though I had hesitated to share my feelings with him, it didn't seem to matter. That night, it was as though Bucky was looking into my very soul and reading my mind. "Penelope," he said as he looked into my eyes, "I've never loved anyone but you." He took me in his arms and gave me a long passionate kiss. This was a special kiss, a kiss a long time coming and I was swept away. Bucky truly loved me and I knew it.

Bucky and I had never shared a real kiss before. We had spent all of our time on the schoolyard and I didn't know how wonderful it could be. All of my defenses were knocked down, all of my fears abated and Bucky and I made plans that night to be together forever. Truth was, if I hadn't embarrassed him by jumping on the motorcycle with Chainsaw Charlie, we would have never been apart. I experienced a sense of relief, maybe I could get through this; maybe my life would work out okay after all.

After Bucky left that night, the pain and horror of Parker's death hadn't been lessened by any degree, but I was now getting the strength to bear it. I was definitely on the mend; I had something to look forward to with Bucky. He and I were finally going to have a chance; the tragedy had brought us back together.

I slept well that night, and the next morning when I got out of bed I looked out the window and found that it was a lovely sunny day. Bucky was at work, and I decided to go to the beach.

I put on my bikini and walked down to the warm inviting sand, spread my blanket and sat down. I watched the birds flying overhead, they were doing tricks and singing; it was as though they were putting on a show just for me. I smiled as I pinned up my long hair and smoothed on slick coconut, tanning butter; then I laid back in the warm wonderful sunshine. I stretched out and tried to relax, but I just couldn't lay still. I was anxious and decided to take a walk to try to settle down. I slowly sauntered along the sandy shoreline, the breeze was gently blowing my hair and the waves lapped over my shiny calves. I watched the water and gazed at the clouds, thinking about everything that had happened to me while living in the city and how much it had changed me. I thought about Parker and how he had been yanked from me so horribly, and now Bucky had come back into my life. I wondered how it would all play out.

I quietly walked along, deep in thought and when I finally looked up, I noticed that I had gone much further than I realized. I had walked all the way out of my neighborhood and onto the public beach.

There were a lot of people on the beach that day, and my eyes locked on to a girl quickly moving through the crowd. When she got closer, I realized that it was Kate. Kate and I hadn't seen each other since our argument about my brother and I could tell from the way that she was stomping toward me that she was still angry. I stood and waited for her to approach... What next?

When Kate got closer she ran the last few feet toward me and yelled, "Damn it Palsy! You bitch!" She jumped and slammed into me, ramming me with her shoulder. I wrapped my arms tightly around her and we both fell into the surf together. A huge wave rolled over us and dragged us into the deep water. Kate and I wrestled about under the water and violent waves, catching a breath whenever we could. We fought the breakers and fought with each other while trying to make it back to land.

We had barely reached a place where we could both touch the bottom when another huge wave slammed us onto the shore. We hit the beach on our knees and the fight went on, Kate and I rolled and thrashed in the sand. A crowd soon noticed and gathered to watch the two bikini-clad girls, sopping wet and covered in sand, wildly thrashing on the beach. They cheered and coaxed us on, screaming and whistling with excitement.

Kate and I were evenly matched; panting and out of breath we broke and stood sizing each other up. Even though the fight looked fierce, not one drop of blood had been shed. Seems that we just didn't have it in us to actually hurt one another.

The crowd wailed for more action, but Kate and I didn't make a move. Then suddenly, at the same moment, we both realized that we were wearing matching bikinis and we both burst out laughing. "I love you Palsy!" we both said at once and hugged each other tightly.

The crowd was disappointed and they kept taunting us, trying to get us to continue the fight, "Boooo... Boooo!" But, the show was over and Kate and I walked away together, arm in arm, I had my best friend back!

When we got back to Kate's car, we exchanged phone numbers and I gave her my new address. I smiled and waved as she drove away; we would never be divided again.

Bucky and I had plans for the evening. I put on a pretty summer dress and made a lovely meal, then waited for him to arrive. I expected Bucky at six, but six o'clock came and went. I called his house at about seven-thirty and there was no answer. The night dragged on and on with no word from him and I was frantic and worried. Had something happened to him? He would never worry me like this, not if he could help it! At about midnight I laid down on the sofa and closed my eyes. I decided to try and get some rest, maybe I needed to be prepared for something terrible.

The sun came up the next morning, and still no Bucky. I called everyone I could think of, and no one had heard anything. I was going crazy, I couldn't stand this; visions of him lying dead and bleeding like Parker, plagued my mind.

What had really happened? I tried to figure it out, there were plenty of other things that could have prevented him from coming over, besides death. Maybe he had merely changed his mind about me. There could be a hundred reasons why I hadn't heard from him, so I tried to calm myself down.

It was about three hours later when I finally saw Bucky walking up the driveway. I took one look at his face and knew that there was something terribly wrong. I opened the front door and sat down on the sofa, I didn't want to be standing when I heard the news, whatever it was.

Bucky came in and sat next to me; he gently took my hand, "Penelope, I don't know how to say this, so I'll just come right out with it."

I sat quietly and listened, even though it was obvious that he had something dreadful to tell me, I was still relieved, at least he wasn't dead and nothing he could say could be as bad as that.

He went on, "I was dating a girl named Karen, we've been on the outs for weeks now, and I went to see her last night to make sure that she knew that it was over between us, for sure this time. I was gonna be with you and I didn't want her making trouble for us. When I told Karen that I was dumping her, she went nuts on me. She was acting so crazy that I couldn't talk to her, so I tried to get the hell out. But when I started to walk out the door, she wadded up a piece of paper and angrily threw it at me. I looked at the paper; it was from a doctor, the results of a pregnancy test, and it was positive." He paused for a moment and took a long breath.

I couldn't believe what Bucky was telling me; my body felt numb as I sat quietly and listened.

"I hoped that maybe she was lying to try and keep me around, so I called the doctor myself and he confirmed that it was true. I didn't know what to do, pregnant with my baby and hysterical, I couldn't just leave her there like that, and I couldn't call you from her house. When she calmed down, we discussed our options. I tried to talk her into getting an abortion, but she won't do it. She knows that I don't want her anymore; she even knows that I'm in love with you, but she doesn't care. She's having the baby and keeping it no matter what, and she expects me to marry her and take care of the kid."

"Karen lives with her parents and they're both violent alcoholics. I'm afraid what will happen when they find out that she's pregnant; they're liable to beat her and kill her and the baby. She's no slut and I'm certain that it's mine, so I can't just walk away from this. But I still want you Penelope; I still want us to be together. The only reason that I was seeing her in the first place, was because you weren't here. Can you accept that I'll have a child with another woman? Take some time and think it over, you can let me know tomorrow."

Bucky got up and started walking sadly to the door.

"If I hadn't come back, would you marry her?" I asked.

"Yes, there would be no reason why I wouldn't."

"You marry Karen and I wish you all the best."

"You don't mean it Penelope; take more time to think it through."

"I don't need more time Bucky, I'm sure."

"Are you certain that you won't change your mind…change your mind after I'm married to Karen and it's too late?"

"Bucky it's already too late; I'm not going to be a part of destroying a child's life. You do the right thing," I said firmly, and pushed him out the door.

Bucky left, and within the hour I had packed my bags and was on my way to the airport. I knew that the decision I had made was the right one, but I had to get out of town before I changed my mind. This girl Karen couldn't go through a pregnancy and raise a child as a single parent, she obviously had no support from her family and Bucky was even concerned that they might kill her. She needed Bucky even more than I did and there was an innocent child to consider. It broke my heart to leave Bucky behind, but I truly believed that it was the only way that I could live with my conscience.

Bucky was a good man, he would make it work somehow, he could give his all to his new family, as long as I stayed out of the way.

On the long flight home, I realized that I was leaving something precious behind. Beneath the struggles and the trials that I had endured while living in the violent city, something else had emerged, something that was true and strong; I had gleaned incredible friendships, based on devotion and trust. I had friends who proved that they would lay down their lives for me, a love that I doubt few individuals ever experience. Some people wouldn't think much of my friends, some of them foul mouthed and crude, but they are truly the finest and the best, loyal to a fault and equal to any challenge. But, most of all I had my Palsy back, and she meant the world to me.

When I arrived home, there was an emptiness that grabbed me fiercely by the heart. Parker was gone and I had to learn to cope with it alone. Bucky was no longer there to ease my pain, and I had nothing to look forward to anymore.

Parker had been buried under the cold dark ground. My cousin Linda Lou told me that she had spoken to Parker's mother at the funeral, and all the woman said was, "Parker sure loved your cousin." It ripped my heart out to hear it, but that was the way that Parker was, he always made sure that everyone knew that he was with the sexiest, most beautiful girl in the world.

After Parker's death, my brother moved to the mountains. He went so far into the wilderness that there wasn't another soul around for miles. He had a big house, his faithful dog, a gun to hunt with, and his truck. That was all he needed. My brother never came down from the mountain; no matter what happened, he would never leave, not even for a single day.

I can't speak for him, but I think that he had had enough of people, and in retrospect I probably should have gone with him.

Bucky and I were over and he had moved on with his new life. Parker was dead and I just couldn't seem to get over it. I missed him terribly, the way he used to pick me up and hold me; he made me feel so special, so safe and cared for. I had not only lost him and the happy life that we should have had together, but I had also lost my dream of a peaceful existence, of no longer living in fear of violence and pain. I now knew that my dream of a peaceful life was just that, nothing more than a dream. I held my head up and didn't say anything about how hard I was taking Parker's death. I didn't think that anyone could possibly understand, because I had only known him for a short time. I never spoke about what had happened between Bucky and I either, as I thought that it made me sound flighty and cheap.

I had to move on. Dad wanted me to go to college, but after what I had been through in school, I couldn't even consider it. I knew of course, that it wouldn't be the same at a college as Junior High and High School had been, but that didn't seem to matter to me. The thought of sitting in a classroom made me feel shaky and nauseous.

I decided to look for work instead, and got a job with an interior designer. I was hired as a color consultant and I did office work as well. I loved my job, and with my artistic ability, I took off. I enjoyed working with beautiful things and found it satisfying, making something special of the mundane.

I buried myself and worked long hours, taking every project I could, just so that I didn't have the time to think, and even worse than that, feel. I missed Parker and I wondered how Bucky was doing, but as long as I didn't stop moving, the pain couldn't catch up to me, I could handle it and no one was the wiser.

The holidays came around way too soon, and before I knew it, it was the night of the family Christmas party. I didn't feel like going, but I couldn't think of a good excuse to get out of it, so I forced myself to attend.

At the party, my cousin Kathy and her boyfriend John announced their engagement. It hurt a bit as I should have been announcing my engagement to Parker at the party as well. But, I was still happy for them and wished them the best.

John was a police officer, and he introduced me to his best friend and partner Kurt. Kurt was tall dark and handsome; he shook my hand and wouldn't let go and said, "Let's get away from the crowd for a moment." I let him pull me away from the others to hear what he had to say. "I believe that I've been invited here tonight to cheer you up, and what a delightful job it will be."

He was so corny that he made me laugh, especially since he was serious. I had never met Kurt before, but knew him quite well by reputation. He was considered the town Romeo and was completely in love with himself. Kurt had had nearly every girl in town; it didn't seem to matter to him how beautiful or special the girl was; once he had her, he tossed her aside. Kurt was out to conquer and when the challenge was over, it wasn't fun for him anymore, and he had left a trail of yearning broken hearts behind him.

Despite his phony charms and seedy reputation, Kurt and I somehow still became good friends. It never ceased to amaze me as I watched foolish women throw themselves at him every place we went.

After the holidays, my parents leased a ranch not too far from town. It had rolling hills and a small lake filled with little green frogs which killed all of the pesky insects, and sang me to sleep at night. There were cats in the barn; big beautiful, full-coated friendly cats. They were excellent hunters and fierce fighters and kept the barn free of rats and mice. The pasture was good grazing and had secure fencing.

That spring, I put out the word that I was looking to buy a horse. A few days later I got a call from Gus, an old horse trader. "I've got a horse here that I'd like you to have a look at," he told me. "He's been raced at the track and he's a beauty. Lucky Loop, descended from that stallion… er, what's his name? That stallion that won that dagblaine Kentucky Derby, you know… Sea Biscuit. He's fine on the ground, but he won't let anyone ride him."

I told Gus I'd be right over, grabbed a few carrots from the refrigerator and backed up my truck and hooked up the horse trailer. I thought it strange that I was doing it; I hadn't made arrangements to pick the horse up, I hadn't even seen him yet, but somehow I knew that he was mine.

When I arrived at Gus' place, Lucky Loop was standing in the pasture hanging his head. I had a carrot in my hand and when I called to him, he came slowly walking over to me. He wasn't hard to catch and was very gentle. I gave him a couple pats on the neck and looked him over; there was nothing wrong that I could see; he just seemed sad. "Gus, who did you buy this horse from?"

"Oh, I picked him up from some old codger north of the valley; his daughter owned the horse and she'd been killed. The old man didn't want to bother with him, he had no interest in the animal and just left him standing alone in a small paddock. I bought him just to see that he'd get better care. That's why I called you, Miss Penelope, I know'd you could give him a good home. Why don't you let me saddle him up for ya and see how the two a-you get along."

I knew how Lucky felt; someone that he loved had died and my heart went out to him. "That's okay Gus, don't bother with the saddle. How much will you take for him?"

It was crazy; I didn't care how much Gus wanted for Lucky Loop, I was willing to pay anything to have him. Fortunately for me, Gus felt just as lucky to find a home for the horse that no one could ride and charged me a fair price. I paid him and then led Lucky to the trailer ramp and he walked right in, no problem. I drove away and took my horse home with me.

When we arrived at the ranch, I pulled up to the barn and unloaded Lucky. I fed him a flake of alfalfa and watched him eat it, then I hand fed him a scoop of grain. I spent the rest of day with Lucky; I talked to him, brushed him and combed his beautiful mane and tail. Lucky was a good looking animal; his coat was a rich chestnut, sleek and shiny and his mane and tail were long and wavy. Luck was built for speed, high in the withers and long-legged, with a deep broad chest.

After spending the day with Lucky, I felt better than I had in a long time. I didn't want to leave him alone in the barn that night, so I made myself a bed of hay in his stall. I snuggled under my sleeping bag, "Good night Lucky Loop." I closed my eyes and peacefully drifted off to sleep, things finally felt right.

The next morning, I released my new horse into the pasture. He bucked like a young colt and galloped like the wind, from one end of the pasture to the other. He was fast, incredibly fast, and feeling good.

I spent the whole day with Lucky again and when I called, he came running right to me. I talked to him and brushed him for hours; our broken hearts were mending.

As the days passed, I spent as much time with him as I could, when I wasn't at work, I was with Lucky Loop, and I slept every night in the barn on my bed of hay. I never got in a hurry to ride him, if I never did it was okay with me, he was my friend.

One night, I was laying in the stall on the hay thinking, "I can't keep sleeping in the barn forever, but I just can't leave Lucky out here alone; I need to get him a friend to keep him company." There had been a few people who had called wanting to sell me horses; I'd have to check it out.

When I walked into the house the next morning, I had a new message waiting for me. It was from an old friend of the family, Tammy, and I returned her call. She told me that she was going through a divorce and had to sell her horses, so I told her that I would be right over.

When I arrived, Tammy invited me in the house and walked me into the trophy room. It was stacked high to the ceiling with shelving that was full to overflowing with ribbons and trophies that the horses had won. These weren't little neighborhood shows that these horses had been entered in; they were in the big time, and I knew that I couldn't afford anything so grand. "Tammy, I don't want to waste your time, I don't have that kind of money."

"Don't worry about the money, come on out and have a look."

We walked into the barn together, and there standing in a stall was a horse looking down at me. He was about eighteen hands tall. He tilted his head to the side and gave me the once-over. I had never had a horse look me up and down before; I felt like I should have dressed for the occasion. This horse was smart! "Who is this woman?" I could see him asking himself. "I've never seen her before, I wonder what she wants?"

I reached out to him to see if he would welcome my attention. He didn't want me to touch his face, but let me stroke his neck. The horse was pure white, his name was Winter, and he had perfect confirmation. That's what he had won most of his prizes for, his beauty. I've seen the mythical Pegasus portrayed in movies and artwork, but none of the horses that played the part ever came close to the stark white coat and perfect symmetry of this animal. I wanted him of course, but knew that there was no way that I could swing it. "He's a beauty Tammy and I'd love to have him, but like I said, I don't have that kind of money."

"Let's not talk about money right now," Tammy answered. "I want to introduce you to Carol Lee, my broodmare; she's out in the pasture."

We walked through the corral and down to the lower pasture. Tammy called out, "Carol Lee," while she waved a brush in the air. "She loves to be brushed, as soon as she sees it, she'll come running."

A moment later, slowly walking up into sight, came a graceful bay quarter mare. When she saw the brush she did come running. She was polite and sweet, an elegant, lady. Carol Lee looked as though she was wearing shiny, black silk stockings on her lovely legs.

Why was Tammy insisting that I see her horses? Maybe she wanted me to keep them for her.

"Well, Penelope what do you think?"

"Tammy, they're incredible and I'm sorry that you have to part with them, it must be terribly painful for you. Is there anything that I can do to help you out?"

Tammy started to cry, she told me that her husband had been cheating on her, and was leaving her for the other woman.

"He's gotten so vicious; he told me that if I don't get rid of the horses by the end of the month he's going to sell them to the slaughterhouse."

"Oh Tammy, surely he doesn't mean it."

"Oh yes he does, he's tired of the divorce dragging out and he doesn't care what he has to do to end it. I'm desperate to find my horses a good home. The man who owned Winter before us abused him, so he won't let anyone ride him but my little, ten year old daughter. If Winter knows you, and you're gentle with him, he's fine, but if someone gets rough, even the toughest cowboy can't control him. People just don't want to take a chance on him because he's so tall and intimidating."

"I want to sell the horses together. Carol Lee has been bred to your Uncle Glen's stud, but I don't know if it took yet. If she is in foal you'll get two for the price of one. "

"I told you Tammy, they're out of my league."

"How much cash do you have in your pocket right now?"

"About three hundred bucks."

"I'll take it."

"Tammy why would you do a thing like that? You're not thinking straight, I won't take advantage of you that way."

"You're not taking advantage of me; I want those horses to have a good home. You'll be patient and gentle with Winter, and Carol Lee will need special care if she is in foal. I know that you have experience with horse breeding and I'll have peace of mind. If my husband wants to threaten me with taking them to the slaughterhouse, that's just about how much he'd get for them. Besides that, whatever I sell them for he gets half, half to spend on his blonde bimbo. I'm not going to see these horses killed, or with some uncaring person because he won't give me the time I need to place them."

"Are you sure that you don't want me to just keep them for you?"

"Absolutely not! I want this divorce over with too, and if my husband wants to be unreasonable he'll get just what he deserves."

I gave Tammy the three hundred bucks and she wrote me a bill of sale.

"I'll be right back with the horse trailer," I said, and I rushed home to get it. I was so excited, I felt that I would burst.

I hooked up the trailer and started back to Tammy's. "Winter will be perfect for Pat," I thought. "I'm sure that he'll like her, she's cute and little like Tammy's daughter."

The horses didn't give me any trouble loading or unloading and I turned them into the pasture with Lucky. They got along famously, just like I knew they would.

I was so excited about my new horses that I nearly forgot about an appointment I had. I quickly got cleaned up and raced off to work.

After finishing with my client, I excitedly hurried home. When I arrived, I opened the gate and drove up the driveway to see Pat already riding Winter. I couldn't believe it, that horse was so tall, I don't know how she even got in the saddle. "Hey Pat, how is he, he give ya any trouble?"

"He's great, somebody spent a lot of time training this horse; he knows more than I do! This is a highfalutin animal, how'd you manage to get him? You turned horse thief on me now?"

"No I was just in the right place at the right time."

Winter had taken to Pat, just like I knew he would; he was a good horse and never gave us any trouble.

That night, I planned to sleep in the house in my own bed; Lucky Loop wouldn't be alone. Before I turned in, I walked out to the barn to check on the animals. I was still having trouble believing that it was really true, but it was; there stood three of the most beautiful horses in the world and they were in my barn. I considered it a miracle.

About a month later, I took my vacation. I planned to work with Lucky and train him a bit, but noticed that he had a small crack in his hoof. I called Harvey Holiday, he had been shoeing the horses in our family for at least thirty years. I used to watch him working the horses when I was a little girl and he fascinated me. I had a mad crush on him for as long as I could remember. As it turned out, Harvey was booked up that day, but he didn't want to disappoint me, so he sent his grandson, Walt, to take care of the horse.

An hour later, Walt pulled up in his old beat-up, pickup truck and unlatched the gate. He looked up the driveway at me and smiled a big toothy smile, then tipped his hat and in that country drawl said, "Howdy, I'm Walter."

Walter was a slow-talking, easy moving cowboy with more charm than any man should be allowed. I liked him right off, and I'm afraid that I was a little obvious.

Walt was just like his grandpa Harvey; he had a way with horses and with the women. He knew it, but it never went to his head; it was just a fact.

Walt knew that I liked him of course, and he let me know right off, "You're too nice of a girl for me Miss Penelope." Then he explained that he liked wild hard drinkin,' hard lovin' women.

I knew that I didn't meet his requirements, and that he was rejecting me, but he did it with so much charm that I wasn't even hurt. I'll tell ya, that man could say anything and make it sound good.

Walt told me that he had a client he wanted me to meet. He said that his name was Larry and that the two of us had a lot in common. He went on to explain that we could go out on a double date and he would introduce us. Well, if Walt was going, I wanted to go, so I agreed to meet his client.

After Walt left, I put a bridle on Lucky; "You've got a brand new pair of shoes, let's go for a little ride and break 'em in."

I didn't saddle him; I thought that it seemed more friendly that way. I hadn't planned to ride Lucky just then; I was barefoot, but for some reason, I knew that the time was right. I grabbed his mane in my hand and jumped on his back. Lucky didn't put up a fuss and try to stop me from getting on, he stood perfectly still for me. "So far so good. Okay Luck, let's head for the hills!" I clicked my tongue and Lucky trotted ahead. I was so happy that he had allowed me on his back that I felt a tear run down my cheek. As Lucky and I happily traveled along the trail, I sang him the same song that I had sung to Buckshot when I was a little girl, and I think he liked it.

It had been a rough winter that year, and when we reached the river, I found that the bridge was washed out. I studied the water; it didn't look very deep, the current didn't seem too strong and the bank on the other side was nice and low. I didn't have my leather saddle on Lucky, and I wasn't wearing fancy boots that could get ruined. I also knew that Lucky liked the water; he swam in the lake in the pasture nearly every day. So I asked him, "You wanna go in the water boy?"

Lucky walked to the edge of the river, touched the water with his nose as if to check the temperature, and then he stepped in and started to cross. The river was deeper than I had expected and before I knew it, it was over our heads and Lucky began to swim. The current got stronger and we were quickly being pushed down river. I held tight to Lucky's mane, "Come on boy, you can make it!"

Lucky was a powerful animal, he fought the current and took us across, right to the opposite bank. The bank was much higher at this part of the river. It had a steep slope that was covered with soft slick mud. The water was deep, but somehow, Lucky still managed to leap up onto the bank. But the ground was slippery, and we began to slide back down into the river. Lucky scrambled, lunging ahead, struggling to get up the slope, but we crashed back into the swift current.

Lucky didn't give up, he kept swimming back to the bank and jumping again and again, fighting to get us up on the shore; the rushing water pushing us further and further down the river with each attempt. We slid down the bank sideways and backwards, it was a real struggle. We were slick with mud and it was hard for me to keep a grip and stay on.

At one point, the riverbank changed, and Lucky found a spot where the ground was more solid and he knew that he could make it. He gave the strongest highest leap he could, and when he hit the bank and lunged ahead, I was lashed back, lost my grip and was thrown off and into the river. I hit a big rock and it knocked the wind out of me. "Lucky!" I faintly called to him.

Lucky flashed his sharp eyes on the rushing river and spotted me, he jumped back in the water, and the current caught him up. He swam after me, his nostrils flaring, forcing the air from his powerful lungs. When he caught up to me I grabbed his mane, then he started for the bank pulling me along at his side. Lucky spotted a sandy beach area at a bend in the river and pulled me to it.

I climbed out of the water on my hands and knees and sat there for a moment to catch my breath. "Damn, getting the wind knocked out of you on land is bad enough, but just try it in the river. That was tough!"

Lucky rubbed his soft nose in my hair and took in a deep breath of my scent. I took hold of the bridle and he raised his head and lifted me to my feet. "Thanks boy." I wrapped my arms around his neck and held him close; I loved him with all of my heart.

"I can't believe it Luck, we're not hurt! Wow! Let's have some fun now."

I jumped on Luckys' back and we hit the winding trails. We were coming around a bend, when we heard something crashing through the brush. A big boulder rolled down the hill and came to a stop right in the middle of the trail, completely blocking our passage. I planned to turn around, but Lucky had other ideas, he took a few quick strides and jumped clean over the boulder! It was a high long jump, but it was easy for Lucky, he was so smooth that I had barely been jostled. It was obvious that Lucky was a trained jumper and I was impressed, but he acted like it was no big deal and just continued to trot happily down the trail. "Guess you didn't want to turn back either did ya, boy."

When Lucky and I reached the top of the highest hill, I got off and we settled under a big tree to take a rest. I leaned back on the trunk and enjoyed the view while Lucky stood over me. I loved being in the hills and so did my beautiful brave horse.

It was already late in the afternoon, when we started back down the slopes. We came to a place where the trails intersected and I took the one heading downhill. A few yards later, I noticed a funny looking, little tree, "Look Lucky, that tree looks like it's giving us the finger." I laughed a little at the unusual sight and Lucky and I went on our way. We never passed the trail that had been blocked by the boulder and I started to get concerned. Then a short while later, I saw the same tree again; uh oh, it was true, I was lost! I looked up and checked the position of the sun; the ground would soon be cool and the rattlesnakes would be coming out. I didn't want to be around for that event; we had to get out of there! I urged Lucky to move a little faster and when we came to where the trails intersected again, I took a different one. Then just like before, I saw the silly little tree. I was going in circles!

I hoped that Lucky could find the way and I gave him his head; "Go home boy, go home!" Lucky soon chose a trail and I thought that he was going in the wrong direction, but I just let him go, he couldn't do any worse than I had. The next thing I knew he had taken us to the soft sandy beach. What a relief! I jumped off of him, and we both took a long cool drink from the river. I sat in the sand for a few minutes and watched the water; it sparkled and glistened as it rushed by. "Lucky look at the river, it's really kinda pretty when you're not drowning in it."

As I was admiring the crystal clear water I noticed that a short distance downriver it spread out and looked like it might be shallow. I got up and

141

took Lucky's reins in my hand, "This time, we're going to try to wade across."

We walked a ways down the river bank and I was happy to find that the water was more shallow there, it didn't go much past our knees. About half way across, I stopped for a moment to rinse the mud off of the both of us and then we waded the rest of the way. "It was much easier this time wasn't it boy?" Lucky shook his head in reply; he knew what I was talking about. I jumped back on my horse and we followed the river to the road.

We were on the trail, on the side of the road headed home, when I heard a horn honking. I could see a car in the distance parked at our gate; it was Kurt.

It wasn't like Kurt to stop by unannounced and I wonder what he wanted. "It might be important, let's try to catch him Lucky, go boy! Yah!" I gave Lucky a kick, he took off running, and when I didn't pull him back, he "shifted" into a faster gear. The speed excited me and I gripped onto Lucky as tightly as I could. "Come on boy, you're a racehorse, let's see how fast you are! Go Lucky! Go!"

I let Lucky run wide open, and he took it all the way; he "shifted" again and again, and went faster and faster! He was like a streak of lightening; the fence posts were just a blur as we raced by!

It had been a long time since I had felt the power and thrill of a magnificent horse beneath me. The two of us galloping ahead together as one, the excitement exploded inside of me! I WAS ALIVE AGAIN!

At that tremendous speed, Lucky and I were fast approaching the driveway and I had to rein him in, "Whoa, Lucky," but he wasn't easy to stop. "Easy boy, whoa, whoa," I stroked his neck, trying to calm him, but he fought me and when we got near the gate he reared up and tossed his head. Lucky was still hopped up, he was snorting, jumping and prancing about, his hooves clacking on the road near Kurt's car.

"Hi, Penelope," Kurt greeted me, "I just stopped by to see the racehorse …wow!" (It's funny how people always seem to think that a horse is beautiful, when it's acting up.)

"Okay Kurt, open the gate and I'll let you have a look at him," I answered, still struggling to gain control of my wild horse.

After Kurt opened the gate, Lucky realized that the fun was over; he finally calmed down and slowly plodded up the driveway disappointed. "Good boy Lucky," I praised him.

When I dismounted, I hoped that Kurt didn't have any foolish ideas about riding Lucky; fast and high-spirited, he was too much horse for Kurt to handle. But just as I had suspected, as soon as he closed the gate, Kurt asked to ride Lucky Loop. I tried to explain to him that it wasn't a good idea, but he kept insisting. "Oh come on Penelope, get real, I just saw you ride him and you're only a girl. I'm a man, how can you possibly think that you can handle that horse better than I can?"

Kurt was so insulting and pushy that I decided to let him try. Lucky was a little tuckered out, and I figured that if Kurt just rode him slowly in the pasture, Luck couldn't run him out on the highway and kill him. "Okay Kurt, you can ride him, but don't let him go any faster than a trot, and whatever you do, don't kick him!"

I decided that it was a good idea to put the saddle on for Kurt so he'd be more secure, and he even protested that, but I ignored him and put the saddle on anyway. When Kurt's foot was in the stirrup and he was ready to mount, Pat came running out of the house. "Wait a minute Kurt!" she hollered from across the yard. She had been looking out the window and saw that Kurt was planning to ride Lucky Loop. Pat knew what a racehorse was; fast, hot-blooded and unpredictable, and this one had a bad attitude besides. "Kurt this horse is dangerous, he could kill ya!" she told him. And then she turned to me, "Sissy what are you doing? You know that Lucky's too much horse for Kurt to handle!"

That was all he needed to hear; big boastful Kurt was insulted and more determined than ever to ride the unruly racehorse. He lashed out at Pat and let her know exactly what he thought of her and her opinion. "I don't know who you think you're talking to little girl," he boasted, "but I've ridden plenty of horses!"

"Kurt, I know in your "extensive equestrian career" that you've never ridden a racehorse, or you wouldn't be so quick to jump on this one."

"It's just an old nag compared to the horses that I've ridden!" he proclaimed.

"Well, I guess that there's just no saying no to ya partner," Pat conceded, "but at least let me show you the emergency thing." Even though she was rightfully angry at Kurt, Pat still attempted to show him a maneuver to stop the horse in the event that Lucky got out of control and ran away with him. She went on to explain, "If the horse runs away with you, don't panic…You hold a rein in each hand, real low, down by his shoulders, and pull his chin toward his chest. Here let me show you."

But mister macho had had enough; he didn't want any part of this little girl telling him what to do. "Yeah, yeah," he quickly dismissed her, not listening to a word she said, and mounted the high-spirited racehorse. "Now girls, pay attention," he gloated, "let me show you how it's done!"

143

And just to show us, Kurt gave Lucky Loop a sharp kick. The horse blew up! He bucked and jumped ahead taking off at full speed, with Kurt screaming at the top of his lungs and hanging on for dear life.

Kurt's screaming faded as Lucky raced away from us. "Oh no," Pat said, "it looks like Lucky's taking him behind the pump house!"

Sure enough, that's right where Lucky was headed. There were pipes that ran between the pump house and the fence at the far end of the pasture, and Luck would have to jump high and wide to clear them all. They both disappeared behind the pump house for a moment and the screaming hushed.

Pat and I looked at each other, "Oh no, he must have fallen off and he's unconscious!"

We started to run for the gate, but when Lucky came racing out the other side of the pump house, I was shocked; Kurt was still hanging on. The "great equestrian" was screaming bloody murder again, his legs were one way, his arms another and he was half way off the saddle. It was a crazy position and hard to describe; it actually would have been a good trick if he had been doing it on purpose.

Lucky wasn't finished with Kurt yet, he really took off in the "home stretch," faster and faster. Kurt still had a hold of the reins and when he pulled back on them, he punched himself in the face so hard that it broke his glasses and knocked him dizzy. Then he dropped the reins and was completely at Lucky's mercy.

Lucky was in a full gallop headed toward the gate; he wasn't slowing down and I wondered if he would jump it too, but at the last second he abruptly slammed on the brakes. Kurt went flying over the horse's head, over the gate, and landed at our feet.

Well, if that was Lucky's plan, it had worked out beautifully! He had given mister macho just exactly what he deserved!

Pat and I were laughing uncontrollably, we couldn't help ourselves. Kurt was furious, he hobbled to his car and stormed off, cursing.

Pat looked at me between chuckles and said, "He shoulda let me show him the emergency thing!"

Once Kurt was well down the road, I tied Lucky to the hitching post and began to brush him. Pat stayed outside with me and helped with the grooming. She stroked Lucky's face and kissed him on the soft nose. "I wouldn't have put up with that jerk either Lucky," she said softly to him.

Pat then looked at me with a gleem in her eye, "How 'bout the two of us take the horses out for a real ride. You're on your vacation; let's pack in for a few weeks!"

Pat and I were always very close, but she was my baby sister, someone that I took care of and protected. The thought of taking her into dangerous terrain was out of the question. "No way Pat, you're still too tiny."

Pat wasn't pleased with my response. "Don't think I can handle it? Why I'm tougher than you; I can take you down any day of the week!" And with that, she jumped on me and knocked me to the ground.

"Why you little half-pint kid!" I shouted in response, "We'll see who's the toughest sister on this ranch!"

Pat and I rolled around, wrestling on the dusty ground. The kid was strong and she nearly had me pinned before I was able to wrangle her off and hold her down for a second. I thought that I had showed her who was boss, but when I started to get up she grabbed me by the leg and strongly jerked me back down. I fell against Lucky and landed under his feet.

The wrestling went on, with Lucky dancing around, trying not to step on us. "Pat, stop it now! Lucky's liable to step on us!"

"Don't give me that crap, a horse ain't gonna step on anybody if he can help it! Does that mean you're wimping out on me?"

Pat had definitely made her point, "Okay, okay, you're tough, I'll take you on the trip! Let's just get out from under the horse!"

I got to my feet and brushed the dust from my jeans. "Turn Lucky loose and let's start getting ready," I said as I walked away shaking my head; somehow this kid had grown up and I hadn't noticed it. I pulled a map from behind the seat of my truck and Pat and I sat in the barn and planned our trip. There were many State Parks to ride and camp in, but they were always full of loud people. We didn't want to deal with that and decided to go deep into the wilderness where there wasn't anyone else around, just us and nature.

Once the truck was packed with supplies and the horses loaded, I started the engine and Pat jumped inside. "The canteens are all filled," she told me, "let's get rolling!"

It was exciting, going on the long trip with my sister. This was the first time that we had ever done anything this daring together; two girls alone in the untamed wilderness.

We drove for hours and hours, through the night and into the next day, past the freeways and paved roads, forging ahead higher and higher into the steep mountains on a battered dirt road. When the road finally ended, we came to a stop. "Well, this is as far as we go in the truck Pat," I said as I looked around, checking out the area. "What'd ya say, we clear the brush on the right side over there behind those trees; they'll make good cover."

Pat agreed and we unloaded the horses to let them graze while we worked. Lucky and Winter were excited as they emerged from the trailer. It was a new adventure and they snorted and sniffed the air, filled with the scents of the high-mountain woods.

Once we had cleared the area, Pat and I were tuckered out, it had been a long drive and it was starting to get dark, so we decided to camp by the trailer. We built a big fire and snuggled in our sleeping bags. It was great hearing nothing but the sounds of nature; no cars, no loud music from the next campsite, no people shouting and no Ranger telling us that we were breaking the rules.

We had a good nights' sleep and were up well before sunrise. We had a hearty breakfast and then loaded our gear on the horses. As we rode up a deer trail the sun was rising, the air seemed alive, and we felt the strength of the towering trees surrounding us.

Pat and I rode Lucky and Winter higher and higher into the majestic mountains; we camped at night by a stream and in the day we traveled deeper into the wilderness. It was an enriching incredible experience, exploring the high-mountain range and being so close to nature.

Late on the fifth day, clouds covered the sun and the sky grew grey; the rain would soon be upon us. Pat and I were looking for a good place to spend the night, when we found a cave not far from the stream. It had a narrow slit for an opening, just wide enough for Pat and me to slide through and get inside. The cave was the size of a small room and the ceiling sloped up and back to a tunnel.

Pat climbed up the rock wall at the back and looked up into the tunnel. "Looks like it branches off to some smaller tunnels, I can see a ray of light, they reach the surface. Let's build a fire and check it out, it should be a good chimney." Once the fire was built, we found that Pat was right, the smoke did vent up through the tunnel; it was a perfect chimney.

Pat and I quickly pushed our gear into the cave and got the horses settled for the night, just as the clouds burst open. I thought that the cave might flood, but all of the water that came in, ran down the rock wall at the low end and then outside. The lightening flashed and the thunder boomed, but Pat and I were cozy and warm; we had stumbled upon the ideal campsite.

The next day, the sun was just peeking out as Pat and I emerged from the cave. Everything was clean and fresh from the cleansing rain, and we breathed in the moist healing air as we slowly stretched and yawned. We were both saddle-sore, and it didn't take us long to decide to take a break from the strenuous riding and relax in our newfound paradise. We took a nice cold bath in the stream, and then gathered wild berries for breakfast, while the horses peacefully grazed on the mountainside. It was a magical day, everything was perfect, there were even two rocks near the stream for us to sit on and relax. Pat and I ate our berries while we enjoyed the stream, listening to the soothing sound of the flowing of the water.

"Ya know Pat, we been camping under some pretty crude conditions on this trip, what do ya say to staying here for the duration?"

"Pat put her head back on her "easy chair." "Sure is nice here, I have to agree with ya," she said, and popped a few juicy berries into her mouth. When she had finished the berries, she stood up and pointed to a big flat rock a few yards up the hill. "Let's roll that rock down here and make ourselves a table, we can have the fire pit right in front of it, make it easier for cooking." The kid had some great ideas and we worked together to make the ideal campsite even better.

For the next two weeks, the two of us hunted and fished and gathered food from the rich forest harvest. Every night we had fresh meat to cook on the campfire, and a variety of greens and berries.

Pat and I had always been close, but it was on this trip that we got to know each other on a different level. No longer a child that I had to mollycoddle, she was a force to be reckoned with; fearless and equal to any challenge, strong intelligent and beautiful; my sister had it all.

Each day in our mountain paradise was better than the last and I didn't want to leave but alas, the dreaded day came when Pat and I had to pack up and go home. But before we did, we made a pact to never tell anyone else about our secret place; if only one person found out, word would be sure to travel, and soon our paradise would be spoiled.

On the way back down the mountains, Pat and I stopped at every turn and notched a tree, so we could always find the way back.

On the drive home, I realized that the trip had done something wonderful for me and I didn't feel the same. I was no longer burdened by the pain of the past and I was optimistic about the future.

SCARY LARRY

The day after Pat and I returned from our trip, Walt called and arranged for the double date to introduce me to his client, Larry. We chose a quiet restaurant so we could talk and get acquainted. Larry was shy and very quiet, unlike Parker and the loud brash bikers that I was used to being around. But when he did say something, it was thoughtful and polite and it impressed me.

Tall and skinny, Larry wasn't my type at all. I preferred a more stout muscular man, but he was a talented photographer, and it was nice to exchange ideas and spend time with a creative sensitive person. I thought it would be interesting to find out what was going on in his mind, I pondered about what wonderful secrets I might find there.

Walt was right, I did like his friend and we had a lot in common, right down to the horseback riding. Larry had a magnificent appaloosa, and said that he enjoyed trail riding as much as I did.

The reason that I had agreed to go on the double date in the first place was so that I could be around Walt. I was surprised, I found Larry so interesting that I barely knew that Walt was even there.

At the end of the date, Larry shyly asked me to go out with him again. I quickly accepted and we were together the very next day. Larry and I got along great, and each date was better than the last. Over the next few months, we went trail riding and on picnics every weekend. It was wonderful spending time with my beautiful horse and my sweet new boyfriend.

We rode through the tall green grasses of the meadows, and climbed the shady forest trails up the hills and into the clearing where we gazed at the vast blue sky. We swam in the rivers and streams and lay in the sun on big hot boulders.

Larry always brought his camera along on our rides, and took photos of me in the glorious scenic surroundings. Because he was a professional photographer, these weren't just quick snapshots used to remember a fun time; they were excellent, worthy to be framed and proudly displayed. Larry was truly a "magic man," he could even make me look good!

Larry covered the walls of his home with my photographs; I was flattered, it seemed as though he really cared and admired me.

On the weekdays, he took me out to dinner and to the movies. He even brought me flowers and candy with sweet loving cards. It was wonderful dating an artistic sensitive man who was so sweet and thoughtful. I felt fortunate to have him, but there was a major problem; I never felt protected or safe when I was with Larry. I knew that if anything ever went down, it would be up to me to handle it, but I hoped with all my heart that the violent times of my life had ended.

One Saturday, Larry and I pulled the horse trailer far up into the mountains. We rode all morning and into the afternoon. When we reached the top of the highest peak, we stopped to enjoy the view. Our horses stood side by side and a soft breeze blew up the slopes through the wild oats; the fragrance was intoxicating. As we looked out over the valley, Larry asked me to marry him.

I was taken completely by surprise, but quickly thought it over; "Larry definitely meets my qualifications, he's sensitive and talented, a soft-spoken gentleman. I haven't known him very long, but Larry's a shy person and if I pass up this opportunity he may never ask me again." I wasn't ready to marry anyone yet, but I smiled softly and said yes. Larry reached over and kissed me, the leather saddles squeaked as we moved toward each other; it all felt familiar and safe.

Larry wanted to get married right away, but I preferred a longer engagement. It had only been a few short months since we had met and I wanted more time to get to know him better. But Larry wouldn't hear of it, and said that he couldn't wait to marry me.

Fact was, I wasn't getting any younger; all of my cousins were married and most of them had already started families and... all of them were wondering what was wrong with me. I definitely felt pressured, but I was very fond of Larry and didn't want to lose him, so against my better judgment, I agreed to the short engagement.

Before the wedding, Larry suggested that we assume the lease on my parent's property. I wasn't sure that I wanted the vast responsibility of the big ranch; I knew how much work it was, but Larry insisted; he loved the impressive beautiful spread.

With Pete already gone and Pat planning to get her own place, my parents agreed.

Taking over the ranch overwhelmed me; I was already carrying a heavy load at work, but with my new husband by my side, I agreed to take it on.

A few short weeks later, it was my wedding day. Larry and I were married at sunrise on the beach with our horses. It was a simple, but beautiful ceremony with just a few people. The sky lit up in brilliant color as the sun rose in the misty air. I rode Winter, my stark white horse. My white flowing, satin gown and vale blew in the morning breeze. The powerful waves pounded on the sand; it was a magical scene. This was it; I was finally getting the peaceful wonderful life that I had always dreamed of!

For our honeymoon, Larry and I took the horses trail riding and camping in the mountains. We slept in the horse trailer with the horses tied to a picket line next to us. The moon and stars were bright and the crickets and frogs were singing. I could hear the horses peacefully munching on their hay. I don't think that many other women would have

149

wanted to spend their honeymoon out camping with the animals, but I did and I was very happy.

Unfortunately, my happiness didn't last for long; Larry's horns came out right away and he let me know that he didn't appreciate my lack of sexual experience. He said that he thought that I had just been pretending to be a nice girl, because it was expected of me. But now that he knew that it was really true, he called me a weirdo. It felt like someone had punched me in the gut.

Chainsaw Charlie had respected my innocence and treated me as a precious jewel; but now, I had married a man who made fun of me because of it. Things were off to a bad start, and I realized that all of Larry's nice acting had been just that, acting.

My family had gone through a lot of trouble for me; they had relocated and re-arranged their lives to see that Larry and I had a good start. I was obligated to follow through with the marriage, even though I didn't want to. I felt like a stupid fool and I didn't know how to get out of it.

It was now obvious that this marriage would be a tough row to hoe, but my life had never been easy. I had been through difficult times before and this would be just one more hardship. So, I buckled down and decided to make the best of it.

It didn't take long before Larry "hurt his back," he never went to the doctor, or made any effort to get any treatment or help for it. It was one of those mysterious kind of injuries that would come and go whenever it was convenient for him.

Not long after this "injury," Larry got rid of his horse; he said that he could no longer ride because it hurt his back. I tried to talk him out of it, but he went to the Livestock Auction and sold the magnificent animal to a complete stranger, for next to nothing. I was in shock! But there was nothing that I could do to stop him as it was his horse.

Before I married Larry, I had believed that he was a good person, unlike the bad boy bikers. I was impressed that he had never done drugs or been in a fight; a nice guy, I thought. Well, Larry didn't need drugs, he drank, and the reason that he had never been in a fight wasn't because he was a peaceful or kind person; no not at all, it was because he was a sniveling coward. Larry picked on animals, children and sick or old people who couldn't defend themselves against him.

It had only taken a few weeks before I found out just how bad he really was, and I realized that I had made an even bigger mistake than I had originally believed. I wanted to divorce him, but I had been raised to take marriage too seriously. Divorce was a sin that my family wouldn't accept.

150

There were no divorces in our family; I would be a disgrace to the whole clan, and Larry knew it. He knew that he had me trapped and I knew it too. I believed that I had no choice; I had to tough it out and hope that somehow things would get better.

As time went on, I became more and more miserable with Larry; there were no more trail rides, no picnics or going out to dinner. All he ever wanted to do was photograph me. Every single weekend he had me posing for him, hour after dreaded hour.

Larry built elaborate sets with special lighting and reflectors. I have no idea what all of the equipment was used for, but he spent more and more money on cameras, lenses, filters and new gadgets every week. Larry bought exotic costumes and lingerie, he experimented with new makeups and had a hairdresser design and fix my hair in different styles for each photo shoot.

Larry loved to photograph me nude; he had orchids and jewels that he used as props for me to pose with. He covered my bare skin with shiny scented oils and had strands of pearls and yards of sheer and satin fabrics that he draped around the elaborate sets and slid over my nude body.

I sat still for hours while Larry painted me with body paints and brushed me with glitter and sparkling frosts. There was nothing obscene or indecent about any of the photos that Larry took of me, as a matter of fact they were beautiful works of art. I had no good reason not to co-operate with him except for the fact that he gave me the creeps. If I even hinted that I didn't want to be photographed, Larry went into a rage as if someone was withholding a drug from him that he was addicted to. My life would be hell on earth if I didn't submit, so to get along with him I did.

Larry had big thick albums full of my photographs, and in his dark room, he blew up his favorite ones. There were huge pictures of me hanging on every wall of the house and the bedroom was covered with erotic, but tasteful nudes.

I thought that it was weird and I didn't like it, but other women were jealous and said that they would do anything to be in my shoes, to have a man adore them the way that Larry adored me.

Women hired Larry to take erotic photos of them. I was hoping and praying that he would become interested in someone else and leave me alone. If he cheated on me, all the better; then by religious law, I could divorce him. But no such luck, my photo sessions went on and on.

Artist or not, there was definitely something wrong with Larry, but no one else seemed to think so. In fact, they idolized him and admired his talent. Galleries featured him at special showings and Larry slid deeper and deeper into his strange fantasy world.

Every second that I was away from the house, I tried not to think about Larry. I buried myself in my job and spent what free time I had with my animals. Every night, when I came home from work, I would have a wonderful parade of horses and dogs to greet me. They ran and trotted alongside the truck, whinnying and barking as I drove up the driveway. I rarely restricted my horses, most of the time they were free to run the limits of the property. In the evenings they would stick their heads in the window to see what I was making for dinner and of course, get a carrot or two.

I had three big Great Danes and an adorable little, white fluffy mutt that just showed up at the ranch one day. I named her Snowball. She was sweet and tiny, but held her own with the much larger animals. She knew that she was my favorite. (But I told her not to tell anyone.)

When we had guests, they always got a big kick out of the evening romp of the dogs and horses. The animals put on a comical performance every night, they ran in circles around the outside of the house, playing chase. Once in a while a kitty would even join in the fun. Usually the dogs would start barking and chasing the horses. Then the horses would turn and chase the dogs, pushing them ahead with their nose if the dogs would stop on the "track." We had huge picture windows on all sides of the living room so you could see the parade all around. The horses made sure to look into the house occasionally to be certain that I was watching their entertaining show. I laughed and applauded to show my approval. I loved my animals and they loved me.

One night, when I came home from work, I was alarmed to see a fire burning in the yard. I raced up the driveway, my heart pounding, only to see Larry in a rage throwing clothing into the flames of a bonfire.

I got out of my truck and went to find out what was going on. When I was close enough, I saw that Larry had all of my old biker clothes in a pile and he was throwing them one by one, into the fire. "You don't love me," he shouted, "you never did! You're too pretty; you only married me because I happened to come along at a convenient time!"

I looked into the fire and there were my black leather chaps and biker boots smoldering in the flames.

Larry picked up my belt with the eagle buckle and swung it above his head threatening me. I stepped back and he started screaming, "Why are you still keeping this? I found it at the bottom of your drawer, you've been hiding it from me! You don't want me; you want to be with a dirty no-good biker! Why else would you still have these things? You wanting to be with scum like that, I just don't understand it! What's wrong with you Penelope? You must be crazy! You're crazy! You're crazy! You're crazy! You're crazy!"

Larry was throwing a fit, jumping around the fire like a demon in hell's flames and accusing me of being the one that was crazy. It was hard for me to take and he was planning to burn my special belt next. I had had the belt since Junior High; the sharp strong wings made it a dangerous weapon and I had depended upon it. I loved that belt buckle; it had saved me many a time.

I was furious! I wanted to knock Larry down, take my belt away from him and beat the crap out of him! But I didn't. I don't know how, but I somehow managed to keep my cool. "Chose your battles," I told myself, "the belt is just an object; you never wear it anymore anyway. It's not worth the trouble."

I was wondering what had prompted Larry to flip out when he suddenly started screaming, "I'm sure that you're very disappointed, you missed your disgusting biker friends today! That's right, bikers; they actually came here to the ranch, to my home looking for my wife! I'm twice the man that they could ever be!" he announced indignantly.

I figured that my biker friends must have been passing through the state and decided to look me up. I pictured the thundering motorcycles pulling through the gate and roaring up the driveway to the house.

Apparently, seeing the rugged burly men must have been too much for the "sophisticated" Larry to handle. He kept screaming, over and over, "I'm twice the man that they are, I'm twice the man, I'm twice the man!"

I decided to leave him alone with his revenge burning, or whatever it was, and I walked away chuckling with a smile on my face. I could only imagine what my biker friends had done to Larry. Perhaps imagining it was more amusing than actually knowing what had really happened.

Life went on, and I continued to concentrate on my animals and avoid Larry as much as possible. As it turned out, Carol Lee was in foal; she didn't have any trouble and dropped her baby in the early spring. I named him Chief Joseph after the Nez Perce Native American Chief. My foal, Chief Joseph, was the grandson of Uncle Glen's, Grand National Champion Appaloosa. The foal had excellent confirmation and a gentle disposition, the product of superior breeding; perfect in every way.

One morning, I got a call from Carl Bascam; I had been hoping to hear from him. Carl was retired and had shown Uncle Glen's horses for years. He was the one who had taken Uncle Glen's famous stud all the way the way to the top. He heard about my colt and wanted to see him, so I told him to come on over.

When Carl arrived, we walked together into the barn. He knew what a good horse was; Carl had been in the show circuit forever. He was greatly respected and his opinion highly regarded.

I watched his eyes light up as he opened the stall door and got his first look at Chief Joseph. He didn't utter a word, approached the colt and knelt down. Chief walked over to him and nuzzled his arm with his soft little nose.

Carl looked at me, "Great disposition, just like his grandfather." Then he gave Chief a couple pats and looked him over. He ran his hand down the foal's back, down his leg and then picked up his hoof. The little horse stood, proud and still. "Great on the ground too; very good." Carl looked up at me and smiled, "Well there's no doubt about it, little gal," he said as he stood up, "we've got a champion on our hands! Guess I'ma gonna have to come out of retirement, can't let an opportunity like this one pass me by."

I was right; Chief Joseph was perfect in every way, my pride and joy. I thanked Carl for coming by and we both looked forward to the excitement of the horse shows.

Later that week, Pat and her friend Lance, invited Larry and me on a canoe trip. I really didn't want to go anywhere with Larry, but I figured that the men would probably be together, and I could spend some time with my sister.

When it was time to get ready for the trip, Larry's convenient back injury hurt too much for him to load anything. He sat and drank beer while he watched me do all the work. He also refused to ride in Pat's Cadillac, because, he said, that the seats hurt his back. We had to take separate cars, as his vehicle of choice was only a two-seater. I offered to drive so he could "rest his back" but he refused; I'm sure so that he could drive erratically and terrify me all the way there, which he did.

Pat and Lance were following behind us in the Caddy. They watched as I got out to pump the gas because Larry claimed that he couldn't bend to pump gas without excruciating pain.

"That lazy, disrespectful, son-of-a bitch, "Lance said, and he got out of the car. He was totally disgusted with Larry and wanted to pump the gas for me, but Pat stopped him, "No, it might just make things worse for Sissy."

When we got on the river, something miraculous happened; Larry's back suddenly felt great! He challenged and raced other canoeists all day long, and was so fast that no one could catch him. It was embarrassing. He was in a frenzy; his eyes were bugged out and he was laughing uncontrollably and acting crazy. When we came to the bridge, it was the end of the trip, but Larry was having so much fun that he wanted to keep on going. It was amazing; he picked up the canoe and carried it, all by himself, a quarter mile to catch the adjoining river.

This feat, a "true miracle," infuriated Pat and Lance. "That Larry is a disgusting lazy pig," Lance growled. "Who does he think he's fooling with his phony back condition? No man has the right to treat a woman like this! That idiot needs to have his ass kicked and that's exactly what he's going to get!" Lance picked up a fallen tree branch and headed straight for Larry.

I grabbed Lance by the arm and stopped him, "Lance, you're right, he does deserve to have his ass kicked, but he's not worth getting your hands dirty."

As much as I would have liked to see Lance beat the crap out of Larry, I couldn't let it go down. I had learned to take fighting very seriously; you never know what might happen in a fight. As far as I'm concerned, every fight is a life or death situation, not to be taken lightly, and certainly not worth the risk over a piece of filth like Larry.

Pat talked to Lance until he calmed down enough to go back to the car and leave. I was happy, at that point, that we had taken the separate cars.

I wondered what was going on with Larry, why he was acting so manic, but I was just grossed out by him as usual.

After his performance on the river, I was hoping that perhaps Larry had tired of feigning back pain, but no such luck. The "miracle" was over as soon as we got home and it was time to unload. It surprised me that he wasn't embarrassed in the slightest, to start complaining again so soon. I thought that he would have at least waited until the next day so that he could claim that soreness had set in.

Larry sincerely thought that he was smarter than everyone else, and that he had us all fooled. He believed that he had found the perfect excuse to avoid doing anything and everything that he didn't want to do, and he wasn't about to give it up.

"Larry, it seems strange to me how you can be fine all day and now suddenly, you're completely disabled again."

"Don't be stupid, Penelope, any doctor will tell you that the back is an anomaly. There is absolutely no way of knowing when it will act up."

"Now that's where you're wrong Larry, I know exactly when your back is going to act up."

Larry had been the one who insisted that we take on the ranch. He enjoyed the benefits and the prestige of living on the big impressive spread. It truly was a magnificent place and Larry liked to show off and brag about it to anyone who would listen.

It was a lot of hard labor keeping things up, and guess who's back hurt him too much to do any of it? I loved the ranch too, but I was struggling to work my full time job, do the housekeeping, shopping, cooking and the ranch chores; ranch work much too heavy for me to handle alone.

One night, a windstorm blew through the valley and in the morning I found that a big tree branch had broken loose and fallen on the barn, caving in a section of the roof. I asked Larry to help me lift it off. He of course, refused, because his "back was hurting."

We were expecting rain and I had to get the roof patched that day or I could lose most of my feed. I climbed on the roof with a two by four, rigged it up as a lever and lifted as hard as I could. The branch started to move, but when the pressure was on, the lever snapped and tossed me off the roof.

I sprained my ankle and ended up with a hernia. The ankle wasn't too bad, but the hernia was serious and I needed surgery to fix it. The doctor told me that I had ripped my insides up very badly and that I needed to have the surgery as soon as possible. He scared me when he said that without the surgery, the hernia would likely strangulate and could kill me. He fitted me with a truss to hold my guts inside, and said that if I had any problems, to go directly to the hospital for emergency surgery.

Considering the shape I was in, I couldn't fix the roof and did the best I could, covering the feed with tarps. I also had to put off training my colt until after I had the surgery, and had the time to heal. Fortunately, there wasn't any hurry, Chief Joseph would come to me when I called him; he was very gentle and tame and I knew that training him would be a breeze.

Early the next morning, before I got up, Larry informed me that he was going to halter break Chief. He, who never lifted a finger to help in any way, was suddenly going to do something nice. I knew better, clearly his motives were sinister.

Larry said that he planned to lasso the young horse and force the halter on him. A colt that young should not be lassoed; it can damage the vertebra in the neck and cripple it for life. When I told Larry this, he said that I didn't know what the hell I was talking about. He grabbed the lasso and ran outside to catch the colt anyway. Chief was tiny, the perfect victim for a fiend like Larry. There was no way that this little animal would be able to defend himself.

I was slowed down a bit by my bad ankle, but I grabbed my crutches and quickly headed outside. I was shocked by how quickly this cruel evil man had taken action. By the time I got out there, Larry already had Chief trapped in the corral and was terrifying him, screaming obscenities and throwing the lasso, trying to catch him. Chief's mother, Carol Lee, was in a panic whinnying and running the other side of the fence line trying to save her baby. Little Chief was frantic, desperately trying to escape from the madman.

I scrambled into the corral to protect him, "Larry! He's my horse and I don't need your help, I'll train him myself, leave him alone!"

"Get out of my way!" Larry screamed, then he ran at me and rammed me full force, slamming me into the fence. I hit so hard that the fence rail broke and I found myself on my back on the ground, broken fence pieces around me.

Larry didn't pause for a moment; the fact that he had struck his injured wife and knocked her through the fence didn't faze him in the slightest. He was still throwing the lasso trying to catch Chief Joseph, to hurt him, to destroy him.

After striking me that hard, I'm certain that Larry didn't expect me to get back up, but knowing what was in store for Chief I had to, no matter how I felt. Larry had wrenched my back and shoulder and I could barely move. I had severe pain in my gut… my hernia! I clenched it with my hand, trying to push it back in, and then I ran on my bad ankle back into the corral. I was furious by this time, I didn't care what happened to me, but Larry was not going to hurt my colt. I was going to protect Chief no matter what it took.

I stood between them again. "Get out of the way!" Larry shrieked wildly.

"No! You're not going to cripple my horse!" I screamed at the top of my lungs. "You stay away from him! Get out of here!"

Standing there, balancing on one foot and holding my insides in with my hand, it was obvious that I was badly hurt. Larry figured that I couldn't fight back and he raised his fist to me.

When I saw that, it pissed me off even more, and I wasn't about to back down. I looked him square in the face, "You dirty son-of-a-bitch, go ahead and try it." I raised my fists to protect myself, as I had done so many times before. "Come on tough guy, if you think you're man enough, go ahead, hit me, you wanna fight let's go!

Even though I was a physical wreck, I was still ready to fight. "Larry's a wimp, you can take him," I said to myself. I stood there, defending my innocent colt, waiting and ready for our tormentor to make his move. But, I was in way over my head; Larry was a man and he was bigger and stronger than me. I was so upset, and in such a hurry to get in the corral and help Chief, that I had forgotten to get a weapon.

Thank goodness Pat pulled up in her big gold Cadillac, just in the nick of time. "Something wrong here?" she asked.

"No, nothing wrong," Larry said in a timid whiny voice.

Immediately, I staggered to the gate as fast as I could and let Chief out of the corral and into the big pasture. He joined his mother and the other horses and they raced off together, dust flying behind them.

Larry walked into the house whimpering, with his tail between his legs.

I took a moment to check; if my hernia had strangulated I would need emergency surgery. I was able to push it back in; thank God I was okay, just sore and banged up.

The next day, I didn't go to work. After being slammed through the fence I was bruised and hurting real bad. That afternoon, while Larry was gone, I hobbled into the pasture and climbed in the manger. I laid back and looked up at the sky; it was a deep shade of blue with little white, fluffy clouds slowly floating by. The horses were nuzzling me with their soft fuzzy noses and tickling my neck. The dogs lay at my feet and the kitty's were purring, pouncing and tumbling about. My little hens were out of the coop scratching the ground and clucking. With all of the beauty surrounding me, I was never more miserable in my life.

I had hoped to meet Prince Charming and live happily ever after, but now my dream was shattered. Larry had taken something away from me that I could never regain.

I thought back to that first night when I had met Larry and how I was looking forward to finding out the magical secrets about him; but everything that I had found was rotten, vile and wicked. The more I discovered, the more appalled I became, and I couldn't let it go on. I knew that I had to divorce Larry no matter what my family or anyone else thought; it was over.

Larry couldn't be trusted with the animals and I didn't dare leave any of them behind. Who knew what unspeakable things he might do to them if I weren't there to protect them. With my injuries, there was no way that I could move out right away, so I made a plan. I would have the surgery as soon as possible, and once I was back to work, find some property and take all the animals with me.

I arranged for the hernia surgery and was trying to find someone to pick me up afterward when Larry heard me on the phone and insisted on picking me up himself. "I'm your husband," he whined, " it's my job."

I didn't want to make matters worse between us, I was trying to get through this thing as peacefully as possible, so I agreed to let him pick me up. I wasn't thrilled to say the least, but everyone else was working that day, and it would have been a big imposition.

I had the surgery and Larry did pick me up from the hospital, but he brought the big old dirty truck that I used to pick up hay and feed. It had heavy shocks and when it wasn't heavily loaded it would actually buck you right off the seat. Larry would never ride in it because it "hurt his back," but here I was witnessing yet another miracle.

On top of the rough ride, Larry drove like a manic, slamming on the brakes and screaming curses at the other drivers. It was an hour drive home from the hospital and it was raining. The windshield wipers and defroster in the old truck didn't work and he should have never brought it. But why pass up this wonderful opportunity to torture me? I was in horrible pain and completely at his mercy; this excited Larry; things just don't get any better for an abuser.

During the trip home, the sky turned black and it began to rain harder and harder. The windows fogged up until we could barely see through the windshield. When I asked Larry to stop and wipe it down, he cleared a spot with his finger, not much larger than the size of a quarter and said, "I don't need to see, I know these roads."

That was the stupidest thing that I had ever heard! "Larry I don't care how well you know the roads, even if you could drive them blindfolded, there are other cars on the road besides you!" I tried to reason with him, to no avail.

I could see that he was deriving a sick pleasure out of my nervousness and pain. I quit wincing and trying to talk to him; I would give him no such pleasure. As bad as he was, I thought that this would have been beyond even him. How did I ever marry a sick monster like this? What was wrong with me?

I don't know how we ever made it home, but we did. Larry wouldn't help me out of the truck because, no surprise, his back was hurting. The truck was high off the ground and I managed to slide down the seat and get out by myself. I made it to my bed, took some pain pills and fell asleep.

In the morning, the rooster was crowing and I felt horrible. "Larry, get up, it's time to feed," I told him.

He was angry, "I can't feed those animals with my bad back!" he yelled.

"Larry, the doctor says that I have to take it easy for two weeks."

"Two weeks! Two weeks!" he kept screaming. "You're good for nothing!"

He was lying at my side, he raised his arm, made a fist and came down with a hard punch to my stomach. The medication had worn off by this time and I felt the full force of the blow. The pain was like nothing I can describe, I thought that he had ripped loose my stitches and that I was going to bleed to death. I couldn't move, it all felt surreal, the pain clouded my mind.

After he struck me, Larry got up waving his arms and screaming at the top of his lungs, "I can't take care of these animals! My back, my back! I'm going to have to kill them! Yes! I'll kill them all! That's a good idea, yes that's what I'll do; I'll kill them all!" He paced back and forth and then grabbed a rifle and ran outside.

I heard a shot and a yelp and I knew that it was Snowball, my little white dog! He had killed her! I couldn't believe that it was actually happening, but this was no nightmare. I heard another shot, and another and another. I struggled to get to my feet but my right leg wouldn't work. I reached and grabbed the top of the dresser by my bed and pulled myself up. There was a belt in the drawer, I wrapped it in a loop around my thigh and used it to pull my leg forward with my hand. I had to stop him!

When I made it to the barn, he was shooting the hens, one at a time. My little hens running in panic trapped in their coop. My dogs and cats lay dead and bleeding on the barn floor.

"Stop!" I screamed in terror as I staggered through the blood. He swung the rifle, hit me in the forehead and knocked me down. I landed on the bloody dead body of my little white dog. I screamed so horribly I thought that my insides would come out. I was hysterically crying, "Snowball, Snowball" and trying to hold her in my arms.

Suddenly, I felt the cold steel of the rifle, Larry had put the barrel in my eye; he raised my head up with it, then in a strange unnatural voice he said, "I... can't... take... care... of... you... either!" He looked insane, his eyes were like black B-Bs and I could see the devil looking at me through them. It was the rattlesnake; I was seeing my nightmare all over again, another murderous demon from the pit of hell. My insides shuddered, but I had to hold it together, I couldn't let fear take me over, or it would mean my life. I knew that this sick bastard wanted to dominate, to terrify me to the breaking point and make me grovel at his feet and beg for my life. If I showed weakness, it would only excite him and escalate the violence. There was no mercy to be had at the hands of this madman.

I took the chance that he wouldn't shoot and grabbed hold of the rifle barrel and pushed it out of my face. I tried to hold onto it, but he yanked it away. I couldn't get to my feet, but from the bloody floor of that barn, I looked him square in the face and I roared, "I'll fight you to the death, you heartless piece of filth!"

Larry stepped back, he wasn't prepared for that reaction, he stood there silently, he was confused as if in shock and he didn't move a muscle. Then he turned away and slithered, with rifle in hand, to the side of the house. I couldn't see where he went; "Maybe to kill himself," I thought.

This was my chance; I had to get out of there. I started dragging myself out of the barn and down the long dusty driveway. If I could just make it to the road, maybe I could get a ride with someone. I heard the front gate open… it might be Larry! I picked up a stick lying in the driveway and dragged myself into the weeds in the drainage ditch, and peeked through.

It was the big gold Cadillac, my sister! "Pat!" I called to her, but she didn't hear me, she had the car windows up. My God, what was she driving into?! Would that maniac kill my little sister next?" I had to stop her! I threw the stick at the car before it got too far away and hit the rear window. Pat stopped, thank God! "Pat, over here!" I called to her.

Pat saw me on the ground and got out of the car. "I just came out to see how you were holding up after the surgery. What in the world are you doin' outside in the ditch?"

"Pat get me out of here!"

Pat didn't ask any more questions, she helped me up and put me in the car.

"Don't pull up to the house!!" I warned, and Pat backed the Cadillac out of the driveway and barreled down the road.

"Pat, Larry shot the animals in a fit of rage, and he almost shot me too."

"My God! All that blood, we better get you to the hospital!"

"No, I'm okay, you know how bad head injuries bleed, most of the blood isn't mine, it's from the dogs and cats. I don't think that he got the horses though, they might still be alive. I didn't put them in the barn last night and when they heard the shots they would have headed for the trees in the high-pasture. But they could be seriously hurt if Larry got a shot off at them before they could get away. We've got to move fast, he might be heading up there right now to finish them off!"

We quickly arrived at Pat's place. "You stay here Sissy, don't try to get out, I'll be right back."

"Pat, whatever you do don't call the sheriff; the law can't help us now. The Sheriff can only let us remove personal property until the judge sorts

161

it out in court. He'll never let us take the horses.

Pat went inside and when she came back out, she had her old six-shooter strapped on her hip and was carrying a wooden box. She threw the box in the seat between us, handed me a towel for my head, and then started up the car and pulled out of the driveway. "We're gonna need the trailer," she said, "and we'll have to fight our way in to get it. You up for it?"

"Looks like I'll have to be," I answered.

"I brought the .357 Magnum for you, it's in the ammo box and here's my gun," Pat pulled it from her holster and handed it to me. "Load 'em both with hollow points, if we do have to shoot that weasel we better make sure that he's dead."

I opened the box and that kid had enough ammo in there to fight a war. At that moment, I was glad that I had a tough little sister and that I had taught her to shoot.

"Sissy, we know he's armed, plus he's got good cover, we'll have to go in blasting."

I knew that she was right. I was prepared to do whatever I had to do to save my horses, even if it meant killing Larry.

The driveway to the ranch was on the right side of the road, the passenger side. When we got close, I shot the latch on the gate. BANG! BANG! It fell loose and the gate swung open... this was it!

"That should get his attention," Pat said. "Now get ready," she drew her gun. "Keep your eyes sharp, he could be hiding anywhere."

The house was to the right of the driveway and we had to drive past it to get to my truck and trailer. We cautiously drove down the driveway and approached the house. Pat screamed, "There's Larry, looking through the curtains in the bedroom!"

"That's him alright!" BOOM! BOOM! I fired two shots over the house. The bedroom window was open, so I knew that Larry could hear me. "Stay in the house, if you come out, I'll drop you where you stand!"

"Okay Pat, go! Get past the house; my truck and trailer are parked by the barn."

"Keep shooting Sissy!" Pat fired a few rounds out the car window. "We've got to keep that weasel pinned down."

BANG! BANG! BOOM! BOOM! BOOM! We opened fire over the house until we were clear.

When we reached the barn, Pat parked the Caddy and we hunkered down behind it, using it as cover. Larry didn't come out of the house and I wasn't surprised.

"We got a break, knowing where he is," I said as Pat and I reloaded.

"Yeah, you're not kidding, that coward isn't going to do anything, he's probably wetting his pants." Pat closed the cylinder of the old six-shooter, "I'm gonna start hooking up the trailer."

"Okay Pat, the truck keys are in the tack room and that ol' .38 Special that Dad give me, get 'em both and don't worry, I've got you covered."

Pat opened the door of the tack room and as soon as she got inside, I heard a screech.

"Oh no!" What was it? I couldn't see what happened! I started scooting myself down the side of the car struggling to get to the tack room. "Pat! Pat!" I cried.

"It's okay," I heard my sister's voice, then she came walking out holding one of the cats in her arms. It was Moe Moe, he was always cautious and spooky, we had found him on the street and I guess it paid off for him, he had survived! Of all of the cats, Pat had always favored Moe Moe and I was glad that she had found him. There was a kitty carrier in the tack room and we loaded Moe Moe up in the back seat of the Caddy.

We enjoyed a moment of happiness, but we were still in danger.

"Come on Pat, let's get the trailer and get out of here."

Pat started the truck and backed it up to the trailer; she got it lined up the first try. Then she cranked down the trailer and hooked up the lights and we were ready to go. Still no Larry.

Pat helped me get in the driver's seat of the Caddy. It looked like we might make it, but we still had to pass in front of the house again. I pulled out in the Cadillac, headed toward the house with Pat in the truck, pulling the trailer close behind me. When we got near the house, Pat and I started blasting; we couldn't let that weasel stick his head up and get a shot off at us! BOOM! BOOM! BOOM! BOOM! Now Larry wasn't the only one armed; he wouldn't like that, not his kind of odds.

We got safely off the property and started down the road, headed for the high-pasture. I was struggling to drive the car, the pain was overwhelming me and I had to fight to stay conscience. My vision was fuzzy and fading in and out. I was still drenched with blood, my own and the blood of my murdered animals. My clothes began to stick to me as the blood dried and hardened. Harsh reality weighed heavily on my mind when we approached the high pasture. Would the horses be there? Were they still alive? What if I found them bloody, suffering and dying? Would I have the courage to put a bullet in their heads to end their suffering? What was I going to face? "GOD HELP ME!" I cried out in agony from the bottom of my broken blood-drenched soul.

Pat and I pulled up to the back gate of the high-pasture and no horses were in sight. I called out desperately, "Lucky, Winter, Carol Lee, Chief!" Anguish overwhelmed me when I got no response.

Pat got out of the truck, "You stay here Sissy, I'll hike out and look for them."

"Watch out for Larry! If you find the horses just halter Lucky, the others will follow him right into the trailer."

Pat headed out and I waited, I waited for what seemed an eternity. Just when I was ready to give up hope, Pat came into sight, headed up the ridge. She was leading Lucky and when they walked a little further, I could see Winter, then Carol Lee with little Chief following close behind. They were all walking in a line, perfectly fine and unharmed. Pat had a big smile on her face and so did I.

Pat loaded the horses in the trailer while I stood guard. "No dogs," she sadly stated. She had still hoped that maybe one of the dogs had made it too. I knew better, I had seen them all lying dead in the barn. I was glad that she hadn't gone in there and seen the carnage.

"We'll take the horses to Byron's they'll be safe there; Larry doesn't know him." Byron was an old rancher friend of Uncle Glen; he loved horses and had plenty of room.

Pat and I made a pact never to tell anyone what had happened that day. We were afraid that if someone in the family got wind of it, they might take matters into their own hands. We didn't want one of our loved ones dead, hurt, or in prison because of Larry, he had already done enough damage. I would have considered it my fault if anyone got hurt because they were avenging me.

I had Larry served with a restraining order as soon as possible. He was to stay away from Pat, the horses and me. I got a call from him that same day. He was calling from the barn phone, I could tell because that phone always had a strange kind of an echo. "He must have broken the phone in the house," I thought and I wondered what he was doing calling me at all, as it was a violation of the restraining order.

I heard him say in his whiney voice, "I don't know why you don't want me around the horses." Immediately, I hung up the phone. After what he had done, how could he possibly not understand why he couldn't be around the horses? Was it because he had so "graciously," not killed them? Was that his warped thinking? Hearing his voice and him asking me such a question made me ill, he was truly a sickening vile creature.

I was reeling from the ordeal, I couldn't stand up straight and had to walk bent over from the pain. I went to see my doctor, "Doc put me back together!" I felt like I was in shreds.

The doctor examined my wounds and stitched up the gash above my eye. He said that because of the trauma that I had suffered, there was no way of knowing how long it would take for me to fully recover. But I would recover, and I didn't need more surgery to repair any of the damage that had been done. The stitches for the hernia had held. That had been my greatest fear, enduring more surgery. I was relieved, but it would still take time.

I couldn't let it get me down. I would take one step at a time, lay low until I healed, then return to work and get my own place as soon as I could. I wanted to get out of Pat's as soon as possible; because of Larry, she was in jeopardy every minute that I was there with her.

The next week, while Pat was at work, I was alone in the house when the phone rang. "Hello," I said, but no one answered me right away. I could hear flies buzzing and I listened more closely... the echo of the barn phone... my God, it was Larry again!

He began his exhortation, "Your doctor called with your blood test results today and I just found out that I'm going to be a father! You know I love you, so why don't you quit overreacting and come home? What's wrong with you anyway? You know that I don't deserve this. The way you're treating me is completely unfair. I realize that you're neurotic, but I'm willing to look past it for my son's sake and take you back. A boy needs both a father and a mother, it's important that we stay together for the child. I'm so excited about this; you just don't know how much it means to me. I'm going to teach him everything I know!"

I listened to every word that Larry said, then I just sat there for a moment in a weird state of some sort of shock, "Quit playing games with me!" I shouted.

"No, it's true you're pregnant," he stated with glee. Just then, I heard a thump like he was hitting something. "Hey! Get away from Snowball you stinking rat! LEAVE... MY... DOG... ALONE!!"

Larry was actually in the barn with the rotting corpses of the animals that he had killed; defending them from the rats and talking to me about being a father!!!

"I'll never have a child of yours!" I screamed in terror and slammed down the phone. Immediately, I got a sharp cramp that put me all the way down to the floor. The rest of the day, and all that night I was cramping and sweating, and in the morning I had miscarried. It was as though the baby had heard what I said, and had given up and died.

I was overcome with guilt; it was unbearable. Just when I thought that I

165

had been feeling the pain of loss in every way imaginable, I found that I was wrong. This was a pain of a whole new level, a level that I couldn't bear.

When I finally calmed down, I realized that it wasn't my words that had killed the baby; it was Larry's cruel punch in the gut. And there was another side to this situation; maybe the baby was lucky, it was safe and happy in heaven and didn't have to grow up with an insane lunatic for a father. I also knew that if Larry's mental problem was genetic, the child stood a chance of suffering from mental illness as well. Could it be that this child had been spared from suffering a tortured life? Perhaps it was for the best. That's what I chose to believe.

But one thing I knew for sure, there was no hope for Larry, no chance of him ever getting well; as far as he was concerned he didn't have a problem, everyone else did. He told people that he was a perfect man and a good catch. That was how he saw himself, when actually he was completely out of his bloody mind…

AND THE BATTLE HAS JUST BEGUN…

TROUBLE WITH A DREAM II
VICTIMS?

AVAILABLE NOW!

This book was brought to you by:
GALVANIZED GROUP INC.

Thank you for buying our book.
Follow us on Twitter and like us on Facebook

Galvanized Group Inc.

We'd love to hear from you: galvanizedgroupinc@gmail.com